Paradise Walk

Also by the Author

Fiction

The Wandering Heart

Nonfiction

Devil on the Deep Blue Sea:
The Notorious Career of Captain Samuel Hill of Boston

Souvenirs of the Fur Trade:
Northwest Coast Indian Art and Artifacts Collected by American
Mariners

A Most Remarkable Enterprise:
Lectures on the Northwest Coast Trade by
Captain William Sturgis

"Boston Men" on the Northwest Coast

Paradise Walk

Mary Malloy

A LIZZIE MANNING MYSTERY

Leapfrog Press
Teaticket, Massachusetts

Published in 2011 in the United States by
Leapfrog Press LLC
PO Box 2110
Teaticket, MA 02536
www.leapfrogpress.com

Distributed in the United States by
Consortium Book Sales and Distribution
St. Paul, Minnesota 55114
www.cbsd.com

Map drawn by Reginald Piggott for Simon Keynes,
University of Cambridge

Monogram: Courtesy of Ann Walsh

First Edition

Library of Congress Cataloging-in-Publication Data

Malloy, Mary, 1955-
  Paradise walk / Mary Malloy. -- 1st ed.
    p. cm. -- (A Lizzie Manning mystery)
  ISBN 978-1-935248-21-7 (alk. paper)
  1. Women historians--Fiction. I. Title.
  PS3613.A455P37 2011
  813'.6--dc23

    2011031232

Printed in the United States of America

For Peg

Let the womman telle hire tale.
Ye fare as folk that dronken ben of ale.
Do, dame, telle forth youre tale, and that is best.
—*The Canterbury Tales*

Time Line

500 – King Arthur (if there ever was such a man) would have lived around this time. His legend blossomed in the twelfth century in Geoffrey of Monmouth's book, *Historia Regum Britanniae* (History of the Kings of Britain), ca. 1138, and Wace's *Roman de Brut* (A History of the British), ca. 1155, and in stories told by numerous later authors.

1154 – Henry II (1133-1189) was crowned King of England.

1162 – Thomas Becket (ca. 1118-1170) was made Archbishop of Canterbury.

1170 – Becket was murdered in Canterbury Cathedral by knights in the service of Henry II on December 29.

1220 – Becket's bones were "translated" into a fabulous new shrine in Canterbury Cathedral on July 7.

1387 – Geoffrey Chaucer (ca. 1343-1400) made a pilgrimage to Canterbury around this date to visit the shrine of St. Thomas Becket, the "holy blisful martir." *The Canterbury Tales* followed soon after and flourished in many manuscript copies; it was first published by William Caxton in 1476 and is still in print today.

1509 – Henry VIII (1491-1597) was crowned King of England.

1538 – As part of his reformation against the Catholic Church, Henry VIII ordered the Royal Commissioners for the Destruction of Shrines to strip the English monasteries of treasure and destroy the relics of saints, including those of St. Thomas Becket at Canterbury Cathedral. Glastonbury and Shaftesbury Abbeys were left in ruins.

1817 – Jane Austen (1775–1817), after writing six delightful novels about walking around the English countryside, died and was buried at Winchester Cathedral.

1911 – Hilaire Belloc (1870-1953), having made a pilgrimage to Canterbury, published a description of his experience in *The Old Road.*

1938 – Alfred Wainwright (1907-1991) completed a long walk through the Pennine Hills, which he documented in an offensively sexist journal that was published in 1987.

1997 – Mary Malloy, the author of this book, walked across England, retracing the pilgrimage of the Wife of Bath.

Path of the Pilgrimage

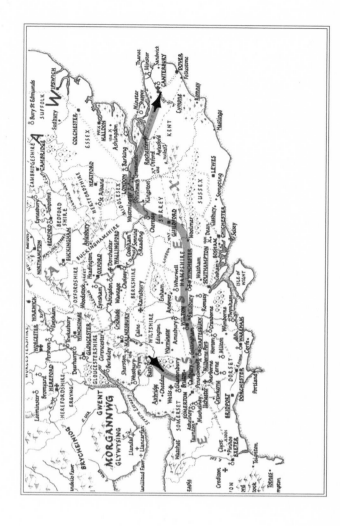

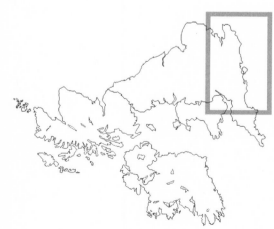

September, 1538

They had to act in secret, and in haste. It was not difficult to haul the wooden cover up to expose the golden shrine; this was a task they had done frequently to bring pilgrims closer to the saint. Opening the sarcophagus, however, was more difficult than any of them had anticipated in the darkness of night and with a desire for silence. Finally, however, they looked upon the skeleton of their saint. It had been laid carefully in the coffin three hundred years before, at the time of its first translation. The long bones of the arms and legs were arranged around the skull, which looked up at them with empty eye sockets from its place in the center of the coffin. When the prior reached in and pulled it out, everyone could see the hole in the crown of the head, where that part of the holy man's tonsure had been severed with a sword.

Four monks arrived with a much plainer coffin, buried in their own churchyard in 1167, the same year their saint had died. Carefully and reverently the two skeletons were exchanged. Three bones from the hand of the saint were kept back, as had been done the last time he had been translated from one tomb to another. The saint had been much taller than the common monk—a man who must have known him in life—but without the flesh, the saint's skeleton could be neatly laid in the smaller coffin.

The prior took the skull of the long-dead monk into his hand.

"What was his name?" he asked.

"He was Brother Osbert Giffard."

"Forgive us Brother Osbert," the prior whispered, kissing the skull, "and look down upon us from your place in heaven. We would not disturb your rest for anything less than to save our saint."

He held out his empty hand to receive a hatchet from one of his monks and gently tapped at the ancient skull until he had created a hole in the crown to resemble the wound of the saint, then he laid the skull of Brother Osbert Giffard, with his other bones, into the shrine of St. Thomas Becket. The sarcophagus was sealed again and the shrine covering lowered into place over it.

The plain coffin was hurriedly returned to the hole from which it had come in the monk's graveyard, though now with a more famous occupant.

"Who will watch this spot and keep the secret of its location?" the prior asked.

"I will," said Thomas Bokland, stepping forward.

Two of his brother monks came to stand beside him, each declaring their willingness to guard the knowledge with his life.

The prior solemnly handed each of them a bone. "Thomas Bokland, William Kent, and Dunstan Hockwold: You must guard this, and the knowledge that it represents, and you must pass it on to one person before you die. In this way, in each generation, three men will know the location of the saint until our holy church is restored in England and the relics of the saint may be returned to his shrine."

William Kent placed the bone of the saint in his pocket. As he walked away the prior stopped him. "Take one of these reliquaries," he said, giving him an enameled box that he had taken from the shrine. "It is a more appropriate home for the Archbishop's finger." William clutched the box to his breast; the smooth enamel was cool to the touch. Along one surface he could feel raised details with his fingertips. He walked quickly to the monk's lodging, where he wrapped the box in cloth and placed it in a linen bag. Then he moved, as ordered, to cheap lodgings near the west gate of the city.

The next day, the monks watched as the bones of Osbert Giffard were pulled from the coffin of Thomas Becket, burned and scattered. The shrine was hacked apart, the gold and jewels that covered it slipped into wooden chests to be shipped to the king, Henry VIII. In their greed and haste the marauding "Royal Commissioners for the Destruction of Shrines" did not even notice that the mortar holding the lid on the sarcophagus was barely dry.

Chapter 1

Lizzie Manning was convinced that if she lived in the same house all her life she would, by the age of seventy-five, have looked at every book on the shelves, no matter how many there were and no matter their condition. But that was before she saw the house of Alison Kent.

Alison's house was full to bursting with books, and with old newspapers and magazines, scholarly journals, marked-up typescripts, glasses of scotch, and overflowing ashtrays— where the long snake-like cylinders of ash indicated cigarettes that had been laid down soon after being lit and never picked up again. It was a curious ancient house, an Elizabethan half-timbered warren of rooms, with good, solid old furniture under the stacks of paper. Lizzie suspected that there might be animals nested in the crumbling thatch, but Alison did not acknowledge in her looks or her actions that anything around her was the least bit unusual. If she recognized that she and her house were eccentric she gave no hint of it.

It was necessary to clear a place for Lizzie to sit, as if the visit was unexpected, rather than an appointment made after almost two months of correspondence. Lizzie could tell that her hostess was scrutinizing her, and information about why she had been invited was parceled out reluctantly and in small pieces. They shared a common friend, George Hatton, who had recommended the American scholar as a competent researcher who might be able to help Alison with a project, but Lizzie still had to prove her worthiness by being sniffed, pawed and licked by Alison's two old hounds, and by a thorough interview. One of the dogs now lay heavily across Lizzie's feet, while she massaged the head and ears of the other.

"I'm not a Chaucer scholar," Lizzie started. George had told her that the job had something to do with a manuscript of *Canterbury Tales,* but he hadn't given her any details of what sort of assistance Alison needed on her project. Her affection for George, and the fact that she had already planned a trip to England, were the reasons Lizzie had agreed to meet Alison. She didn't think there was enough overlap in their interests and expertise to make a collaboration realistic, and she had a pretty fair idea from Alison's behavior that her hostess didn't think so either. She must love George as much as I do, Lizzie thought as she waited for a response.

Alison was abrupt in her answer. "I can handle the literary end of the business."

"Of course," Lizzie said quickly, not wanting Alison to think she had implied any criticism of her scholarly credentials. "I know you are an English professor." She didn't know what to say next. It was difficult not knowing what the agenda was.

Sitting back in her chair, Lizzie perused the room as she waited for the older woman to decide when and how much information to share. It was a fascinating place, filled with wonders, and she looked about her curiously. Shelves crammed with books rose almost to the ceiling on every wall, and furniture filled most of the open spaces on the floor. The thing of greatest interest was an enameled box that sat on the table in front of her, and Lizzie could not keep her eyes from returning to it again and again. She had seen one like it before, with its dull gold sheen against a brilliant blue enamel.

"You may look at it if you like," Alison said, gesturing at the box. "I can see you are curious about it."

Lizzie thanked her and leaned over to examine the object before her. Though it had a substantial look as it sat on its four golden feet, she thought she could probably lift it easily with both hands. The lid was not flat on the top, but had two panels that met at a peak. Two scenes were visible on the side of the box that faced her. Along one of the long panels of the lid, a man was being laid into a tomb. On the side of the box were four golden figures, captured at the moment of a murder.

Taking a deep breath, Lizzie adopted her curator voice. "It is Limoges enamel, I believe."

Alison nodded.

"And depicts the martyrdom of Thomas Becket," Lizzie continued. She looked up to see that Alison was smiling at her.

"Very good," the other woman said. "How did you know?"

"Partly from recognizing the incident," Lizzie answered, pointing out the central figure in the bishop's mitre, and the armored knights attacking him with raised swords. "And partly from having seen a very similar reliquary at the Victoria and Albert Museum," she continued. "I think they bought it from Sotheby's not too many years ago."

"It was 1996," Alison said. "And the museum paid four million pounds for it."

"A lot of money," Lizzie acknowledged. She had suspected the value of the piece when she first spotted it lying next to Alison's ashtray. The hound at her feet stood up and sniffed it, as if he knew what they were talking about, then turned and gave it a quick polish with his tail.

"I suppose you think I should sell it or donate it, given its value," Alison said.

"Not necessarily," Lizzie answered. "If you need money, it could certainly bring you some, but the thing itself is so beautiful and of such historical interest and importance that it might as well be you who loves and appreciates it as someone else." She couldn't help thinking that Alison looked perfectly comfortable in her surroundings and didn't seem to need much beyond a good housekeeper.

Alison was clearly pleased with the answer. She took a small golden key from a drawer in the table and gave it to Lizzie, inviting her to open the box.

The age and value of the artifact made her somewhat hesitant, but Lizzie found the key fit perfectly and turned easily. There was a satisfying click as the lock opened. Her hesitancy now replaced by curiosity, Lizzie put her hands around the box and with her thumbs on the two front corners of the lid, pushed it open and looked inside. She could see a leather-bound volume stuffed with extra pages. There was also a small scrap of dark cloth, a bone, a scallop shell, and two round pieces of glass that looked like they might be lenses from an old telescope.

The book probably held the manuscript she had come to talk about, but the bone and the cloth were the things that captured Lizzie's attention. She tried to control the excitement in her voice as she asked Alison how long the box had been in her family.

"I don't know exactly how long," Alison answered, "but at least several centuries."

Lizzie took a deep breath before speaking. "Is it possible then, that these are actual relics of Thomas Becket?"

"I'm sure that whoever put them in the box believed them to be, but even if the bone has been there since the box was made, there is no guarantee that the relic is authentic." She pulled the bone from the box and held it up to Lizzie. "It is certainly a human finger bone, and I suspect it is from the hand of Thomas Becket, but we can't be positive, as there have been charlatans making substitutions and selling forgeries almost since the day he was murdered." She put the bone back in the box and pulled out the book. "Chaucer makes good use of one such faker in his character of the Pardoner in *Canterbury Tales.*"

Lizzie had recently re-read the book in preparation for this meeting, and smiled as she thought of the character who sold chicken bones as relics of saints, and pillow cases as the mantle of the Virgin Mary. She touched the stiff fabric at the bottom of the box.

"Is this his blood, do you suppose?"

"There are good descriptions of people mopping up his blood and brains with towels and then cutting them up for distribution."

Lizzie picked up the box and looked closely at the exterior detail. The heads of the various people depicted on it were applied separately from the enameling, in what looked like gold. Along the crest of the lid, a decorative frieze held several semi-precious stones.

"A box like this, so beautifully made, and using such expensive materials, was certainly intended for a very special relic," she said. "Blood, brains or bones would certainly all qualify, and Thomas Becket was the most important of the English saints."

"His martyrdom at the altar of Canterbury Cathedral is compelling drama," Alison said, nodding at the depiction of it on the box.

Lizzie returned the box gently to its place on the table and looked at Alison, who held the small book and was now ready to talk about it.

"This is a very early edition of *Canterbury Tales*," the old woman said. "Made by William Caxton around 1483; it is one of the first books printed in English."

Lizzie could not help but think of the tremendous value of that small volume, possibly worth as much as the reliquary at auction. She did not want to ask for it and waited until Alison removed the manuscript pages from it and handed it to her. It was a small book, fitting easily into Lizzie's hand. The binding was loose from having had those extra pages stuffed into it for so many years—maybe even since the book was new, Alison told her.

There was no introduction or title page and the first line was familiar: "WHAN that Aprille, with his shoures soote. . . ." As she leafed through the book, Lizzie saw several charming woodprints illustrating passages from the book, including one that showed the pilgrims sitting around a table sharing a meal that included wedges of cheese and the head of a boar. She could make out the text in only the most rudimentary way; she had struggled through Middle English texts, including this one, when she was in college, but the archaic language was coupled here with a heavily inked old-English typeface that was almost as foreign to Lizzie as any other unfamiliar language.

"George told me you had a manuscript of *The Canterbury Tales*," she said. "But this early printed edition is just as interesting to me."

Alison reached out to take back the book, which she put down on the table casually, as if its age of more than five hundred years was not impressive. She picked up the sheaf of loose hand-written pages that lived inside it and gently touched the top page; this was clearly, to her, the greater treasure.

"There *is* a manuscript," she said, "but it is not by Geoffrey Chaucer." She gave Lizzie a searching look. "When I confided to George that I was having trouble finding someone to help me with an important project, I told him that my greatest concern was that I did not trust the people around me, and I did not know how I could trust a stranger." She hesitated for a moment, and then said quickly, "George said that I could trust you."

As she reached out to receive the manuscript, Lizzie studied her companion. She was a handsome woman, with a strong square jaw and blue eyes that had faded with age. Her white hair was pulled back into an elastic band at the nape of her neck. Lizzie found that she was warming to the woman as her crust came off.

The manuscript was made up of several dozen pages, neatly folded and covered from edge to edge with a small script similar to that on the printed page, but with a greater fluidity. Lizzie carefully turned over page after page; several words were obscured where ink had come too quickly off the quill and left a black spidery-edged blotch. The last few pages were covered with lines and squares that looked rather like elaborate games of tic-tac-toe.

"I can't read it," Lizzie said apologetically. "What is it?"

Alison sat back in her chair and lit a cigarette. She contemplated Lizzie and Lizzie contemplated her back. It had been a long time since she had seen someone smoke so casually, without any apology or explanation that she was quitting soon. The older woman inhaled deeply and then set her cigarette into an ashtray on the table beside her. She was a tall woman, and seemed stiff as she pushed herself up from her chair and went to a sideboard where she poured herself a glass of scotch and gave it a quick blast of soda with an old-fashioned siphon.

"Do you want one?" she asked Lizzie, holding up the glass.

Lizzie nodded and Alison made her an identical drink before returning to her chair. It was good scotch, strong and peaty. Lizzie wasn't sorry that Alison had cut it with the soda, which was nice and fizzy, though her husband would have hated to see such a good whiskey diluted.

"I'm going to trust you," Alison said.

The eyeglasses perched on the end of her nose were small enough that Alison mostly looked over them, but now she tilted her head back to see Lizzie more clearly. Lizzie met her eyes calmly, curiously. She took a sip of her drink and let the fire of the alcohol sit for a moment in her mouth as she waited for her hostess to speak again.

"There are certain parties here in England, and in the larger world of Chaucer scholarship, who would love to get their hands on what I have here," Alison said finally. "I am concerned about protecting it until I can publish it myself."

People unaccustomed to the world of academia might have been surprised by such a suspicious approach to the work of an author dead for six hundred years, but Lizzie understood Alison's concerns perfectly. Professional reputations, promotions and job security were all tied to original scholarship, documented and shared in publications. She assured her companion that she could be trusted to keep Alison's information confidential until she was ready to share it.

"This is the diary of a woman who made a pilgrimage from Bath to Canterbury in 1387," Alison said, taking the manuscript. "She was a weaver from Bath and her name was Alison. I am named for her."

"Dame Alison?" Lizzie asked. "Like the Wife of Bath character in *Canterbury Tales*?" Even as she said it, she realized the potential importance of those old pieces of paper. "Do you think she could have been the basis for the character in Chaucer's work?"

Alison continued to give her the same steady look. "I'm certain of it," she said.

The importance of the diary was now obvious, but Lizzie still didn't know what role she might play in any work to be done on it.

"If I don't have expertise in the topic, how can I help you?" she asked.

"I need a smart and clever researcher," Alison said, watching for Lizzie's response. "Someone who might have new and original ideas on an old topic." She leaned forward in her chair. "And someone who can walk for me."

"Walk for you? Where?"

"Across England," came the answer. "From Bath to Canterbury to retrace the pilgrimage described in the diary."

The request was so completely unorthodox and unexpected that Lizzie hardly knew what to think of it. "Isn't that like two hundred miles or something?" she asked.

"Something like that."

Lizzie laughed. "I think I could do the first part of what you describe," she said. "I am a smart and clever researcher, but what made you think I could or would walk two hundred miles?"

Alison sat back again and shrugged. "It was George's idea," she said. "Frankly, when I saw you today my first thought was very similar to yours. You don't look like much of a walker."

Lizzie was offended by the comment. She was not, in fact, much of a walker, but she didn't like to have it be observed so casually by someone who was still almost a stranger to her. She put her arm across the plump roundness of her midsection as Alison continued.

"I don't know what George was thinking. Ordinarily he gives me such excellent advice and recommendations."

Lizzie took a long swig of the scotch. "Just because I am not in the habit of making long walks doesn't mean I'm not capable of it," she insisted impulsively.

She knew it was a mistake to make such a brazen declaration without considering the implications, but she could not help herself. It was not that she felt she needed to protect some image of herself as an example of physical strength or prowess; she had no pretensions to anything of the sort. She prided herself on being an intellectual—for her it was long stretches in the library and at the computer, not long rambles in the country. Maybe it was the strength of the scotch, or the personal nature of the challenge, or the obvious importance of the work, but even acknowledging the mistake of impulsiveness, Lizzie felt suddenly compelled to accept the strange job.

"When would I start?"

The look on Alison's face was a mixture of surprise and amusement. "Are you saying you would actually do this?"

"Yes," Lizzie said, nodding her head to convince both herself and her hostess. "Yes, I think I might." She asked again about the schedule. Her husband, Martin, had been commissioned to complete a work of public art in Newcastle. They were in England over the Christmas holiday to finalize the details, and planned to return in the spring when he would begin the work in earnest. Lizzie would teach the winter term at St. Patrick's College, and had arranged to take a sabbatical for the spring term to be in England with Martin. She had thought she would spend the time working on a book on museum collections, but every minute that her mind turned to the idea of Alison's project, with all its physical and intellectual challenges, the more she thought it was meant to be.

"When would I need to start?" she asked again, explaining her teaching schedule to Alison.

"The original pilgrimage began in the last week of April and took a month," Alison said, the tone of her voice making it obvious that she was not yet convinced that Lizzie was the right person for the job.

Lizzie pretended not to notice Alison's tone. "Of course," she said with a broad smile, "Wan that Aprille. . . ."

"There would be preliminary work," Alison said cautiously.

"I could be back here by the middle of April. Would that be enough time?"

Alison still hesitated. "George said you had an eye for detail, and that would be extremely valuable to me." She paused. "I need someone who will notice details in the landscape, in villages and churches, and be able to tie them to descriptions in the text."

There was a long silence as each woman considered the direction the conversation was going, and the implications of Lizzie undertaking the pilgrimage. It would put them in close contact and it would require that they trust each other.

Lizzie was the first to speak, asking Alison why she had not undertaken the project herself.

"I have a bad hip," Alison said matter-of-factly. "It's too

bad I didn't discover this manuscript twenty years ago, because I *was* a good walker."

Ignoring the insult implied in the comment, Lizzie asked if the route could not be retraced by car.

"Parts of it, of course," was the answer. "And I have driven back and forth to Canterbury dozens of times. But some parts of the path lie along ridge tops and through forests. They are not accessible by car."

Lizzie imagined herself out on a high ridge in the English countryside. In the hour they had talked she had gone from being skeptical about the project to having an earnest desire to undertake it.

"I'd like to do this," Lizzie said. "George was correct; I am the right person for this job."

When Lizzie left the house an hour later a deal had been struck between the two women. All that was left was to explain to her husband that she would be walking across England, and then to do it.

Chapter 2

George Hatton was very traditional in his celebration of Christmas. In his house, Hengemont, only the housekeeper, Helen Jeffries, was more observant of the details that defined the holiday. As they drove up the long drive, Lizzie saw that the familiar face of the house was illuminated by candles in every window.

"I wonder how long that took Helen," her husband wondered. "And how often she has to replace them to keep them lit?"

Lizzie answered that she was glad they had arrived at dusk, so that Helen was probably still on the first round of candles.

Her feelings about the house and its occupants were filled with complications, contradictions and confusion. Even though she had known the place and its people for only a year, she had developed deep and passionate relationships, of love and hatred, with George Hatton's sons Edmund and Richard.

Lizzie was related to both George and his servant Helen through her Irish great-grandmother, who had worked in the house and secretly wed the heir when she became pregnant. His parents swiftly annulled the marriage and the unfortunate girl was shipped off to America. These were facts that the descendants had only learned in the past year, and it had been a time of enormous tumult. George's oldest son, Richard, lost most of the family's fortune in bad investments and killed himself in the aftermath. Lizzie had had no love for Richard, who tried to poison her, but she dearly loved Helen and George, and especially George's younger son Edmund, with whom she shared a warm bond. When she received the invitation to spend Christmas with the Hattons and the Jeffries, she did not think that she could refuse.

The knowledge of the relationship between her family and George Hatton's family had been a burden to Lizzie in the last year. She struggled with the fact that she knew something about her father's parentage that he did not. That his grandmother had chosen to keep it a secret through the whole of her long life seemed important to Lizzie, and she did not see how she could just blurt out information that would fundamentally change her father's past and his notions of his identity. The subject was much on her mind when Lizzie was called to be with her father after a stroke debilitated him in September.

"Is there something on your mind?" he had asked her one night, rousing from sleep. It was past midnight and Lizzie was taking turns with her mother and siblings to sit with him through the night. His speech was slightly slurred from the stroke, but Lizzie understood the question and knew that he sensed her discomfort.

She didn't know how to answer; she didn't want the relationship of his grandmother and the Hattons to be the last thing she ever spoke to him about. "I love you," she said, reverting to the easiest phrase on her list of things that must be said.

Her father began to laugh but it quickly turned to coughing and Lizzie rose from her chair to stand beside his bed. She put her hand on his. "Sorry," she said, "I didn't think it was so funny."

He squeezed her hand. "It wasn't funny," he said, wiping his mouth with a handkerchief. "It just wasn't what I was expecting. You looked so pensive," he continued. "As if you were waiting to tell me some enormous secret."

She pulled the chair right up to the bed and put her elbows on the mattress, holding his hand between hers. "If I had a big secret, would you want me to tell it to you?"

"Now?" he said. He looked as if he were ready to laugh again, but controlled the impulse to keep from coughing. "Now, when I'm dying and can't do anything about it you are going to tell me your secrets?" He smiled at her and reached his hand up to touch her cheek. "If it has anything to do with sex, money, religion, drugs, arrests, secret marriages or unwanted pregnancies, I don't want to know," he said, struggling to get through the long list.

Surprised at how close he had come to the truth in several categories, Lizzie pulled back a bit.

"What?" the old man insisted. "Did you have an abortion?"

"Of course not," Lizzie answered quickly. She took his hand again to reassure him. "And I'm not even talking about myself."

"Is this one of your sisters then?"

Again Lizzie quickly assured him that it wasn't. She was regretting having brought up the topic at all when her father said, "This isn't something about your mother, is it?"

"Oh God no," Lizzie said. "What could you be thinking?"

"Well, what are *you* thinking," he asked.

It was clear that he was getting agitated and Lizzie did not see how she could get herself out of the awkward conversation easily. "I learned something about your grandmother when I was in England," she blurted.

Her father relaxed instantly. "My grandmother?" he said with a smile. "Don't worry about her." He closed his eyes as if in thought, but after a few minutes passed Lizzie began to think he might have gone to sleep. She remained motionless, her hand held to the bed by the weight of his. Perhaps he *had* known his grandmother's story, she thought. Maybe *he* was the one who kept the secret all those years, not she. He opened his eyes again.

"What were we speaking about?" he asked.

"Nothing important," she said softly.

He turned to rest his gaze on her face. "It was my grandmother," he said. "And anything I need to know about her I can learn from her soon enough."

Lizzie felt a tear run unbidden and unexpected down her cheek.

He suffered another stroke and died a week later. Lizzie had told no one else in her family about the relationship with the Hattons. To them, they were simply people for whom she had worked as a researcher, and with whom she had developed a close relationship.

Only Martin knew the whole story and his voice brought her out of her reverie.

"I wonder if it's possible that the candles are electric?" he mused. "Most of the ones you see in Boston are."

"We will find out soon enough," Lizzie said, driving to the back of the house.

Her first entry into the house the previous January had been through the grand main door that brought visitors into the base of the medieval tower, the oldest part of the house, but she felt more comfortable now going to the kitchen entrance. There they found Helen, wiping her hands on an apron as she came through the door and extended her arms to greet them. She gave Lizzie a warm embrace, with all the affection of family, and Lizzie hugged her back.

"Come," Helen said, ushering them directly into the kitchen. "Come and stir the pudding. I can't put it in to cook until everyone in the house has stirred it." She handed Lizzie a wooden spoon and instructed her to give a good stir to the concoction in a large ceramic bowl, and then took the spoon from her and gave it to Martin.

"It smells wonderful," he said as he turned the spoon around and around the bowl, scraping the sticky mixture from the sides into the center. "What is in it?"

"Fruits of various kinds, raisins, and citrus peel, which I have been marinating for weeks in brandy," Helen answered. "Flour, sugar, almonds, eggs, spices, and suet, which I think most Americans find unappetizing, but is necessary to the success of any good pudding."

Martin wasn't sure what that was, but was unfazed when Helen defined suet for him as the hard fat of a cow or lamb. "We use something very similar to that in Mexican cooking," he said. "Manteca—and my mother puts it into wonderful donuts called *roscos de manteca.*"

He was interested in hearing the whole process of how the batter was put into the old pudding molds and lowered into boiling water to cook. Helen was explaining that the process would take the whole night, when Lizzie, fearing they would never leave the kitchen, asked if Edmund had arrived.

"Indeed he has," Helen said, taking off her apron. "I'm

sorry Lizzie, you must be anxious to see them, and he and Sir George are waiting for you."

Helen turned to Martin as she took Lizzie by the arm. "Come back if you want to help me make the posset. It's our Christmas Eve drink and I think you will find that recipe interesting too."

He assured her he would return after he greeted the hosts, and they proceeded through the house to the library. Helen had brought a forest of greens inside; evergreen boughs and holly were entwined around the railing of the grand staircase and laid out on every windowsill and mantelpiece. Lizzie stopped at the bottom of the staircase and looked to see her old friends in the paintings—they had been an important part of her experience when she lived here the previous January.

The reunion with the Hattons was tinged by memories of the losses of the last year, not only Lizzie's father and George's son, but also the collection that had first brought her here as a researcher, and had been subsequently donated to the British Museum. The doors to the empty museum cabinet were closed and a Christmas tree stood in front of them. Lizzie glanced toward it but made no comment. The tree was a nice touch, she thought, and wondered which of them had thought of it.

After a few minutes of conversation, Martin made his excuses and returned to the kitchen, where Helen's Christmas preparations intrigued him. He knew that Lizzie would want to catch up with her old friends and that he wasn't needed for that part of the reunion.

"I'm sorry you won't see Lily while you are here," Edmund said, bringing up a subject that Lizzie had hesitated to address.

"She's with her mother for Christmas?"

Edmund nodded. He and his ex-wife shared custody of their daughter, and she would consequently spend the holiday in London.

"I'll miss being Father Christmas and putting her presents in the pillowcase at the end of her bed," George said sadly. "The holiday is always better when there is a child in the house."

This was not, Lizzie thought, a good way to begin a Christmas visit; happy memories of past holidays often led to morose feelings in the present.

"I suppose you already know," she said, changing the subject, "that I met with your friend Alison yesterday and am going to walk across England for her."

This was news to Edmund, who instantly perked up and asked for details. George actually laughed. "I wasn't quite sure how serious she was about that when we first talked," he said. "She has really convinced you to do it?"

"Not quite. She seemed rather unconvinced that I could do it, and I consequently had to persuade her to *let* me do it." It occurred to her, as she said it, that Tom Sawyer had gotten his fence painted in exactly the same way.

Edmund needed to be brought up to date on the details and they were deep into the conversation when Helen and Martin arrived with a tray of hot drinks.

"Ah, the posset," George said. "It's a Christmas Eve tradition and no one makes it better than Mrs. Jeffries."

"It's a terrific recipe," Martin explained to Lizzie as he handed her a steaming mug. "It's made with milk and sugar, cooked up with bread to thicken it, and then poured over ale."

This description did not seem promising to Lizzie, but the drink was hot and sweet, with a tang from the ale, and flavored with cinnamon. "It's delicious," she said to both her husband and Helen, "just the right thing for a cold night."

As the group drank, Martin leaned casually toward her and whispered, "Helen has invited us to go to Mass with her family at midnight."

When George asked her a few minutes later if the two of them would join him and Edmund in the Hatton family chapel at midnight, she was confused about how to answer. The season of peace was the cause of much public discord and personal conflict, she thought. She asked about her friend Father Folan at the Catholic church, and when she learned he had been transferred to a different parish, decided to go with the Hattons to their ancient chapel, which was more familiar to her.

Lizzie had thought that spending Christmas at Hengemont,

with their quaint and charming English traditions, and with people who were related to her, but with whom her history was too short to include the regrets and irritations that were part of sharing holidays with close family, would amuse her and warm her spirits and be different enough that she wouldn't notice so much that her father was now absent from the planet. But the Hattons had their own disappointments and felt keenly the absence in their circle of Edmund's daughter Lily, who would come down to Hengemont later in the week, and of Richard, whose death had been preceded by so much fear and meanness.

The youngest man in the house was now Peter Jeffries, Helen's 24-year-old son, and Lizzie asked about him when Helen brought the posset in with Martin.

"He and Henry are setting up the Yule log in the main hall," Helen explained. Her husband kept such a low profile in the house that he wasn't generally seen unless one looked for him.

After a toast with the hot mugs, Lizzie excused herself to go and greet them, taking her drink with her. Martin followed.

This room was the oldest in the house, and Lizzie's favorite. It had been the hall of the castle when Hengemont consisted only of the tower.

Henry did not speak often, but when he did it was usually interesting.

"Keep your eyes open as you walk to the service tonight," he said, nodding at Lizzie, "at midnight the sheep in the fields all turn to the east and bow."

"And bow?" said his son. "I always thought you told me they turn to the east and baaaa!"

They all laughed. On this particular Christmas, the servants in the house had more to celebrate than the master, with all his losses.

Near midnight, Lizzie and Martin walked with George and Edmund across the frozen yard to the chapel that stood just outside the stone wall that defined the property. As they entered, a girl from the village gave each of them an unlit taper, and George led the group down the center aisle of the church to the front pew, which had been the Hatton family's place to worship for almost nine hundred years. Martin went in first, then Lizzie, Edmund and George, who sat on the aisle to greet the citizens of the town as they passed. In past centuries, their ancestors had been the serfs and servants of his ancestors, and even with the breakdown of the old aristocracy and the inevitable loss of his fortune, he was still treated with respect by everyone in the church.

Lizzie watched this with interest. She shared those ancestors with George, but the obeisance that he continued to receive from people in a lower hereditary social class was uncomfortable, even distasteful to her. She turned her head to look at Edmund and saw that he was watching her.

"Are you reading my thoughts?" she asked.

He nodded. "You are rather transparent on this topic," he said. They had spoken of it several times when she was previously at Hengemont.

Martin leaned forward to catch their conversation. George was speaking softly to an old woman, and held her hand gently.

"Are you wondering if I will continue this tradition of greeting the rabble when he is gone and I sit at that end of the pew?" Edmund whispered.

"I am, quite simply, unable to see you in that position," she whispered back. "I can easily see you, as a doctor, speaking consolingly and supportively to anyone and everyone, but you know this idea of inherited position bothers me."

"Poor Lizzie," he said, patting her on the arm. "It's your blood too."

"Ah, but mine has been polluted by the rabble."

"Diluted, maybe."

They both laughed quietly and she put her hand on his.

Martin moved again to catch her eye and she smiled at him. She knew he was somewhat jealous of her relationship with Edmund; she moved her hand and Edmund withdrew his.

Lizzie leaned toward her husband and pointed to the bronze plaque that he had designed at her request and mounted on the stone wall of the church. There were hundreds of candles burning on the altar, and several evergreen trees covered with small white lights. The golden metal of the plaque caught the lights and reflected them back, shimmering softly against the darkness of the interior of the chapel.

"It is so beautiful," she said. "I am happy to see it again."

There were carolers at the service, and a nativity play, but the most moving moment of the night was when the priest came down and with his large candle lit George's slim taper. George turned to his son to pass the flame, then Edmund turned to Lizzie and lit her candle from his. Their eyes met and she saw the reflection of the flame flicker there before she turned to her husband and lit his candle from her own. He also looked deeply at her, the flame caught in his warm brown eyes. From candle to candle, the light was passed around the church until the interior glowed. Lizzie looked up to the rafters and down to the stones of the floor, and moved her eyes around the monuments to dead ancestors and wondered that she could share blood, not only with George and Edmund, but with a few hundred dead, memorialized and entombed here over the centuries.

On Christmas Day their small party sat at one end of the massive oak table of the great medieval hall of Hengemont. Helen had decorated the mantle of the big stone fireplace in which the Yule log burned, and a Christmas tree stretched up beyond the height that any of them could reach, and yet was still dwarfed by the size of the room, with its ceiling details disappearing into the gloom high above them.

There was something of a gloom around the table as well. The most comfortable topic of conversation turned out to be Lizzie's upcoming walk, and the research project on the Wife of Bath.

"Last year, the Christmas pantomime in Bristol was *Canterbury Tales,*" Edmund said after several minutes of talking about the route of the pilgrimage.

Lizzie expressed her surprise. "It must have been watered down a lot," she said. "None of the stories are appropriate for children."

"The panto wasn't considered a children's event when I was young," George said. "It was an opportunity for the laboring classes to take a jab at their betters, and they frequently did so in the rudest way possible."

"Be careful, Father," Edmund said, winking at Lizzie. "'Betters' is one of those terms that must be used with caution around Lizzie."

George looked uncomfortable and Lizzie blushed with embarrassment. Edmund was usually not so ungracious.

"But you are right of course," Edmund continued, "it was very much reduced to the bare bones of the story."

Martin asked what story was being told in this year's pantomime and Edmund answered that it was "Hansel and Gretel."

"Much better," George said ironically. "Children and cannibalism. Who could possibly object to that?"

Each of his three companions had a witty remark to make, but all remained silent in deference to the others.

Chapter 3

Lizzie and Martin returned to Boston in time for the New Year, and she began her winter term at St. Patrick's College the following week. On her first day back on campus, Lizzie headed to the library to see her friend Jackie Harrigan, who would be a good sounding board as she devised a reading list on the Wife of Bath, *Canterbury Tales,* and the biography of Geoffrey Chaucer.

Jackie was sitting at her post in the reading room. Around her a few scattered students were looking at reserve readings for courses and making last-minute decisions on registration. She didn't look up when Lizzie came into the room.

"Excuse me, Ma'am," Lizzie whispered loudly as she approached Jackie's desk. "Can you tell me about the middle of English?"

Jackie kept her hand on the book she was reading and looked up, ready to correct her exasperating interruption. When she saw Lizzie she smiled.

"Professor Manning," she said, closing the book. She raised her hand and gave Lizzie's a hard slap. "When did you get back?"

"Just a few days ago."

"And how was the holiday in England? All villagey, I imagine, with chestnuts and pantos and Father Christmas and wassailing."

It occurred to Lizzie for the first time that she had had no wassail, nor even heard the word mentioned when she was at Hengemont. "Hmm," she said, "no wassail. But all those other things and a fairly intriguing wassail substitute called posset."

"Doesn't it bother you that they insist on saying Happy Christmas instead of Merry Christmas?"

"Not in the least," Lizzie said. "And did you have a *happy* Christmas?"

"I don't know, does anybody these days?"

"Not the folks at Hengemont. They are feeling their losses this year. Death and divorce do take their toll on a family."

Jackie nodded ruefully. "Too true," she said.

"But now we are in a New Year and that gives us all hope," Lizzie said cheerfully. "Merry New Year to you, my dear friend!" She leaned over and kissed the librarian on the cheek.

"And a *Happy* one to you," Jackie returned.

A student stepped up to put a book on the desk, and said a quiet hello to Lizzie. After he left, she began to explain her upcoming project to Jackie. Though she trusted her friend, she did not tell her about Alison's manuscript. Unlike herself, Jackie had a wide circle of correspondents in the field, and even if she had not sworn an oath to Alison, Lizzie would not want to put her in the position of having to keep a secret about such an important find.

"I am going to walk across England," Lizzie said, blurting out the news without any preamble. "A literary scholar has hired me to retrace the pilgrimage of the Wife of Bath."

"What?" Jackie said in complete surprise.

"Please," Lizzie whispered, putting a finger to her lip. "Library voice!"

"What?" Jackie said again, equally loudly. "The Wife of Bath? Do you remember the awful story she tells in *Canterbury Tales?*"

"Of course," Lizzie insisted. "I'm not a cretin, and I just reread it a few weeks ago."

"It is awful!"

In her short discussion with Alison in Bath a few weeks earlier, the story told by the Wife of Bath in Chaucer's work had never come up. It wasn't part of the manuscript and so it clearly wasn't on Alison's mind at the time.

"In fact," Jackie continued, "the first time I read the book I thought how awful it was for Chaucer to put *that* story in *her* mouth. When we read about her in the prologue she's an impressive independent woman for her time, she has her own income from being a fine weaver, she's had an active sex life with multiple husbands, she's traveled all over Europe and the Mediterranean, and she's very well read—though Chaucer mocks her for that."

"So it is the story she tells that you object to and not the character herself?"

"Yes, of course," Jackie said. "In fact I wrote a paper in grad school speculating that Chaucer must have had a real woman as his model. He fell in love with her and when she rejected him, punished her by making her into a caricature in his book and having her tell a raunchy story where a rapist creep gets rewarded for his deed by a bunch of women who should have known better."

Lizzie stared at her in astonishment. It was very hard not to confide to her right then that there very likely *was* such a woman, and she had left a document. She decided to contact Alison and ask if she could bring Jackie into their circle.

"And Chaucer was a rapist," Jackie added, not noticing Lizzie's response to her last speech. "Did you know that?"

"I did not," Lizzie said, emphasizing the last word. "Is all this in the paper you wrote? And if so, can I have a copy of it?"

"It is and you can, but I will have to dig through my files to find it. I wrote it so long ago that the electronic version is on a diskette that I can't even play anymore. I'd have to go to the Science Museum to find an old computer to read it."

"But you have a paper copy?"

Jackie said that she did and promised to find it for Lizzie. "I should have it by Thursday," she said. "Are we on for lunch? It's a long time since we've all been in town at the same time."

"Geminiani's at noon," Lizzie answered. "I'm looking forward to it."

Chapter 4

When her business allowed it, Rose Geminiani always joined Lizzie, Jackie, and their friend Kate Wentworth, for their weekly lunches at her restaurant. Consequently a table for four was spread and waiting for them, with a bottle of wine already opened to breathe, and a fresh basket of bread. The day was cold, so the three women from St. Pat's walked quickly across the bridge from Charlestown, where their small campus was located, to Boston's North End, where Rose's restaurant was tucked into a small storefront on Prince Street.

"Happy New Year!" Rose shouted as she saw her friends come through the front door, stomping the snow off their boots. She raced across the restaurant to meet them, simultaneously wrestling them out of their coats and hugging them.

"Everyone, tell me what you did for Christmas," Rose said, speaking fast as she sat them at their table. She waved away a waitress, saying, "It's okay, Tina, I'll order for them." She poured wine into each glass and proposed a toast that they would each have an adventure in the New Year.

"Well, Lizzie already has hers scheduled," Jackie said, matching Rose for speed of talking and launching into a description of Lizzie's proposed walk.

"No fair!" Rose interrupted. "Lizzie had the great adventure last year!"

Lizzie touched her glass to those of each of her friends. "I'm hoping this won't be quite so adventurous," she said with a laugh.

"No death threats?" Jackie teased.

"Absolutely no death threats are anticipated."

Rose and Kate pressed her for details and she explained quickly about the offer from Alison Kent.

"You are going to walk how far?" Rose asked, shaking her head with disbelief when Lizzie answered.

"I don't remember the details of *Canterbury Tales*," Kate said. "Can one of you give me the short version?"

"It was written at the end of the fourteenth century and describes the travels of a group of people to Canterbury on a pilgrimage to visit the tomb of St. Thomas Becket," Lizzie started.

"They met at a tavern in London and decided to travel together," Jackie continued, "and their host suggested that they amuse each other by telling stories along the way."

"Ah yes," Kate said, "I remember now. There were some *very* naughty schoolboys in 'The Miller's Tale.'"

Rose's attention had been divided between listening to the conversation and supervising her staff, but Kate's comment brought her fully back to the discussion. "I remember that story too. It wasn't on the reading list at St. Angela's but it managed to make the rounds!"

"We all read that as comedy when we were in high school," Jackie said, "but it isn't clear that the sex in that story was consensual."

Her friends all knew that this was potentially the launching point for a lengthy discourse on the disempowerment of women in literature, a subject they had discussed for many hours at this very table. Rose was disinclined to hear it again and said that she needed to check something in the kitchen. Lizzie remembered that Jackie had written a paper on Chaucer's treatment of the Wife of Bath character and asked her if she brought it. Jackie reached into her bag and pulled out an old typescript, held together by a rusty staple.

"Is this the original manuscript?" Lizzie asked with surprise. "I'm amazed you kept it this long."

"You are a librarian to the core," Kate added. "Not only did you save the thing for twenty-some years, but you were actually able to retrieve it!"

"And you will all be glad I did," Jackie said as Kate reached to take the paper from her hands.

"You got an A on it, of course," Kate said, reading the comment on the last page. "A particularly original and insightful essay. Excellent!"

Jackie grabbed it back and handed it to Lizzie. "You already knew that I was a brilliant student. Now let Lizzie benefit from it."

Rose returned to the table with salads. "Are we still talking about some feminist interpretation of *Canterbury Tales*?" she asked as she passed a plate to each woman.

"As a matter of fact, we are," Lizzie answered. "Jackie wrote a paper in college about the Wife of Bath character—the one whose path I will follow."

"Do we like her or not?" Rose asked as she returned to her seat.

"We mostly like her," Lizzie said, "but not the story she told."

"So let's hear the story."

"May I tell it?" Jackie asked Lizzie. "I have reviewed it again since we spoke about this earlier."

"By all means," Lizzie said, making a gesture with her hand.

"Wait," Rose said. "Let me get the pasta, more wine, and arrange for the coffee to come silently at the appropriate moment so that the story doesn't get interrupted."

When all the preparations had been made, Jackie cleared her throat and began.

"Back in the old days before Catholicism killed all the elves and fairies, a lusty bachelor knight from King Arthur's court raped a young virgin whom he encountered near a river. His crime was discovered and he was sentenced to death. The Queen—who must have been Guinevere, but she is not mentioned by name in the story—stopped the execution and gave him a chance to save himself. He had to return to the court within one year and answer the question: 'What is the thing that women most desire?' He went off on the quest, traveling around the countryside, asking the question of everyone he met, encountering a group of fairy maidens along the way, and finally meeting a horrible old hag."

Jackie stopped to take a few mouthfuls of food and Kate

asked why every woman above the age of thirty in fairy tales was either a witch or a hag or both. "I think I'd recognize a hag, of course, because she would be ugly and poor, but is that it? Does she need to be evil?"

"No," Jackie said, wiping her mouth with her napkin and taking a sip of her wine. "Ugly and poor pretty much does it, but the kicker in this case is that she is the only one who knows the answer to the queen's question."

"Does she tell the lusty knight?" Rose asked.

"Not at first," Jackie continued. "She made him agree to take her back to court with him and, if she can provide the right answer, to give her whatever she asks for. Off they go then, like some ticking bomb in a Bruce Willis movie, with the hours and minutes racing down to the end of his allotted year."

"And of course they make it just in time," said Rose.

"Of course," Jackie said, "and, as expected, she knows the right answer."

The women at the table all leaned forward. "Okay," Kate said, "let's have it, what is the thing we most desire?"

"Let me," Lizzie said, lifting her wine glass. "The thing we most desire is to be masters of our husbands!"

There was an anti-climactic moment of silence.

"That's it?" Kate and Rose asked simultaneously.

"What else?" Jackie said facetiously. "As the Wife of Bath tells the story, everyone in the court has a moment where they slap themselves on the head and say 'Oh my God! She's absolutely right!' 'Why didn't I think of that?' et cetera."

"What does the hag want from the knight?" Kate asked.

"I hope she said that he should get his balls chopped off for raping the girl," Rose added.

"Oh no," Jackie said dramatically. "The hag insists that the knight marry her!"

"Oh for God's sake!" Rose said. "How offensive is that! She wants to marry the rapist?"

Lizzie told them that the worst part was yet to come. "The knight and just about everybody else in the palace is ready to barf. I mean, he may be a rapist, but she is even worse, being all those really awful things like ugly, poor, low class, and old. But he's a gentleman, so he does it. That night in bed she harangues him about what a jerk he is for being so shallow, insensitive, and snobbish, which seems to be exactly what he deserves, but then the story goes awry. For no reason whatsoever, the old hag turns into a beautiful young maiden and gives him a choice, 'Would you like me to be beautiful by day and ugly by night?'"

"Thereby allowing him to show off a babe to the court, but being required to have sex with an ugly broad," Jackie added.

"Or would you have me beautiful by night and ugly by day?"

"Thereby insuring good sex, but risking extreme embarrassment in front of his pals."

Lizzie finished the story. "He, finally having learned something, says 'You choose.' And then, Hooray! That was the right answer, so now she will be beautiful all the time!"

Rose and Kate were outraged at the outcome.

"That is a horrible story, I absolutely hate it!" Kate said, throwing her napkin onto the table.

"And I will go back and read 'The Miller's Tale' with fresh anger," Rose declared with a wink. "How did the other pilgrims like the story?"

"They loved it," Jackie said. "'You go girl!' they shouted. 'You certainly do know a lot about relationships between men and women!'"

"As the company was made up almost entirely of men and nuns, they pretty much had to rely on the Wife of Bath for a woman's wisdom on relationships," Lizzie explained.

"She had been married five or six times," Jackie said, finishing her glass of wine and accepting a refill from Rose.

By now, Rose had opened a third bottle of wine and a fairly bawdy discussion followed of what women really desired most. With each answer they laughed louder until all the other diners had either left the restaurant or moved closer to hear more clearly.

Chapter 5

During the weeks leading up to her departure for England, Lizzie read the Wife of Bath portions of *The Canterbury Tales* again in a side-by-side translation from Middle English to modern English, and a mountain of scholarly criticism on the text and its sources.

Kate stopped into her office one day with a gift and a request. The gift was a book called *A Pennine Journey: The Story of a Long Walk in 1938*, by Alfred Wainwright; the request was that she be able to join Lizzie for some portion of the walk. The walking part of the project was, in fact, much better suited to Kate than Lizzie. Kate was captain of St. Pat's research vessel, *St. Brendan's Curragh,* and was a runner and adventurer. She was very fit, and undaunted by the prospect of a walk of a few hundred miles.

"This guy devised a walk across England that I have frequently considered following," Kate explained as Lizzie opened the book, "from St. Bee's Head to Robin Hood's Bay."

She had a road map of England, which she laid across Lizzie's desk. "This path goes across a much narrower part of England than you are walking, but I thought you might like to see it."

"The names alone are enough to capture the imagination," Lizzie said, looking as Kate traced her finger along the route.

"Here is Bath and here is Canterbury," Kate continued, putting a finger at each end of Lizzie's path. "What intermediate points will you stop at?"

Lizzie regretted that Alison had been so mysterious about the details.

"I'm not sure," Lizzie said, "as I am not in charge of the

itinerary, but I imagine at least every place that has a medieval cathedral, so Glastonbury, Salisbury, Winchester and London."

Kate pulled dividers from her bag, a standard tool of a navigator, and measured ten miles along the key with the two points of the instrument. Then she walked it across the map. "You'll have to make eight or ten miles a day to do this in a month," she said. "If you start, say, on April twentieth, that would put you in Salisbury around the fifth of May." She snapped the dividers shut and put them back in her bag. "I'll join you there!"

The advantage of having someone along who was good company, experienced at navigating and an efficient planner was clear to Lizzie, but she balked at accepting.

"I'm afraid my pace will be so much slower than yours," she said apologetically. She knew she really should be out walking every day now, but with the snow and all. . . .

"Don't worry about that," Kate said kindly. "I feel that having you as my personal guide to history and literature will make this much more fun than doing the Wainwright walk with anybody else!"

Lizzie thought about it. "Well, if you don't join me until the middle part, I will hopefully be accustomed to the business when you arrive."

"This guy probably won't be your model," Kate said, tapping a finger on the Wainwright book, "but he talks about what it is like to walk a pretty good distance every day."

"I will read with interest!" Lizzie said. "Thanks for this."

"Tell me more about the nature of a pilgrimage," Kate asked. "You know that I was raised by heathens." Kate's family had been in New England for generations and Lizzie knew for a fact that her grandfather had been a Unitarian minister.

"You probably have actual Pilgrim ancestors!" Lizzie joked, "though I'm sure they never let any saints' bones into Plymouth."

"I think they were more into allegorical pilgrimages, like the one in *The Pilgrim's Progress.*"

"Yuck," Lizzie said. "That book was such a disappointment."

"I only read it because the March sisters liked it in *Little Women*, but it was very very dull, especially for a 12-year-old—which I was when I first tackled it."

"A good pilgrimage requires the bones of a saint," Lizzie said.

Kate asked her what bones were in England and Lizzie was sorry to report that none of the bones that would have defined the pilgrimage of the Wife of Bath survived. "One of the things Henry the Eighth did at the time of the Reformation was to send around a gang of pillagers to destroy all the relics and it is a real shame because they had some corkers."

She described some of the relics that had been viewable in England in Chaucer's time. Bones were the most popular, often held and displayed in reliquaries that were shaped like the body part from which they had come, with heads, arms and hands being the most popular. "You would not believe how many heads there are of John the Baptist!" Lizzie said to her friend. "There are something like ten heads in various collections around the world, plus teeth and other bones, and even the block on which he got his head chopped off."

"I hadn't realized there were so many fakes around so early."

"Many, if not most of the relics in medieval times were fakes. It wasn't until five centuries after the time of Christ that relics began to be venerated, so who, for instance, would have saved pieces of the true cross, or the head of John the Baptist? Or the manger in which Christ was born? There were pieces of that all over England in the Middle Ages. Before Becket's murder in Canterbury Cathedral, they already claimed to have the table of the last supper, the stone from which Christ ascended into heaven, and the *coup de grace,* a piece of the clay used by God to make Adam!"

"Who would ever have believed any of that?" Kate scoffed.

"I think wanting to believe is a big part of it," Lizzie answered philosophically. "These objects have power because we imbue them with meaning through faith and imagination."

"But that doesn't actually make them either real or powerful."

Lizzie agreed this was so.

"I begin to understand the Reformation tendencies of Martin Luther and Henry the Eighth," Kate said. "These things had really gotten out of control."

"But that doesn't mean that relics have gone away. People still crave a tangible connection to fame. Hair clippings from pop stars get sold on eBay for incredible prices!"

"How do you even know that?" Kate asked, astonished.

Lizzie laughed. "How do you *not* know it? It seems to me that news like that is everywhere!"

Kate had a collection of sand and shells, collected from places she had sailed, and Lizzie said that was a collection of relics too. "They are relics of places and experiences," she said. "And it was common to sell pieces of famous ships when they got broken up," she added, thinking of other maritime things. It reminded her of an exhibit at the Maritime Museum in Greenwich that she had seen on her last trip to England.

"Now that I am warming to the subject, I have just realized the relics that are still in England," she said enthusiastically. "Just because the bones of saints are gone does not mean that the British have lost their desire to seek the magnificent and the historical in the tangible. In Greenwich, I saw the coat that Admiral Nelson was wearing when he was shot at Trafalgar, the bullet that killed him, and his bloody socks."

"I guess there might have been a Nelson cult after his death that could have been something like the Becket cult that flourished earlier," Kate said thoughtfully. "They were both martyrs to their cause."

She asked Lizzie if the lack of relics would make her pilgrimage less meaningful.

"Not at all," Lizzie answered. "I'm in this for the historical adventure, not the religious experience." She added that the Wife of Bath had probably not undertaken the pilgrimage as a religious exercise either. "None of those jolly tradespeople in *Canterbury Tales* were particularly holy or reverent, just the opposite! But the pilgrimage was a legitimate way to see the world. It was an excuse for travel within a well-developed and acceptable framework. It was like a guided tour with published itineraries, specified routes, souvenir shops, and travelling companions. It allowed a woman like the Wife of Bath to travel by herself in safety, without losing dignity or blemishing her character."

"Well then, 'Onward History Soldiers!'" Kate said, starting to sing.

Lizzie stopped her before she could get too far in extemporaneously rewriting the old hymn. "I hope that won't be our theme song while walking," she said.

"Do we need a theme song?"

"I'm not sure," Lizzie said, "I will probably sing while walking by myself, but we can still put a duet to a vote for that portion of the walk when you join me."

"I'll vote for a Beatles song."

"I will ponder my choice in the weeks to come," Lizzie said, but she could not, for the rest of the day, get Kate's damn hymn out of her head.

Chapter 6

There was a bridge under construction in her house when Lizzie arrived home. Her husband, Martin Sanchez, had an international reputation as a painter and had been commissioned to create a mural on a public building in Newcastle-upon-Tyne, the great industrial city in the north of England. For several months he had been putting together the various elements that identified the city, including coal mines, ships, trains, fish, a castle and several British footballers, captured running out of the painting and onto the street, where he planned to paint their feet just emerging onto the sidewalk. He had included a crate of his favorite ale among the cargo piled high on a pier, and now he was sketching in the arch of a bridge, which framed the whole work and tied the disparate images together.

"I love it!" Lizzie said as she plopped into her favorite chair and looked up at the expanse of paper on which he worked.

"Unfortunately, I've completely lost the light, but I have to finish this section of the bridge while I have it clearly in my mind."

Martin's studio rose two stories high on the back of their South Boston row house. It had windows almost from floor to ceiling on three walls, but the short winter days were frustrating him.

"Are you on schedule with the work?" Lizzie asked him.

"Mostly," he answered. "I think I have everything in it that's going in it, but I need to look over my notes again from all the various conversations I've had with folks in Newcastle over the last year, and just make sure one more time that I'm not missing any of the components that people thought were important." He spoke into his work as he added details to the riveting of the bridge, but Lizzie was used to talking to his back after so many years of watching him from this position.

"Do you need this light?" she asked, moving the lamp on the table near her so that she could take a first look at the Wainwright book Kate had given her.

"Hey!" Martin said quickly. "Put that back! I need it where it was."

Lizzie angled the shade back up to the paper where her husband was working.

"Just a bit to the right," he said. "That's it." He never turned around.

"I'm going off with Alfred Wainwright," Lizzie said as she left the room. She thought she heard a grunt of acknowledgement, but couldn't be sure.

Lying on a couch in the living room with a cup of tea and a warm afghan, Lizzie opened the book again. "Tell me about making a long walk," she said as she leafed through the pages. Wainwright was a stylish writer with good descriptions of the English countryside, but he quickly made Lizzie realize just how ignorant she was of the undertaking to which she had committed herself. This doyen of walkers traveled some twenty miles a day, in the process climbing, crossing and descending ridges of 2000 feet. He knew his pace so well, he claimed, that after a careful study of the map and the landscape, a quick glance at his watch would tell him his exact position.

From the day she had so insistently demanded that she could do this thing, there had always been some doubt in Lizzie's mind about her ability to actually complete a two-hundred-mile walk in thirty days, but she had pushed those doubts aside with bravado because the project sounded interesting. Reading the account of someone who actually knew what he was doing made her see clearly that she did not.

She called Kate. "Yikes!" she said. "You were right that Mr. Wainwright cannot be my model." She paused, twirling a long strand of hair around her finger. "Can I actually do this?" she said finally. The question sounded more plaintive than she intended.

"Of course you can," Kate answered without hesitation. "I

thought you'd like the book because he describes the sort of paths we'll be on."

"I guess I hadn't realized quite how serious the English are about this stuff."

Kate began to describe a group she knew of that worked hard to keep access open to the ancient footpaths in Britain, even as private property owners increasingly objected. "There is a society of ramblers in England that tries to get people out on each of the paths every year," Kate explained, "just to insure that they remain accessible to the public."

Lizzie remembered the "Public Footpath" signs that delineated paths she had walked on near Hengemont. Some of them went along the edges of cultivated fields or grazing grounds of animals. "Wainwright said that he was afraid of getting into a field with a bull, and now so am I," she wailed.

Kate laughed. "That was seventy years ago and I think the terrain was a bit wilder."

"You know that he wore a flannel suit, complete with vest and tie, he carried no other clothes, and slept in his suit at least twice?"

"Yeah, but you don't have to. I have to admit that I haven't read the whole book. I've known of it for a long time though."

"I have no idea what my pace is."

"That's okay. This isn't a race and it will be your primary occupation for a month."

"I'm glad you're coming along," Lizzie said, her voice full of emotion.

"Me too! The more I think about it the more excited I am at the prospect."

Lizzie returned to the book and quickly skimmed the rest of the text, her fear and frustration turning to anger. She sat up and put her feet on the floor, reaching into her purse for a marking pen, and highlighted several passages where Wainwright described what he thought of women. He had never, he wrote, "witnessed genuine enthusiasm in one of them." (Sometimes there was the "pretense of it" but the "divine spark" was missing.) In another passage he wrote, "it is the comparative deficiency in intellect that makes woman's claim for equality with man pathetic."

The sound of Martin in the kitchen brought her to her feet. "Listen to this," she called as she moved to find him. "Alfred Wainwright says that women are 'strangers to dependability' and 'have not the rigid standards of men, nor the same loyalty.'" She made little rabbit ear gestures with two fingers to identify the quoted passages. "He wrote this in 1938! It is as if nothing changed in the six hundred years since Chaucer!"

"Isn't this the man you said you were going away with?"

"Not anymore!" She tossed the book onto the kitchen counter. "He is banished to the rubbish heap, as he would say. My God! What English women have had to put up with for the last thousand years!"

"What is that, my love?" Martin asked.

"English men!" She described the conversation at lunch. "The story the Wife of Bath tells in *Canterbury Tales* is really bothering me, especially since I am about to literally follow in her footsteps. But Jackie has an interesting take on it, and even wrote a paper in college about how Chaucer might have been punishing a real woman by putting that story in her mouth."

"Did you tell her about the manuscript journal?"

Lizzie pushed herself up to sit on the kitchen counter as Martin prepared their dinner. "Alison absolutely swore me to secrecy. Jackie has no idea how close she is to the truth—that there was an actual Wife of Bath."

"Does Alison know that I know?"

"She does." Lizzie reached out to touch Martin with her toe. "But she isn't worried about you because you don't know any Chaucer scholars. Jackie, on the other hand, corresponds with bunches of them. I sent Jackie's paper to Alison, though, and asked if I could bring her into the sacred circle." She left her perch to set the small table in their kitchen as she saw Martin put the final touches on dinner.

"I've been reading *Canterbury Tales*, too," he said, deftly turning two pieces of fish onto plates and adding rice. He pointed with his elbow and told her there was a salad in the refrigerator.

"And what do you think of it?"

"Chaucer clearly didn't think much of the church, despite

the fact that half his characters are in the clergy and all of them are on a religious pilgrimage!"

"I read in a biography that Chaucer once beat a friar and was fined two shillings as punishment, so he wasn't exactly a reverent man, but it still seems amazing that he got away with being so disdainful of the Catholic Church."

"Ha!" Martin laughed. "That must be why friars live up Satan's 'arse' in the book!"

"That is a particularly compelling image," Lizzie said. She complimented him on the fish before continuing. "One has to keep in mind that the fourteenth century was a really a low point for the church, with lots of false relics, dubious indulgences, rich bishops, and fornicating priests. It was also when there were two competing popes, so it isn't that surprising that people, even the most faithful, must have begun to have doubts."

"The most troublesome story to me is the one told by the prioress, who is a rich old hag and a raving anti-Semite, despite the fact that she runs a convent. Her description of the horrible Jews, who murder innocent little Christian children just to throw their bodies into muck heaps, is absolutely disgusting."

Lizzie agreed that it was the most offensive story in the book. "But all the clergy come off badly. The monk is rich, the pardoner is a crook, the friar is a womanizer, and the summoner is a drunken blackmailer."

They ate in silence for a few minutes.

Martin was the first to speak again. "Chaucer was kind of a creep, wasn't he?"

Lizzie looked up at her husband. "Is that it? It's true that the more I read the angrier I get." She paused. "But perhaps that is his genius—that his themes are so human that we are still battling the same bad behaviors. It's pretty impressive that he is still getting such a rise out of us six hundred years later."

"I have to admit, some of it is hilarious," Martin said sheepishly. "The 'Summoner's Tale' is a great big fart joke!"

"Rose Geminiani said that at St. Angela's High School 'The Miller's Tale' got passed around under the desks because they weren't officially allowed to read it."

"Ah, 'The Miller's Tale,'" he said, smiling. "Chaucer did tap into a deeply perverse part of the adolescent brain with that one."

"So the poor hate the rich and visa versa, schoolboys are constantly thinking of sex, men mock each other by throwing around fart comments, powerful people make deeply offensive racist remarks about people they almost certainly don't know personally, men degrade women, and the Catholic Church is in trouble. It actually sounds quite modern!"

"And probably has since it was first written. That may be its enduring quality."

She reached across the table and put her hand on his. "Thank you for this conversation," she said. "I feel better about Chaucer."

He turned his hand over and held hers. "And the Wife of Bath?"

"I really want to love her."

Martin squeezed her hand. "You will. Chaucer doesn't have the final word on her. She left her own version of the story, and now you get to rediscover it."

Chapter 7

When she entered Alison's house the second time, both the house and its owner had less of a Havishamian feel to Lizzie. There was still a mountainous landscape of books around the perimeters of most of the rooms, but there seemed to be more space and fewer papers in the interiors. Lizzie had tried to argue over the phone that she thought she should stay at a hotel when she was in Bath, but Alison insisted that she must stay in the house with her. The general cleanup must have been for her benefit, Lizzie thought, and she appreciated the effort. The rooms she was given were certainly comfortable. The ceilings were low and the path to get to them went up and down several small staircases, but the bedroom was cozy, the study was airy, and the bathroom had a big claw-footed tub that looked comfortable for a long soak.

It wasn't long after her arrival that the scotch came out and she found herself back in the familiar chair. The Becket reliquary was no longer on the table, and there was no sign of either the early Chaucer edition or the manuscript journal of Alison's ancestress, but a plain black binder had a label with Lizzie's name on it.

"Let's get straight to work," Alison said, handing the binder to Lizzie.

It was evening and already dark outside as they sat at the small table. Alison asked Lizzie if she needed to rest from the time change, but she had spent a few days in London with Martin before they went off to their respective jobs, and she was ready to work. She opened the binder and found a typescript of the journal and a road map of the South of England, across which Alison had drawn a route in red.

"I translated the journal from Middle English for you. It isn't word for word, but I think it captures something of her language."

Lizzie turned over a few pages and found descriptions that fairly leapt off the page, of verdant hills and wooly lambs, of the smell of new-mown hay and the peaty smoke from cottage hearths, and of the sounds of distant bells and of wind rustling new leaves in a spring forest.

"Lovely," she said, looking from the page to her hostess. "Either she or you has a wonderful turn of phrase.

"It's probably a combination of the two of us," Alison responded. "As I said it isn't word for word but it will guide you through the landscape. That is the only copy," she added. "I made the translation as I went and typed it on a typewriter, so there is no chance of anyone else seeing it unless you let it out of your hands, and I cannot stress enough how important it is to me that you not let that happen."

Trying not to be rude, Lizzie asked if there was really a danger that someone might try to steal it.

"Indeed," Alison said pointedly, "someone already has."

When Lizzie asked for more details, Alison told her about her discovery of the Becket box and its contents.

"My father was very ill for a long time," she began. "He had for years told me that there was a family secret that he needed to tell me before he died, and that he left clues to its discovery in case he wasn't able to." She seemed sad as she recounted her father's descent into Alzheimer's and his eventual inability to distinguish fact from fantasy. "He became paranoid about protecting this secret, whatever it was," she explained, "and developed elaborate hiding places around the house where he secreted important documents and cash, but also train schedules and worthless circulars from stores. He lost his ability to distinguish what was valuable from what was not." She described how she had, in the ten years since his death, found piles of things all around the house, tucked into corners, hidden behind or under loose boards, and even pushed into canisters of flour and sugar. "He especially liked to hide things among and in books, and he ruined a number of very good books by cutting holes in the pages to hide things."

At the mention of the books, the two women simultaneously looked around the room. Lizzie didn't want to embarrass Alison, but despite the tragedy in the story, when their eyes met she had to stifle a smile. The number of books in this room alone bordered on absurdity, and as she thought of the rest of the house, with its book-lined corridors, and bursting shelves, the idea of ever finding anything hidden in a single volume struck her as hilarious. The older woman did what Lizzie had worked to hold back, and gave an explosive laugh that was contagious. The two women laughed hard until Lizzie could feel her eyes watering.

"There are a lot of books," she said when she could finally catch her breath.

"Yes there are," Alison admitted.

"Where did you find the Becket reliquary?"

Alison stood and gestured to Lizzie to follow her, wiping her eyes on her sleeve as she walked. They went to a part of the house that Lizzie had not yet seen, and through a low door into a dark room.

"Wait until I turn on the light," Alison said, walking ahead. "There is no overhead light here." She pulled a chain to turn on a green-shaded desk lamp and Lizzie took in the space.

The room was dominated by a big desk with leather chairs on opposite sides. An ancient fireplace, big enough to sit in, looked like it had not been warm in years, and the room was lined with the ubiquitous shelves of books

"This was my father's study," Alison said. "From the time I was a child it was my favorite room in the house; we often sat here and talked of so many topics. He was a real historian, an amateur astronomer, and a lover of literature." Her tone turned regretful. "When he became sick he wouldn't even let me enter, and after he died I avoided coming in here."

She walked behind the desk and put her hand on a shelf at shoulder level. "Until two years ago. We were hiring a new faculty member at the University and the leading candidate was to give a lecture on *The Canterbury Tales,* so I came in here looking for a copy of the book that I could review in advance. My father collected multiple editions of Chaucer."

Lizzie stepped over to the shelf. There were at least twenty different editions of *Canterbury Tales,* bound in vellum, leather, cloth and paper; some had the title stamped in gold along the spine. They took up one full section of shelving, one end of which was bisected by a short board to allow the smallest volumes to be stacked on two smaller shelves.

"When I came to find a reading copy of the book," Alison explained, "I wasn't really interested in these small copies. They tend to be the oldest and are both valuable and hard to read, but I was being methodical and so I pulled each one off the shelf and thumbed through it." Even as she said it, she began to transfer the small books from the shelf to the desk. She pulled Lizzie closer beside her. "And look what I found," she said, tapping on the back of the shelf. "The shelves here are not only half as high, but half as deep as the others."

It was not an elaborate hiding place, simply two pieces of wood, with one joined to the other at a right angle along the center line. The larger of the two formed the false back wall, the other the small shelf. Alison pulled it out easily and showed Lizzie the Becket reliquary sitting on the shelf behind it; the gold and enamel glowed in the reflected light of the desk lamp.

Lizzie couldn't help making a sound as she drew in her breath in surprise. The box and the book inside it were each enormously valuable. How many decades had they sat quietly on the shelf without anyone knowing of their existence?

"I had seen stories in *The Times* about the Becket box that the Victoria and Albert Museum purchased," Alison said, continuing her story, "so I knew what it was and how much it might be worth." She turned to Lizzie. "It is, by the way, not commonly known that I have such a valuable item in my house, and I hope that situation will continue."

"Of course," Lizzie said in response.

Alison replaced the board and the shelf. "The box even had the key in it. I expected that the edition of *Canterbury Tales* hidden in it was probably special, but I didn't then have any idea how special it was. I decided to bring it to the lecture and see if our visiting scholar could tell me something about it. It still had the manuscript pages tucked into it."

Lizzie listened intently as she handed the small books, one after another, to Alison.

Alison talked as she filled the small shelves. "It was the first time I met Dante Zettler and I handed it over to him, without any suspicion of its value, either historical or monetary."

"Dante Zettler?" Lizzie asked. "He's the Chaucer scholar?"

Allison nodded as she continued. "He was interested in the Caxton Chaucer, of course, but he also quickly realized the potential importance of the manuscript. He asked if he might borrow it to study it, and I was cautious enough to refuse, but I later found him at the copy machine, making a copy of it. I don't even know how he got it; he must have taken it from my satchel when I wasn't looking."

"What a sneaky bastard! Were you able to get the copy he made?"

"I think so. I caught him and was furious, but he is, as you note, a sneaky bastard. He insisted that he had simply misunderstood me and repeatedly declared his innocence."

"I hope you didn't hire him!"

"I'm sorry to say that we did. He has a very engaging manner, and his father is a famous literary scholar, which was influential to some of my colleagues who don't know anything about literature."

"That explains his name, I guess."

Alison made a derisive harrumphing sound. "Yes, all the children in the family are named after authors. My colleagues thought that was charming!"

Lizzie had looked up Alison on the website of the University of Bath, and knew that the college didn't offer much in the way of English Literature. "It's not a large department, is it?" she said carefully.

Allison told her that there were only five people who were literary scholars in a larger department of Modern Languages.

"We began as a technical college, we don't have the grand old buildings, and English Literature doesn't even have its own department; most of the students in our courses are foreign students. Dante thought he would be here for a year at most—an interim step on a fast-tracked career, but the economy has been so bad that most colleges have frozen hiring so now he is rather stuck here and it clearly isn't the place he wants to be. He is depending on a book he is writing to propel him up to the next level." She put her hand again on the shelf with the multiple volumes of Chaucer. "His book is on Chaucer's sources for *Canterbury Tales,* and now that he knows that I have a manuscript by a woman who might have been the model for the Wife of Bath, he cannot publish without it."

"Because if he does, and you then come out with your own version of the work, he will look like a chump."

"I had a different word in mind, but yes. His book without this source will quickly be dismissed." She smiled slyly. "He has asked me for it very politely, he has begged me for it, he has demanded it, he even tried to get me drunk. If he had not stolen it out of my purse to copy it on that first day I met him, I might have let him see it by now."

"Well, in my opinion he *is* a chump and this important work is better done by you."

As they returned to their working space in what Lizzie came to call Alison's "den," Lizzie asked her new friend about her own decision to stay at the University of Bath. "Why didn't you move on to another institution where there was a real department in your field?"

"Because I am so tied to this house," Alison answered. "These days I know people who commute from Bath to both Oxford and Winchester, but forty years ago it just wasn't done, and during the period when my father was so ill I never felt I could be far from home." She poured them each a scotch and eased herself into her chair.

For the next hour they drank liberally and talked openly. It was clear that whatever issues Alison had once had about trusting Lizzie were now resolved. She had not had a female confidante for decades and the conversation turned quickly from professional topics to personal ones.

"How do you know George?" Lizzie asked curiously. This was something she had wanted to ask on her first visit, but Alison had been so stern then, and by the time she arrived at Hengemont, the gloom of Christmas had already descended and she couldn't bear to ask George for more details about their friendship.

"George Hatton and I were engaged in college."

This was news that took Lizzie completely by surprise. "Spinsterish" was how she would have defined Alison when she met her. The comparison to Miss Havisham was more apt than she thought, though Lizzie instantly gave herself a mental smack for even thinking such a thing.

"I see the news surprises you," Alison said, watching Lizzie's face as she digested the information. "I was very much in love with George, and he with me."

"Why didn't you marry?"

"My family is Catholic and his parents objected," she said, lighting a cigarette. "Well, so did mine actually, but his put up the bigger stink about it."

"I thought we had done away with those prejudices."

Alison sat, her scotch in one hand, her cigarette dangling from the other, like an old-fashioned movie star and looked at Lizzie, who was beginning to wonder if she was an alcoholic.

"The monarch still can't marry a Catholic, but pretty much all other things are supposed to be equal now. In the fifties, however, there was still a lot of latent hostility."

"Do you know that I am related to George?"

"He told me something about it, but I don't know the details."

"His great-uncle got my great-grandmother pregnant," Lizzie explained. "She was a servant in his house and he married her."

"Oh my good gracious!" Alison exclaimed. She set her cigarette in the ashtray and slapped the arm of her chair. "That must have shaken the foundations of Hengemont!"

"His parents instantly had the marriage annulled and shipped her off to America by herself."

Alison seemed disappointed. "Well she had three disadvantages from their perspective, of which being Catholic was probably the least of them. I assume she was Irish, and she was a servant, and those would have been insurmountable barriers. Class and nationality still divide us."

When Lizzie told Alison that her great-grandfather had committed suicide after his wife was sent away, the old woman was clearly upset by the news.

"The family learned nothing from that, did they?" she asked sadly. "George's father treated me like the ultimate pariah, questioned my ethics, my parentage, and called me a whore, a gold digger and a Papist."

"He would have known about the suicide of his uncle. How could he separate you and George?" She didn't want to add how disappointing George's behavior was. How could he have allowed himself to be persuaded?

Alison seemed to read her thoughts. "Don't blame George, though he was weak. We were young and he simply didn't see how he could separate himself from his family. Do you know he lost two brothers in the War?"

Lizzie nodded. There was a memorial to them in the family church at Hengemont.

"He thought it would kill his mother, and his sister was mentally ill and seemed really to rely upon him. I think he thought that they needed him more than I did." She finished her drink and set the glass down with a clunk on the wood of the table. "He told me I was so strong and they were so weak." She looked at Lizzie as if expecting her to say something.

"What a load of crap," Lizzie blurted; it was all she could think to say.

"That's what I thought. I didn't speak to him for the next forty years."

Lizzie knew that George had married someone else and had three sons. She suspected that it must have been after he was widowed that he sought out a new friendship with Alison.

"Was your family that different from his in terms of money and position?"

"Not in terms of money, we had piles of it. My grandfather built a textile mill just as the woolen industry was taking off in England. But the Hattons are very proud of being able to trace their aristocratic lineage back a thousand years."

"If the Wife of Bath is your ancestress, you must have a family tree that goes back at least six hundred years."

"Don't think my father didn't fling that at George at the right moment. He grew up with the advantages of money and education and had adopted the manner of the aristocracy, though he didn't have the titles. Even though he never would have let me marry George unless he converted, my rejection by the Hattons hit my father hard."

"Would you have considered converting?"

"Never. And it's not because I am such a strict believer in the doctrines of Catholicism. The Kent family stayed true to their beliefs through centuries of persecution. It would absolutely have killed my father and grandfather if I had even considered leaving the Church. Their faith defined them, as it did their ancestors back to the Reformation."

The conversation turned to textiles. Lizzie thought it was interesting that from the Wife of Bath almost to the present, cloth had been woven into the lives of the Kents.

"Cloth and Catholicism," she said, almost under her breath.

Alison looked at her in disbelief. "That is exactly how my father described my family: cloth and Catholicism. He used to say as a joke that if he ever had a crest, that would be the motto."

"Well it is very apt."

"I can't believe you said that. My grandmother actually wove him a fictional coat of arms with that motto on it. Let me get it." She pushed herself up from the chair as she spoke and walked stiffly to an ancient closet.

"I had it framed for my father at one point," Alison explained, reaching into the back of the closet to pull the object out. "But we never found the wall space to hang it."

She returned to Lizzie and handed her a light frame with an intricate woven picture; there was no glass and the fabric was covered with dust. When she realized this, Alison took it back and tapped the frame several times against the back of Lizzie's chair, then gently brushed at the image with the hem of her skirt. When she gave it back to Lizzie there was a recognizable coat of arms of a loom and a cross. A shuttle with a trailing thread was woven into the design, in the act of producing the motto.

Lizzie left her chair to look at the weaving in the light of a pole lamp in the corner of the room. She tilted the shade until the light caught the still-vibrant colors.

"This is woven?" she asked. "I would have thought it was needlepoint."

"My grandmother was an expert weaver," Alison said.

"That's obvious," Lizzie said. She was impressed not only with the exceptional quality of the work, but with the cleverness of the design. There were numerous visual puns, most of which must have referred to inside jokes that Lizzie didn't understand. In each corner was a monogram.

"This is my grandfather," Alison said, pointing to the top left corner. "D. K. for Daniel Kent." She moved her finger to the right and said "and this is my grandmother. She designed the M.K. signature for her work when she was known as Maggie Kerry, and was able to keep it when she married my grandfather and became the more formal Margaret Kent." Her father's monogram was in the lower left corner and in the bottom right was an A over a W. The A had a flat line at the top, in a style much older than the others.

"Is this for your mother?" Lizzie asked.

"Goodness no," Alison said, taking the piece back and looking at it again. "I don't think my mother was even in the picture when my grandmother made this. That is an homage to our Wife of Bath. That is how she signed her work."

"I thought her name was Alison Kent."

"It was, after she married Roger of Kent, whom she met on her pilgrimage. Prior to that she referred to herself as 'Alison the Weaver,' or simply 'Alison Weaver,' but she continued to use this monogram on her work."

"I love that!" Lizzie said enthusiastically. "I love that she had a signature that is still recognizable six hundred years later, and I love that your grandmother, also an expert weaver, used it to acknowledge her."

"She was an Irish immigrant," Alison said. "Like your great-grandmother. She came here to work in my grandfather's mill."

This was a story of interest to Lizzie and Alison was happy to share it. Her grandmother had been a remarkable woman, she said. Even as she stood all day at the loom her brilliance was recognizable. She had ideas about how to improve production and especially how to make the work more tolerable for the workers. She invented an ear covering to protect against the ferocious noise of the looms. She had ideas about carding and spinning as well as weaving, and thoughts on the orientation of the factory so that the stages of production were better connected through the plant. Day after day she marched up the wooden stairs from her loom to the office where Daniel Kent supervised his mill and told him her ideas. At first he rejected them outright. She was, after all, just an immigrant girl. But over time, as he considered them in unexpected moments, he found that almost every suggestion she made was worth adopting.

He asked her if she would be his secretary, but she refused. She had ideas about design, and wanted to experiment with different ways to set up a loom to achieve them. At her request, he provided her with a loom and watched with fascination as she worked on it day after day and long into the night. He knew the mechanics of weaving, but not the art of it, until he learned it from her. As her ideas and designs were incorporated into the production in the mill, the quality of the woolens became known all over England and he became rich.

"At this point in the story you are probably expecting the marriage and the happy ending," Alison said. "But she was a canny one, was my granny. She once told me that when my grandfather first mentioned that he would like to make all her dreams come true, she told him that the thing she wanted most was a real education, at Oxford University no less."

"Did Oxford accept women when your grandmother was a young woman?"

"There was a college there, St. Hugh's that sought out poor but talented female scholars, and that is where she went. By that time, of course, my grandfather was pretty madly in love with her and went up to see her on weekends; he married her as soon as she finished her degree."

In this house, Alison explained, Maggie Kerry Kent became fascinated by the story of Alison the Weaver, and scoured the place for evidence of her. It was she who first recognized the monogram as a signature in scraps of textiles, and used it to identify other works by her medieval predecessor. There were a number of fragments of cloth, and several large rolls of medieval tapestry, all marked with the distinctive monogram.

"Are they still in the house?" Lizzie asked, curious to see

anything made by the woman who was the subject of their scrutiny.

Alison shook her head. "Granny felt very strongly that other weavers could benefit by seeing the work. She gave all the fragmentary textiles to the Victoria and Albert Museum."

"And the rolls of tapestry?"

"That is an interesting story," Alison said. "She went over them very carefully and did some restoration of places where moths had gotten at the wool. When my grandmother died, my father and grandfather decided to donate them to St. Hugh's College at Oxford in her memory and they were still hanging there when I went there."

Lizzie could not help interrupting to ask Alison about her own education, but her hostess very quickly returned to the story she thought was more important.

"I paid to have them restored a few years ago and the conservators said that they are definitely Flemish from the turn of the fifteenth century, so though they bear the familiar monogram, they weren't actually woven by our Wife of Bath."

"But they still have her signature?"

"On each of the four panels." Alison described the panels, each about four feet wide, which depicted towns and landscapes all over the south of England, populated by tiny people and animals. "The conservators thought the panels were meant to be stitched together to make a single continuous piece, and that is how it is hanging today."

"I'd like to see it," Lizzie said.

"I thought we might drive to Oxford either tomorrow or the next day," Alison responded. "The best way to get to know our subject is to look at all the things that were of interest to her, and many of the towns that she describes in her journal are pictured on it."

The connection between a manuscript and an object was just the sort of thing Lizzie loved to explore and she quickly expressed her enthusiasm to see the tapestry as soon as possible. When they agreed to go the next day, Lizzie asked Alison why their weaver would have put her monogram signature on something she didn't actually make.

"The conservators thought that she might have drawn the

original cartoons on which the weaving was based," Alison explained. "She wasn't a tapestry weaver, which we know from the fragments of her work at the Victoria and Albert Museum, but no one in England really wove tapestries at that time."

"So she commissioned another artist," Lizzie said thoughtfully. "Fascinating."

It had been a long, interesting and productive evening of conversation. Lizzie was eager to move forward on the project, but she could feel her eyes drooping with exhaustion, and Alison looked tired as well.

"What shall we call her?" Lizzie asked as she began to gather her things and prepare to go to her own room.

"Who?" Alison asked.

"Our Wife of Bath," Lizzie answered. "I think we need to distinguish her from Chaucer's Wife of Bath, even if he based his character on her, and it is too confusing to call both you and her Alison, so I'd like to have another name by which we can know her."

They stood silently for a moment as each woman pondered this idea.

"AW sounds too modern and too much like a restaurant," Lizzie said, rejecting her own suggestion as soon as she made it.

"How about 'The Weaver?'" Alison suggested.

"The Weaver," Lizzie repeated, then repeated it again. "I like it, not only the sound of it, but the implication that her story will be woven as we work."

Alison looked pleased at the thought. "A name *and* a metaphor. How perfect!" She smiled at Lizzie and touched her softly on the arm. "Thank you, my dear. I look forward to sharing this adventure with you."

"And I with you."

Lizzie went off to her small bedroom and climbed into bed. Though she was physically exhausted, her mind continued to work and she could not resist pulling out the transcript Alison had made of the Weaver's journal. It was a different account of the Wife of Bath's pilgrimage, similar to Chaucer's in its general outline, but varying widely in the details. The

Weaver was intelligent and well read, pious, but adventurous; she took advantage of the pilgrimage as a chance to travel. Recently widowed for the second time when she left on her pilgrimage, this Alison met a new husband on the road to Canterbury. The story moved through the English countryside and Lizzie finally fell asleep with her feet on the Pilgrim's path.

Chapter 8

The day began with maps. Alison had cleared the desk in her father's study and spread several maps across it. Lizzie found her there when she came downstairs. The most detailed were the Ordnance Survey maps, which had a scale of one kilometer to the inch and were perfectly designed for walkers—a map that was a yard across only showed twenty-some miles. Every road and house was illustrated, though the details that Alison immediately began to point out to Lizzie were the dotted lines that indicated the public footpaths.

Lizzie needed a jolt of caffeine to set her up for a conversation like this so early in the morning, and having had none, thought Alison was talking about their trip to Oxford. It was only when she realized Lizzie's confusion that Alison remembered her duties as hostess and offered to bring Lizzie coffee and toast.

While Alison fetched the comestibles, Lizzie looked at the maps. In the course of tracing the Weaver's pilgrimage, she would walk from one end to the other of more than a dozen maps, a daunting prospect. She took the road map of southern England from the folder Alison had given her the day before and compared scales to get her bearings. Each of the Ordnance Survey maps represented a small piece of the country map. She began to look closely at the first of them, which included Bath and the Mendip Hills. The concentric lines that indicated changes in altitude hit her forcefully. She had been picturing herself strolling along straight well-defined paths on a level landscape when, in fact, on the very first day she would have to go up and down some very steep hills.

Alison returned with a tray as Lizzie steeled herself for the prospect of leaving the comfort of this house and spending a month on the road. She pulled several of the maps out of the way as Alison set the tray down and poured her a cup of coffee.

"Oh good," Alison said, handing Lizzie the cup. "I see you're looking at the first map. I thought we should just go over the route of your pilgrimage before we head to Oxford, and then we will be able to talk about it while we're in the car." She had made an appointment for one thirty with the librarian at St. Hugh's College and it was only a bit more than an hour to drive there.

Lizzie agreed. She took the larger map of England and looked at the route Alison had drawn out in red, and then figured out how much of it was covered by each of the survey maps.

"Can I write on this?" she asked, gesturing at the map.

"Of course," Alison replied. "That is your copy, I put that route on for you and you're free to add anything you like to it.

"I assume this route is based on descriptions in the text?"

Alison took a bite of toast and nodded.

Lizzie took the typescript out and leafed through it. "Can I write on this too?" she asked, holding the book up to Alison.

Permission was immediately granted.

Page by page she began to look at descriptions of towns and compare them to names on the map. Bath, Wells, Glastonbury, Castle Cary, and Shaftesbury were the main stopping points in the first part of the trip. Then came Salisbury and Winchester, great cathedral towns that would have been important stops for any pilgrim. Guildford was on the way to London and Southwark, where the opening to *Canterbury Tales* was set. From there the path was familiar from Chaucer's text: Rochester, Sittingbourne, Boughton-under-Bleen and Canterbury, with overnight stops at Dartford and Ospringe. Back and forth from text to map, Lizzie marked the places where the Weaver had traveled more than six hundred years earlier.

"It is wonderful that the names are still recognizable," she said. "When I was in Boston I downloaded several maps of this region from different time periods, and the persistence of names was one of the most remarkable things I noticed."

Alison asked about these other maps and Lizzie opened her laptop and quickly showed her a dozen, from a manuscript of 1250 through the Industrial Age, when new features like bridges and mills began to appear, to early twentieth-century road maps, from before the modern system of motorways was built.

Their appointment with the librarian at St. Hugh's was the only thing that could have dragged them away from their interesting discussion. Lizzie was expecting to drive them to Oxford in her rental car and was surprised when Alison walked past it to the garage and pulled open the doors to reveal a sports car, a classic MG from the 1960s.

"I've had it since I was in college," Alison explained. "I suppose I should give it up with my bad hip, but it feels like surrendering to old age."

It was clearly an effort for the old woman to climb into the low-slung car, and Lizzie felt all the exposure of sitting on the left side of the car with no steering wheel in front of her. Her immediate fear that her host would drive like a maniac was put to rest as Alison brought the car carefully out of the drive and onto the main road. She quickly and comfortably brought the conversation back to their earlier subject, making a comment about her pleasure in finding that Lizzie was a map lover.

"It's more than that," Lizzie explained. "I consider maps to be one of the most important tools I use as a historian. In them you see how humans understand the world around them and how they have altered the landscape for their own benefit." She talked a bit about how different kinds of maps showed not only changes in political boundaries, but changes in land use as well. "We can tell from maps when forests were cut for fields, how rivers were diverted to run mills or for irrigation, and how the human population shifted from rural places to expanding cities—and that's just the most obvious stuff."

"Here be dragons!" Alison said, referring to those places on medieval maps, as yet unknown to Europeans, where mysterious dangers were thought to lurk.

"Exactly!" Lizzie responded enthusiastically. "Those little extras on maps sometimes give us the greatest insight into how the people who made them understood their world." She held up the modern road map of Britain, which she had been using to follow their route. "I'm sorry that this is becoming such a relic. With our reliance now on electronic navigating systems, I find that many of my students don't even know how to read a map; they never use them. Except in my classes," she added. "They may understand them as historical texts, but I'm not sure they could find their way from Bath to Oxford."

With little mid-morning traffic, they made good time and arrived in central Oxford around 11:30. "I thought we could have lunch at the Randolph," Alison said, negotiating through the crowded streets to the front of the elegant hotel. On the opposite side of the street was the Ashmolean Museum, which Lizzie had visited several times in the past.

The crests of the individual colleges that made up Oxford University were mounted high on the wall of the dining room and Alison pointed out the blue crest of St. Hugh's.

"Was it the first college at Oxford to accept women?" Lizzie asked.

Alison answered that the first was Lady Margaret Hall. "It opened around 1880, I think, and the first Principal was Margaret Wordsworth, the niece of the poet. Within ten years she decided to found a new college for women, particularly to make an Oxford education available to poor women, and my grandmother was in one of the first classes."

"I imagine the Romantic poets were prominent in the curriculum," Lizzie said.

"Of course," Alison said. "That's where I came to love them. It steered me into my life's work." She spoke a bit about her own time at St. Hugh's College and the advantages she had always felt from being educated there.

When Lizzie was in Boston, Jackie had given her copies of all of Alison's articles on the Romantic poets, and the book she had written on Samuel Taylor Coleridge's *Rime of the Ancient Mariner*. Lizzie was happy to find that she liked Alison's interpretations of the literature; she grounded the works of the Romantics in the context of British expansion and the Industrial Revolution. As they sat at lunch in Oxford, Lizzie told Alison that she had read her book on Coleridge.

"You did? My God, it's almost as ancient as the mariner himself. I didn't know you could even buy it anymore, but I'm impressed you checked me out so thoroughly."

"You know that no good researcher would take on a job like this without checking out her collaborator." She looked up at Alison, who gave a nod of agreement.

"But I would have found your book interesting even without knowing you," Lizzie continued. "The influences of Captain Cook's voyage narratives on the development of that poem were very convincing."

"It was an interesting time," Alison said. "And of course Coleridge and Wordsworth were particular friends."

Lizzie told Alison that she had memorized a Wordsworth poem in high school, and proceeded to recite it in a dramatic voice, gesturing with her hand into the air in front of her. "Oft I had heard of Lucy Gray," she intoned, "And when I crossed the wild, I chanced to see at break of day, the solitary child." She paused and looked at Alison, whose patient expression seemed to indicate that she had heard similar interpretations hundreds of times before.

"I certainly hope it isn't all you've read of Wordsworth."

Lizzie smiled while she wracked her brain for anything else she might remember of the famous poet, but found nothing. "Lucy Gray has an appealing creepiness," she said, hoping Alison wasn't too disappointed in her. "Those little footprints in the snow disappearing on the bridge."

The waiter arrived with lunch just in time to save Lizzie from showing her true ignorance of the Romantic poets.

Chapter 9

St. Hugh's College was several miles north of the center of Oxford, and as they walked between the twin gatehouses, Alison pointed out features of the architecture to Lizzie. It was substantially newer than the majority of Oxford colleges, but its design was reminiscent of the medieval campuses, with a central green space surrounded by residential and academic buildings.

As an active alumna and generous benefactor of the college, Alison was well known to the gatekeeper and he greeted her warmly. "Mr. Moberly is expecting you at half past one," he said, "and will meet you in the reception area of the Main Hall."

It was only a few steps from the gatehouse to the door of the building that housed the dining hall, chapel and a conference center. "The library was originally in this building," Alison told Lizzie, "but a new library building had already been built before I came here."

When the Kent family made a gift of the tapestry to St. Hugh's, it had been their intention that it would hang in the library, but the new building had too much natural light for the fragile textile, which had already faded somewhat at the time of its restoration. It now hung in a reception room in the interior of the main building.

They arrived fifteen minutes before their appointment and Alison took Lizzie directly to where the tapestry was hanging. The room had wood paneling up to waist height, and then a dark red wall stretching up to a high ceiling. The most prominent colors of the tapestry were the greens and blues that ran up and down the edges of the panels in an exuberant burst of foliage. The red dye was more faded, but the color of the wall picked up what was left, and the rust-colored faces of deer could be seen peeking out of forests.

"Oh my God!" Lizzie exclaimed enthusiastically when she saw it. "You didn't tell me it was a map!"

"It only appears to be a map at first," Alison explained, "because there are named towns on it, but when you look closely, you'll see that there is no sense to the geography."

Lizzie scanned her eyes up and down each of the four panels, and back and forth across their combined width. It was a very large piece, sixteen feet across and some ten feet high. In the top left corner was a wonderful depiction of a town on the top of a steep hill, labeled "Shaftesbury." The bottom right corner showed a medieval London, with walls and bridges and a prominent Thames River. Vignettes along the panels had key features that identified the individual properties of towns with castles and cathedrals. Rivers snaked through many, and a path in faded gold linked them up and down each panel.

"It's a strip map," Lizzie said breathlessly. "And it has been put together in the wrong order."

Alison stepped up close to her. "Do you mean the Weaver put them together in the wrong order?"

"No," Lizzie said softly. She pulled the folder from her bag and pulled out the typescript journal. "No, what she did is completely marvelous." She turned and looked at Alison. "It was the conservators who erred."

Michael Moberly, the college librarian, joined them at that moment and overheard the end of their conversation. After the necessary introductions, he asked Lizzie to explain what she meant.

"This is a strip map of a pilgrimage from Bath to Canterbury," she said.

Like Alison, he began to explain that the Flemish artists who wove the tapestry had had no conception of English geography, and had put the various places on it in an almost random order. "Even Englishmen had only a very sketchy idea of what our island looked like at that time." He smiled condescendingly at Lizzie, and made a remark about how charming those old Flemings were in their idiocy. He pointed out various towns that were at different latitudes, implying that she was not unlike those charming old Flemings in her knowledge of English geography. He had a very satisfied smirk on his face as he finished and turned to wink at Alison.

Lizzie savored the moment. She gave a slight condescending laugh and her own self-satisfied smirk.

"Alison," she said, preferring to address her friend first. "You may remember that among those maps I showed you this morning was a very early manuscript strip map. It was made by Matthew Paris in 1250." She turned to Michael Moberly. "I'm sure you know his famous manuscript at the British Library." He indicated that he did.

"One of the problems modern people have with looking at old maps is our bias that north should always be up," Lizzie said. "That isn't the case here, so latitude doesn't matter. This is a map that shows the road from Bath to Canterbury and only places along the road are shown. Since the path proceeds in more or less a straight line, the orientation is constantly changing."

She pointed at the top of the second panel. "There's Bath," she said, "and from there one would proceed along a path that would take you through Wells and Glastonbury," two places that were linked by the golden line. "Shaftesbury should come next." She pointed to the top of the first panel and proceeded down it, "then Salisbury and Winchester. The last panel in this configuration shows Guildford and London, but the one that begins in Southwark and proceeds down the road through Rochester to Canterbury should be presented on the far right."

The expressions on the faces of her two companions showed when each of them realized the logic of her argument.

"It is her pilgrimage," Alison said, her voice filled with awe.

"It is indeed," Lizzie said. "This is the illustration of her journal."

This was the first time that Michael Moberley had heard about either pilgrimage or journal, and inquisitiveness and acquisitiveness were barely disguised in his voice as he asked for more details. Would the library be able to obtain a copy of the journal if it was associated with the tapestry? He didn't quite ask for the journal outright, but Lizzie could see that it wouldn't be long in coming. Alison very quickly told him that she and Lizzie were still working on the research for a project that might link the two items and instructed him to keep the information confidential until she knew more about it.

"Will we be sending the tapestry back to the restorers to be correctly mounted?" he asked.

Alison told him that she would pay to have the correction done, but not until her current research was completed.

"May I at least describe this new information about the map in the newsletter of the college?" he asked.

When he received another negative response, he reminded Alison that there would be a Chaucer conference at Oxford at the beginning of the next month. "People there might be interested in a map and journal of a medieval pilgrimage to Canterbury, and I could arrange for you to make a preliminary announcement about your project."

This seemed like a great opportunity to Lizzie. She regretted that she had given Moberley so much information without thinking, simply to put a snotty twit in his place. He now knew that the tapestry was a map of a pilgrimage and that there was a journal that documented it; Dante Zettler knew that Alison had a Chaucer-era journal kept by a woman from Bath on a pilgrimage to Canterbury. If Alison was to control the way this information was delivered to her colleagues and the public, she needed to present some part of it soon. A preliminary announcement at a Chaucer conference was the perfect opportunity.

She looked at Alison and tried to read in her expression whether the same thoughts were working their way through her brain. The lines on her face seemed deeper as she pondered and her eyes moved from Moberley to the tapestry and then to Lizzie, where they settled.

"Will we be ready to make an announcement in just a few weeks?"

Lizzie nodded. She didn't want to discuss any details in front of the librarian, and it was clear from Alison's behavior that she didn't want to give anything more away either. The possibility that their Weaver had been the model for Chaucer's Wife of Bath was a claim neither would make without more research.

Alison turned her gaze back to Michael Moberley. "That is an excellent suggestion," she said briskly. "Sign us up to present an announcement on a medieval pilgrimage, documented in a text and a tapestry."

"Should it say any more than that?" he asked. "Do you want to include dates or the name of the pilgrim?"

"Not in the title," she answered. "We'll figure out the details in the next few weeks." She asked him if he had prepared the pictures she ordered, and he produced an envelope.

Lizzie had been wondering why Alison had made an appointment with Moberley and this now explained it. Though he was involved in the world of Chaucer scholarship, Alison clearly did not want to confide in him about the Weaver's journal.

As he handed Alison the envelope, he explained what was inside. "There is one of each of the vignettes, one of each panel, and one of the tapestry as a whole, though now we know it is not quite as it should be." He turned to Lizzie and gave her a deferential nod of the head as he said this, like some gentleman in a Jane Austen novel abiding by rules of behavior demanded by good breeding rather than personal inclination.

Alison was rather good at that game too, and after she thanked him properly she dismissed him with a polite wave with the back of her hand. She was already pulling the photographs from the envelope.

Lizzie extended her hand. "Thank you for your time, Mr. Moberley," she said, adding that she looked forward to seeing him again at the conference.

Alison clearly did not want to speak any more about the subject with him and looked with concentration at the photos as he moved away.

"I have been meaning for some time to get copies of the photographs that were taken when the tapestry was restored," Alison said, handing a small stack of pictures from the envelope to Lizzie. "Digital images don't allow enough close detail. With these, we can get right down to the stitches if we want."

They compared the pictures to the tapestry and talked their way along the route of the map.

"Now that you have pointed out how this strip map works, I can't believe I never saw it before," Alison said, complimenting Lizzie. "I told you in December that I was hoping to find someone who could look at things in a different way and you have already more than earned your salary with this!"

"That will save me a lot of walking!" Lizzie said with a laugh.

"On the contrary. It makes the walk that much more necessary," Alison said seriously. "In order to compare what you will see in the landscape with what our Weaver documented here."

"Of course it will," Lizzie said. "With the journal and these images I will have a lot to inform me as I retrace the pilgrimage."

One by one they held the photographs up to the tapestry and compared the vignettes of villages. They were clearly meant to capture specific features of each location, and though there were numerous castles and churches and roads and walled towns, each was unique. Her first destination was Wells, a city with a cathedral that had dramatic "scissor" arches that the Weaver had incorporated into the images of the building. Lizzie hoped she would be able to recognize other pieces of this ancient fabric in the places she visited along the route of her pilgrimage. When she felt she would be able to remember the tapestry from the photographs, Lizzie carefully slid them back into the envelope and the two women returned to Bath.

As they drove into the city, Lizzie looked again at the hills that lay beyond. She referred to the road map on her lap. Wells had to be the first stop. It was clearly described in the journal and illustrated on the tapestry, but it meant backtracking to the west before she put her steps firmly on the road east to Canterbury, and it meant crossing the Mendips. They looked mountainous.

When they returned to Alison's house, Lizzie set herself up in the study and began to collate the resources, looking at the journal entries, the Weaver's strip map, and the Ordnance Survey map of each section along the route. She looked at the road from Bath to Wells as the Weaver had illustrated it and began to wonder about how she had described and illustrated the hills. The photograph of the tapestry was clear, but Lizzie could not quite determine the meaning of some of the lines on it. Could they be compared to the elevation markings on the more modern map?

"Do you have a magnifying glass?" she asked Alison, hoping to get more deeply into the details.

They were in the library, sitting on either side of the partners' desk that Alison's father and grandfather had shared.

Alison began to pull the drawers out on her side. "I'm almost certain that I saw one here at one time, but it might have been on your side."

Lizzie opened the top drawer and found two pieces of a broken lens, which she pulled out and laid on the table. "This larger one might work," she said, sliding it over the top of the photograph, but it wasn't big enough.

"If you can use that kind of lens for the job, then there are two in the Becket reliquary," Alison said. She rose and went to the corner bookshelf. "I was meaning to pull out the original manuscript for you to see again anyway." The small books from the shelf were quickly handed to Lizzie and piled on the desk, and Alison pulled out the board that hid the reliquary.

"I'm glad to see this again, too," Lizzie said as Alison set it on the desk in front of her. "I never really had a chance to study it closely." She put out a finger and gently slid it along the smooth surface, then around the gold embossed head of one of the murderers of Becket, which was applied onto the enamel. She opened the box and took out all the contents, laying the bone carefully on the wood of the desk, then the stiff scrap of fabric, the scallop shell, and then the two lenses. Alison took the Caxton edition of *Canterbury Tales*, with the inserted journal of the Weaver.

Lizzie picked up the two lenses, one in each hand, and held them up in front of her face with the slightly larger one behind the other.

"I think these are from a telescope," she said. "I thought

so when I first saw them in December, and now that I look closer I am even more convinced." She put them back on the table and picked up the two pieces of the broken lens. "And this looks like one too."

"My father ground his own lenses," Alison said. "He learned how when he was at Oxford. There was an astronomy society there, and he maintained the interest and his connections with those men all his life."

She had spoken to Lizzie of her father during their roundtrip to Oxford. He was the oldest of four children, all of whom, girls and boys, spent some of their childhood in various jobs in the mill. The family's growing fortune had allowed his parents to educate them well, and he, as the oldest, inherited the business and the greatest part of the fortune. Alison's mother was also from a large family, with little money but substantial aristocratic pretentions.

"I'm impressed that he had both the theoretical knowledge and the practical skill to pursue it," Lizzie said. She moved the largest of the lenses over the top of the photograph of the area of the strip map that illustrated the road from Bath to Wells. Certainly the Weaver had marked hills.

She sat back, unwilling to tell Alison of her doubts about her ability to get through even the first day of walking. Now that the start of the pilgrimage was only a week away, she acknowledged again how much she did not know about what she was doing. She held the lens in her hand and rubbed her thumb across the concave surface of the glass, and then around the outer rim. There was a slight roughness, which stood out against the perfect smoothness of the rest of the lens. She held it up to her eye and saw that there was a small inscription: CC 7/7.

"Are you sure your father made this lens?"

Alison assured her that she was certain of it. "Why do you ask?"

"Because it seems to have someone else's mark on it." Lizzie held the lens across the desk for Alison to see where her finger marked the lettering incised into the glass.

Alison took it from her, but the letters were too tiny for her to read. "Are you sure this isn't just a scratch?" she asked.

Lizzie took the other lens from the desktop and was about to hand it to her friend to use as a magnifier. As she picked it up, she felt a similar rough place along the edge and another inscription: StM 12/29.

"Well this is strange," she said, reading out the letters to Alison. "If it isn't a signature, could it refer to a particular telescope that it was made for?" She looked up. "Do you have any of his telescopes?"

"All his scientific instruments are still in this room, as far as I know."

Lizzie had already noticed a fine old sextant on one of the shelves, and Alison pointed to several wooden boxes that she thought held instruments. A quick search revealed four telescopes and several additional lenses, but none of them were marked, and there was nothing on any of the telescopes to indicate that it had a special name or number.

"Why do you think these particular lenses are in the Becket box?" Even as Lizzie spoke, Alison was asking her a similar question.

"Is it possible that he observed something special with these lenses and marked them as souvenirs of the occasion?" Lizzie asked.

"Like what?"

"I'm not sure, maybe a comet or star or something?" Neither could remember having heard of any such celestial phenomenon with the initials C.C. or St. M., and the dates weren't meaningful to Alison. After several minutes of discussion, they determined that whatever they were, they weren't relevant to the Weaver's pilgrimage, so they returned them to the box and went back to the journal.

Chapter 10

Alison and Lizzie spent the next several days poring over the journal, comparing it to the images on the tapestry, and looking at both ancient and modern maps to determine the route. They realized as they marked the path along the Ordnance Survey maps that two other literary themes were constantly intruding on their work: Jane Austen had lived at several places along the route, albeit three hundred years later, in the late 1700s, and sites associated with King Arthur unrolled across the south of England from Mount Baden, one of the Mendips—which was said by some to be where King Arthur fought the Saxons.

The latter topic had a connection to their project, as it was in King Arthur's court that the "Wife of Bath" set her tale.

"There is plenty of critical scholarship that has already been done on Chaucer's use of Arthurian sources," Alison said one day to Lizzie, "and on where the 'Wife of Bath's Tale' comes from. I don't intend to deal much with that, if at all, in our work."

"But the Weaver has a mention in her journal of Arthur's tomb at Glastonbury," Lizzie said. "So we'll need to prepare a note on it to go with our annotations to the text."

"I hope you realize that the so-called tomb of Arthur was a great medieval hoax," Alison said, a hint of frustration in her voice. "I get so tired of hearing people talk about Arthur as a historical rather than a literary figure, but you are right, of course, we will have to include a note about it." She made a gesture with her head to an area of shelving over her right shoulder. "There is a section here of different versions of the Arthur texts if you would like to take on that topic."

"Of course," Lizzie said with enthusiasm. She had loved the story since she had seen the Disney movie "The Sword in the Stone" as a child, avidly read Thomas Malory's *La Morte de Arthur* in high school, and had probably seen "Monty Python and the Holy Grail" more often than any other film; she could quote numerous passages from it. That Alison did not consider Arthur to have any basis in a historical character was a surprise to her, but she could sense that a conversation on this topic would be better after she had gained more background, and she decided to choose some of the books from Alison's collection and bring them with her when she retired for the evening to her room.

With the discovery that the tapestry illustrated a strip map of the Weaver's pilgrimage as described in her journal, the structure of the book that Alison would write on the topic evolved very neatly. She said she considered Lizzie her collaborator on all aspects of the work, and the two of them were dividing up research tasks.

The most difficult problem was how to convincingly connect the Weaver to Geoffrey Chaucer, who was not mentioned by name in the journal. Even without that connection, a book linking the tapestry map to an actual fourteenth-century journal would be a remarkable achievement, but Alison was convinced that her ancestress *was* the Wife of Bath. Before Lizzie identified the tapestry as a map of the journey, that idea had steered the project, but now she seemed to waver.

"I don't want to diminish the importance of the Weaver's works by overstating the Chaucer context," she told Lizzie one day. "If the reception of the book gets dominated by a debate over whether or not the Chaucer connection is supportable, then I will be disappointed."

"I assume you would not mention this unless you thought there were scholars out there who *will* argue against it."

"Of course there are!" Alison said pointedly. "That's their job, the Dante Zettlers of the world. He will be the first in line to say that the Weaver was not a source for Chaucer; he will build his reputation on it."

Lizzie asked Alison to lay out the evidence for her so that she could see the strengths and weaknesses in the argument for a correspondence between the Weaver and the Wife of Bath, and Alison began by reminding Lizzie of the structure of *Canterbury Tales.*

"There are three different passages that deal with the Wife of Bath," she said. "The first is the glimpse we get of her when all the characters are introduced in the 'Prologue,' the second is the prologue to her own tale, the third is the tale itself. We learn that she is, first and foremost, an excellent weaver; she has been married five times, her socks are red, she has ample hips, she rides astride and wears spurs, she loves to laugh and gossip, she has travelled very widely, and she has a gap between her front teeth, which everybody says was a sure sign of promiscuity." Alison added that the last part was ridiculous, of course, but it was an old literary shorthand to let physical features denote aspects of a person's character.

"When the Wife of Bath introduces herself to her companions and her readers, she tells of her relationships with her husbands—beginning with the first when she was twelve years old—and compares her personal experience of love to what she has read in several books."

Lizzie interrupted to ask Alison if she had read Jackie's paper from college. "She deals specifically with the way that Chaucer presents the Wife of Bath's relationship to books. She was meant to be hilarious to the knowledgeable reader because her interpretation of what she has read is completely unconventional—and therefore laughably wrong. There is a bit of a nudge and a wink to the reader as we make fun of her for it."

"Your friend's paper was very perceptive," Alison responded. "I read it last night. Her notion that there might have been a woman who influenced Chaucer, and whom he treated cruelly in the text, hit close to home, I must say."

"Weird, isn't it. I'd like to tell her about the journal because I think she might be helpful on some of our research questions; she is an extremely astute librarian."

It was Jackie's perspective on the Wife of Bath that most intrigued Alison. "Most people dismiss or condemn the character because she is crude," she said. "And that is what I most wanted to rescue the Weaver from. But your friend Jackie isn't bothered by straightforward sexual talk; in fact she seems to admire it. What she doesn't like is that Chaucer made the character seem stupid."

To Lizzie, the combination of crude and stupid seemed the worst possible flaws the author could inflict on his character, especially as she was one of the few independent female characters depicted in the literature of the age.

"But the definition of what is vulgar has certainly changed in six hundred years," she said, "and modern readers do not necessarily see an openness about sexual behavior in the same way as Chaucer intended."

"That is certainly so, but I am more interested in *his* motives than the interpretation of readers today."

Lizzie had to admit that in that case the Wife of Bath was extremely coarse. Not only did she express a willingness to have sex with any man at any time, but she mentions in delightful medieval terms how they praise her sexual anatomy. "I love the word she uses to describe her genital region," Lizzie said, laughing to Alison. "Her 'quonium!' And she calls it the 'beste that mighte be!' In its own day that certainly must have been exceedingly vulgar."

"Today we could use the word with impunity," Alison responded. "Nobody knows what it means!"

"If they did, we'd have to refer to it as the 'q' word!"

Lizzie had tried to maintain a serious demeanor through the conversation, but now her composure failed and she gave a honk of laughter.

"This conversation might be even more interesting with a glass of scotch in my hand," Alison said, pouring her ubiquitous drink into two glasses and handing one to Lizzie. The slight buzz it brought on made Lizzie laugh even more boisterously.

"I'm going to write a romance novel," she said enthusiastically, "and use the word quonium! No more of those silly euphemisms like 'mound of Venus' or 'gateway to Paradise!'"

"Those aren't even particularly poetic," Alison complained. "I've often thought that I could write a fairly racy novel—under a pseudonym of course—with metaphors that get the heart pumping." She took a swig of scotch and laid the empty glass on the table with a clunk. "She exposed the nest that lay between her silken thighs," she said with a gesture of her hand, "and the sacred bud opened to greet his throbbing manhood."

Lizzie was slouched down in her chair and she slapped at her leg with hilarity as Alison described ever more graphic displays of semantic gymnastics. "You are mixing some metaphors," she said after a particularly splendid offering.

Alison acknowledged that Lizzie was right. "Perhaps when we are finished with our present collaboration we can move on to a novel," she said. "I think between us we could fill it with wonderful allusions to nastiness and you can correct my metaphors."

The conversation devolved from there. After each had downed another scotch and soda their metaphors were no longer metaphors and they were speaking so crudely that Chaucer would have blushed to hear them.

"Do you think," Lizzie said finally with a great sigh, "that maybe the Weaver and her circle of women friends sat in this very house speaking forthrightly about their quoniums, and Chaucer actually captured something about her that was real?" She paused, and then asked Alison if it would bother her if they somehow found that that part of the description was true.

"After our raunchy language tonight I could hardly condemn her for the same behavior, but you know of course that she didn't live in this house, so if she discussed her sexual escapades it wasn't here."

That had not occurred to Lizzie. "I guess I should have known that your house isn't quite that old," she said. "But since the Weaver's work was found here by your grandmother, I made a rash assumption that it was always here."

"This house was built in the reign of Mary Tudor, when Catholics gained their positions back, and my family had some money to spend. We were wool merchants then."

"So still the cloth and Catholicism motto?"

"Yes indeed. Someone involved in the building of this house was interested enough in the old fragments of cloth to collect them and bring them here, but I think that many more must have been lost."

"Where was the original house?"

"It is described in an old deed as being near the northwest corner of Bath Abbey, so it was probably right on top of where the restored Roman baths are. There were remnants of several looms found in the excavation, so it seems there was a concentrated community of weavers at that spot during her lifetime, and Bath was pretty well known for being a center of the business." She gave Lizzie a wink. "Cloth and Catholicism."

The hour was late and as they made their plans for the next day, Lizzie expressed an interest in seeing the site where the Weaver had lived.

Chapter 11

Jackie once again proved her usefulness when Lizzie opened her email the next morning.

"I found an interesting article for you in *Nature* from 1998," it began. "Some scientists, who ordinarily use computer models to trace the DNA family trees of biological specimens, teamed up with some Chaucer scholars and they analyzed all the surviving manuscript versions of the Wife of Bath's Prologue with very interesting results."

She went on to describe the methodology of the research. Eighty-eight manuscript copies of *The Canterbury Tales* survive that were made before 1500. They are all different, many are just fragments, and 58 of them include the Wife of Bath's Prologue. The most important of these manuscripts, and the ones most often used as sources for published editions, are the Ellesmere manuscript at the Huntington Library in California, and the Hengwrt manuscript at the National Library in Wales.

"The Ellesmere is perhaps the more famous," Jackie wrote, "because it includes wonderful little portraits of the pilgrims, painted in the early part of the fifteenth century. We looked at these before you left."

The purpose of the elaborate computer project was to see if it was possible to find Chaucer's "last, best" version of the Wife of Bath's Prologue from the *Tales,* which were unfinished at the time of his death.

The researchers concluded that the Wife was most outrageous in the earliest versions and thereafter was, according to Jackie's source, "really a woman struggling to keep her appetites within the confines of Christian marriage. . . . She is still outrageous, but with hankerings after respectability . . . arguably a more subtle, more satisfyingly rounded portrait."

Lizzie printed the message and took it instantly to Alison. "How do you like this?" she asked. Jackie had included a link to an article in the British newspaper *The Independent* from 1998, which summed up the research.

> A scientific analysis of the Wife of Bath's Prologue has revealed that Geoffrey Chaucer changed his mind about a key passage in the tale that has blackened the lady's character forever. The passage, where the Wife of Bath says she satisfies her sexual appetite with whatever man she can, was meant to have been deleted from a working draft of *The Canterbury Tales* but was instead copied into subsequent manuscripts after Chaucer had died.
>
> The 26 lines in the passage turned the Wife of Bath into a "monster of carnality" according to scholars, but Chaucer had a change of heart over his original description of her character, say scientists.

This was interesting news for Alison.

"Do you like Chaucer better for having at least thought about cleaning the character up a bit?" Lizzie asked her.

"Perhaps."

"There is still the tale she tells though," Lizzie said. "That may be the cruelest thing of all that he did to her."

"There has been scholarship on that as well, of course, and some debate if the tale we now associate with her was the one Chaucer intended for her to tell."

They talked of these things as they walked that morning around Bath. Alison pointed out to Lizzie those parts of the place that survived from ancient and Roman times, and from the age described in Jane Austen's novels in the late eighteenth century.

"Unfortunately, most of the medieval parts of the town have been so altered as to be unrecognizable, so you are not seeing much of Bath as it was known to the Weaver." She explained that the abbey had been so extensively renovated over time that little of the original fabric was visible, and the whole impressive and elaborate structure of the Roman Baths had been excavated in the nineteenth century, after sitting under other buildings for more than a thousand years. "The Weaver probably lived right on top of all this and didn't even know it was there."

They had spoken of Jane Austen when they looked at the maps to plan the route and now spoke of her again. Alison had often taught her books and Lizzie had read them ardently since she was in high school. She was pleased to think again about Austen's first and last novels, *Northanger Abbey* and *Persuasion,* which were largely set in Bath. They had lunch at the Pump Room, where Austen had set so many scenes of elegant people drinking the sulfurous water that bubbled up from the Roman baths beneath them.

"The surviving architecture makes it so easy to imagine myself here with Anne Elliot or Catherine Moreland," Lizzie said, mentioning two of her favorite Austen heroines. "I'm sorry we can't feel that with the Weaver and her age."

"You don't feel it here," Alison said. "But you will along the path. The cathedral at Wells and a street near it are very well preserved and will give you a wonderful sense of that past."

It was a reminder that Lizzie must be soon embarking on the walk. In the next few days, she and Alison scouted several places by car to see how the paths looked. They acknowledged that much of the route taken by the Weaver would have been along what were now the paved roads, but Lizzie was unhappy at the prospect of walking on them. They looked dangerous to her. Generally just over one lane wide, they were bound by a high hedge on each side and there were enough curves that the visibility ahead was seldom more than a few car lengths. Add to that the fact that the steep shoulder, or "verge" as Alison called it, was covered with a prickly vegetation, and that people drove very fast, and Lizzie felt that she would be safer if she could stay on the footpaths.

"Obviously we don't have enough information for me to follow the Weaver's tracks exactly," she said. "If there are some places where you think it is necessary for me to be on the road I will, of course, walk there, but I would prefer not to."

"My objective is to explain to modern readers the process of this pilgrimage," Alison answered, "and to prove that the Weaver traveled the path. We can make some logical assumptions about how she traveled between places, but we can only speak with certainty of those places either mentioned in the journal or shown on the tapestry; everything else is speculation."

"And she had a horse," Lizzie added. She was reminded of this by an illustration from the Ellesmere manuscript that Jackie had attached to her email.

The few days remaining before Lizzie's departure went rapidly. She and Alison scouted as much of the first few days that could be done in a car, and Alison pointed out where the footpaths left the road to go across fields. At the road end they were well enough marked, but Lizzie wasn't convinced they would continue that way once she had tromped out of sight of the road.

The evening before her departure, Edmund and George joined them for dinner and once again the maps came out and she and Alison traced the path with them.

"If you are traveling down this road through Inglesbatch, I see you have a 'piggery' to pass through," Edmund said with a smile.

Lizzie did not smile back. "That looks a lot more amusing if you are not about to walk through it in an expensive pair of the finest walking shoes ever made."

"Would you like a companion on your first day?"

This was not the first time that Edmund had offered to accompany her on her walk, but as much as she would have enjoyed his company, she felt that the uncertainties of the first few days should not have witnesses. "In a few weeks I would love that," she answered warmly. Rejecting his company did not mean that she was unwilling to enumerate her fears for what might happen to her on the walk. "The number of ways that I could get hurt are many," she said. "I could get bitten by a dog, gored by a bull, hit by a car, stung by a bee—"

Edmund interrupted her. "That last one I can help you with," he said, handing her a package. "I made up a first aid kit for you and it can help with some of the minor scrapes and bruises, and with an allergic reaction if you have one." He reminded her that she could call him on her cell phone and he could be to her within hours. "No matter where you are, no matter what time it is," he said. He made her acknowledge him. "I'm serious," he repeated, "any time."

She thanked him, knowing he would rescue her if she needed it, but she hoped she wouldn't.

The next day, Lizzie marched out the door of Alison's house, put her feet on the road toward Wells, and began the adventure she had anticipated and feared for months.

Chapter 12

Lizzie was not so naïve as to believe that all the public footpaths in England would be paved, but she had allowed herself to indulge in some fantasies of hard-packed dirt paths, possibly shaded by boughs arching overhead. She was, consequently, disappointed to find that for her first morning there was almost no path at all that could be found on the Ordnance Survey map to take her from Inglesbatch to Chewton Mendip, the halfway point to Wells. Determined as she was not to walk on the roads, she decided to depend on local knowledge and consequently when she arrived in Inglesbatch she asked a couple working in their garden about local footpaths to Chewton Mendip.

"You can just walk right along this road and you'll be there," the woman answered.

Lizzie explained that she was trying to avoid the road, and though the Inglesbatchians were clearly perplexed by that, the man took the map from her, determined to help. He pointed to a curve in the road and told her to go straight at that point "past the piggery, turn into the field and then cross it down to the stream to pick up the path. If you walk along the stream you'll find a proper bridge."

She spent a few minutes chatting with the couple before she left them. They had a small farm and a B&B, and they pointed out their seventeenth-century stone barn and described the problems of fitting modern farm machinery into it. They were the first farmers Lizzie met in England and they set a very high standard of intelligence and historical knowledge. There was nothing the least bit rural or provincial about them and the fact that they seemed skeptical of the whole walking enterprise gave Lizzie pause. When she could no longer delay her departure by discussion she adjusted her pack, and set off toward the piggery.

She felt good, strong. The countryside had an exotic quality that was exhilarating and the weather was perfect for walking. When she got to the curve of the road there was no indication of any kind of a public footpath, and two mangy dogs came out of nowhere to bark at her. Still, she was upbeat and energetic. Even the piggery failed to darken her day, though the road was thick with a deep, black, swiney muck. The Mephisto walking shoes that she had paid $300 for in Boston were now worth about three bucks, she thought as she approached the field described by the farmer.

There were actually two fields, a nearer one populated by horses, and another beyond with tall grass; they were divided by a fence and ran down a steep slope to the stream shown clearly on the map. As there was nothing to indicate a public footpath, Lizzie hesitated to walk through the horse field, as it was so clearly private property. The wild and uncultivated look of the next field on made it seem like it must be freer of access to the public and for that reason she chose it.

The grass was knee-height, slick and steep, with an unseen and uneven footing. On the downhill climb Lizzie found that her pack made her unsteady. She tried once to grab onto a fencepost for support, but the fence itself was made of barbed wire and was no help. In trying to avoid grabbing the barbed wire she missed her footing and fell. It was only when she had struggled almost to the bottom of the hill that she fully comprehended the implications of the barbed wire fence. She would have to climb over it to travel along the stream in the right direction.

Near the stream, a small tree offered something to hang onto as she tossed her pack over the fence and followed. This, she thought, as she scrambled gracelessly across, was the reason that she wanted no witnesses until she better knew her strengths and weaknesses. Only the horses were there—their big dark eyes looked at her disinterestedly, as if awkward women commonly dropped into their field from that fence and that tree.

There was no path. There was only thick vegetation and a muddy stream bed, but in the distance was the bridge she had been promised and to that beacon she made her way, assuming that there must be a recognizable path associated with it at either end, and for a time there was. The progress of the day alternated between moments of frustration and moments of bliss, with more of the former than the latter. Once she found that she had circled around to a place she had already passed more than an hour earlier. She found that some of the footpaths were blocked by electric wires, which she covered with the Ordnance Survey map and clambered across. But she also passed through a small wood carpeted in bluebells, and at that moment she pictured the Weaver, ambling through these same woods on her way to Canterbury.

There was a great golden rooster on the steeple of the church in Priston, which Lizzie admired as she passed through that town. Between there and Timsbury was a real path, well worn by the tread of many feet. Lizzie nodded at several local people, mostly women, as they made their way from one village to the other to shop or visit. One of them wore a woolen skirt and sensible shoes and when she reached the ubiquitous two-step stile, which made it possible to pass into or out of a field without letting the livestock loose, she was unhesitant in making the climb.

Lizzie turned back to watch her and saw the crowing cock on the Priston church as it caught the afternoon light. Thereafter she turned around several times again as she walked down a gentle slope, until the golden rooster sat on the crest of the hill, and then disappeared. The weather was cool and misty, the countryside beautiful. Jane Austen had once written that England looked better through mist than sunshine, and Lizzie was reminded of a favorite episode from *Pride and Prejudice,* when Elizabeth Bennet trekked across the countryside to visit her ailing sister Jane at Netherfield. When she arrived at the house, the hem of her skirt was covered in mud, which scandalized the Bingley sisters, but the glow in her cheeks after that walk led Mr. Darcy to fall in love with her.

"Mr. Darcy," Lizzie said under her breath. There were a

number of sheep around her and a frisky lamb seemed to answer with a high bleat.

She felt that the Ordnance Survey map, on which she had depended with such confidence from the comfort of Alison's study, was failing her. She was hungry and tired, her feet were wet and aching, and though it seemed like the path she was on was evident on the map, she had been lost enough times on this, her first day, to have real doubts about her current location. If she was where she thought she was, then there was a pub at the top of the next rise. She climbed hopefully and was rewarded with a lovely old place called The Stars.

Sitting with a pitcher of water in front of her, a pint of cider on the way, and the promise of ham and cheese, Lizzie felt herself sink into the padded seat beneath her and relax. She stripped off her shoes and socks and stretched and wiggled her toes against the flagstone floor. She believed she had conquered the worst of the hills. Chewton Mendip lay along this road and she was within a few miles of her destination. When she finished her meal she marched on and found the B&B that Alison had arranged for her.

Martin was waiting for her call and wondering how the day had gone, and when she called him she described it with less drama than she might have were she not so bone tired.

"Do you feel like this will help with the book you are working on with Alison?" he asked.

"Not yet," she said honestly. "I am so out of my element. But I think I will make an adjustment that will allow me to slow my mind down to a walking pace, and then there will be things to learn."

He asked her to describe some images for him, and she told him of the animals she had seen: cows, dogs, sheep in profusion, and one golden cockerel. "Tomorrow I will get to Wells," she said. "We know the Weaver visited there, so I am thinking of it as the first day of actual work."

"Today was the preamble?" He laughed at his own joke as he said it, and she felt good hearing his laugh. They spoke for several minutes about his work on the Newcastle mural. When she hung up she walked to the window of the room in which she was staying. The sun had not yet set, though the day had been long and she was completely exhausted. Below the window was an old swimming pool that the family running the B&B had turned into a fishpond and water garden.

She lay on the bed and thought about how much of the English countryside would still seem familiar to the Weaver, and even more so to Jane Austen. There was a quality to the countryside that, while not quite "timeless," seemed continuous. Despite the fact that most of the population in England lived in cities, it was still the rural districts that defined England both to its own population and to the romantic outsider, like herself. The small farms, stone walls, hedges, and livestock; the ancient barns set in their lush green rolling landscape; the small farmhouses that had been continuously occupied for centuries, all contributed to the feeling that the place and its past were inextricably woven together.

Lizzie opened the first aid kit that Edmund had made for her to take some aspirin for her aching feet, and found a card tucked inside.

"I am so glad to know that you are back in England," he wrote. "I have thought often of pilgrimages since we spoke of this at Christmas. I can give you no advice from personal experience, but I did find a good Biblical passage, Jeremiah 6:16. (Admittedly I didn't find it by reading the Bible but by searching online!) It advises you to ask for help, which I hope you will.

Stand at the crossroads and look,
Ask for the ancient paths,
And where the good way is,
And walk in it,
And you will find rest for your soul."

Chapter 13

There was no way to avoid walking on the road the next morning and Lizzie was disappointed as she went over the map with Betty, her hostess at the B&B. Her feet were still sore and when Betty offered to drive her a few miles to a bridle path that led into Wells, Lizzie accepted. While this was a clearer path than any of those through the fields of yesterday, it was still hard going. The decline was steep and the surface was first muddy and then rocky, but the views through the mist were idyllic. It was a soft cool day and the air was filled with the sounds of birds, some like the jingle of a tambourine, and one like the honk of an old car horn. The steady sounds of sheep and cows added to the chorus.

To her left as she descended was a woodsy patch with bluebells pushing up through the carpet of leaves. To her right, a broad pasture swept down to a farm in the valley below, and a mirror image of fields rose on the other side. Lizzie breathed it all in, thinking that it would be impossible to romanticize the picture to be more idyllic than it was. Even the loamy smells—part earth, part poop—added to the sense that this was the best of nature as Anglo-Saxons envisioned it.

She was inspired to sing the oldest song she knew, "The Twa Corbies," an ancient English ballad. "Down in yonder green field," she sang, full voice, "there lies a knight, dead 'neath his shield." A chorus of "baaaas" accompanied her. She stopped singing to listen to the song of the sheep; she had never noticed before that they bleated at different pitches and with differently pulsed bleats. Many of the big ewes in the field had twin lambs, and a pair of them moved along in unison with her.

The distance to Wells by this route was only about three miles and it was still morning when she found herself walking along the north side of the cathedral. Five people stood looking up at the clock on the wall of the building and Lizzie, with that curiosity that always comes from finding people looking upward, joined them. It was just a few minutes to eleven and the small crowd was waiting to watch the clock chime. Lizzie sat on a low stone wall and watched as two armored knights, mounted above the clock face, alternated chopping with their axes eleven times upon a bell.

"Wonderful!" she said.

A man beside her turned and asked if she had seen the clock from inside. "There's a jousting match!" he said enthusiastically when she told him she hadn't.

She determined that she must be at the clock inside when it struck noon, and proceeded around to the front of the building. Lizzie was unprepared for the sheer gloriousness of Wells Cathedral. She had known nothing about it before she began working with Alison on their project, and had read about it only as they began the background research. The Weaver captured it in the tapestry, however, and Lizzie would have recognized it from that. Across a vast expanse of grass, the broad west face of the cathedral rose up, covered with medieval stone carvings of angels, saints, bishops, kings, knights and noblemen. It took her breath away. She had read that the statues were originally brightly painted, but the color had worn off over the centuries and they were now a warm brown color.

Inside it was just as wonderful. Dramatic crossed "scissor arches" define the end of the nave, and the near-noon light coming through the medieval stained glass on the overcast day, heightened all the lines and shadows. Lizzie worked her way slowly down the long nave to the transept—where the shorter section of the church crossed the longer. There, at noon, she was ready with a small crowd to witness the chiming of the clock.

There was a sign explaining that the original works of the clock were now ticking away at the Science Museum in London, but its complex representations of the universe and the phases of the moon, and the carved mechanical figures—all dating from the Weaver's time—was splendidly original. Every fifteen minutes, a door opened in a wooden tower above the clock and four horsemen rode out, two in each direction. One unlucky combatant had been knocked off his horse every quarter of an hour for six hundred years. A carved man sitting in a sentry box above and to the right of the clock banged out the hours on a bell in front of him with two hammers, while simultaneously kicking his heels at two additional bells under his chair.

Lizzie found the effect so wonderful that for the two hours she spent in the Cathedral she returned to the clock every fifteen minutes to see the endless drama played out again. Unlike at Bath, where the Abbey seemed a jumble of additions and renovations, most of the original fabric of Wells Cathedral survived. All the major components were in place before the Weaver made her pilgrimage, though she would have come here not as a pilgrim, but simply as a reverent Catholic and a lover of beauty.

In their research of the place, Lizzie and Alison had discovered that Wells had no significant relics in medieval times, and consequently few pilgrims. A portion of the church was built to hold the relics of a local bishop, but he was never canonized and the reliquary remained empty. Nonetheless, the Weaver had come here—a portion of the interior of the Cathedral was illustrated on the tapestry, and there was a reference in her journal to having made "an offering in honor of my kinsman, Bishop de la Marchia, so recently called to God."

This was on Lizzie's mind as she walked the long axis of the nave up one side and then turned and ambled back down the opposite side. There were three tomb chests along the aisle on this side of the church, each with the effigy of a fourteenth-century bishop. Unlike the dramatic effigies she had seen of crusader knights in other churches, the features of these old clerics were mostly worn away. Noses, ears and fingers had long ago been chipped off, as had edges of fabric and anything else that protruded beyond a flat surface, but six centuries of wear had smoothed the rough spots.

Some of these men might actually have been known to the Weaver, Lizzie thought. Certainly these three tombs were here during her lifetime. She walked slowly around them, looking closely at the marks on the surface of each. The carved stone man in the middle lay full length upon his box, his mitred head slightly elevated on a patterned pillow, his now illegible hands folded in prayer. There was a small placard on the column nearest him that identified him as "Bishop de la Marcia." He was the man for whom the Weaver left a memorial tribute when she visited here; she had called him her "kinsman."

Lizzie went again to study his face, disappointed that everything in his features that might have resembled the Weaver was worn away. She looked at the lumps in the stone that had represented the shapes of his nose and lips and eyes. His bishop's mitre had some detail left, and a pattern in the carved fabric could still be slightly distinguished in the pillow under his head, but his face was disappointingly indistinct.

She looked more closely at the pillow. At one time there had been a clear pattern there, carved to represent a woven fabric, and painted to bring out the details. There was at least one leaf still faintly visible, and the curve of a stem or vine that passed beneath it. Lizzie quickly took off her pack and grabbed the photographs of the tapestry. The frieze along the edge had a design of leaves and vines that looked similar, though the pattern on the stone was so worn that she couldn't be sure if it was the same. She read the entry in the journal again as Alison had transcribed it: "Welles. Here I made an offering in honor of my kinsman, Bishop de la Marchia, so recently called to God."

In the tapestry, Wells Cathedral was represented by an interior view, a recognizable portion of the nave with the high scissor arches on the left, bounded by a section of the right aisle with the three box-like tombs. Lizzie took the image with the greatest detail from the envelope of pictures, and looked again at the way the three small tombs were illustrated. She took the flexible magnifying lens she had brought for this purpose and looked intently at how the middle tomb was represented in the tapestry. Beneath it was a ribbon identifying

"Bishop de la Marchia," and on the side of the tomb itself, in tiny stitches, was the Weaver's mark: the "AW" monogram with the flat-topped "A."

Lizzie took a deep breath and held it. When she and Alison had gone over each of the tapestry pictures they had missed this. She walked around the tomb again, looking carefully at each of the sides of the base, and then came back again to the bishop's effigy. Running her eyes, and occasionally her fingers, along the vestments, she searched for details that she had not detected on her first casual observance. She slowly scanned each inch of the mitre and the pillow, which had clearly been carved with patterns representing fabric. Moving around the head, she examined every scratch in the stone. On a corner of the pillow, almost under the ear of the effigy, she saw the mark. Blurred by the years, it was nonetheless recognizable as the Weaver's "AW" monogram.

Reaching out her hand, Lizzie felt the ridge of the letters in the stone with her fingertip. The Weaver had stood in this exact spot. She had caused this mark to be put here, for what purpose Lizzie did not yet know, but certainly it had been done by her intent.

"Here I made an offering in honor of my kinsman, Bishop de la Marchia, so recently called to God," Lizzie said softly. Had the Weaver paid for this monument? Had she commissioned a stone carver as she had commissioned the Flemish tapestry weavers?

It occurred to her that Alison should know about this as soon as possible, and she grabbed her bag and hurried out through the front door of the Cathedral, dialing her cell phone as she went.

"Alison," she said quickly, barely giving her friend time to answer. "I have found something at Wells Cathedral. How soon can you get here?"

"I'm glad you called," Alison responded, not grasping the urgency in Lizzie's voice. "I was wondering how you are after your walk yesterday."

"Fine," Lizzie said impatiently. "I'm in Wells and I have found something at the Cathedral that you must see right away. Can you come here?"

The conversation went back and forth a few more times before Alison completely comprehended Lizzie's request. "What have you found?" she asked.

"I would really rather show you than tell you."

Again there was a back and forth for clarification before Alison agreed that she would come. "I'll meet you at the Cathedral in one hour," she said.

Lizzie went back inside to wait. The cathedral did not have permanent pews, but there were folding chairs scattered around and Lizzie took one to the tomb of Bishop de la Marchia and sat beside it. She read that portion of the Weaver's journal again, though there was nothing about Wells Cathedral beyond that one line about making an offering in honor of her kinsman. Nor did a thorough examination with her magnifying lens find anything else of interest in the tapestry picture of Wells Cathedral. Her curiosity piqued, however, Lizzie moved the lens to the image of the next destination along the route, Glastonbury Abbey.

There again was the mark, in tiny stitches. The intricate illustration of the monastic compound at Glastonbury had another of the Weaver's monograms—an "AW," woven almost imperceptibly into the stone of the foundation.

Lizzie was so intently concentrated on the image that she jumped when she felt Alison's hand on her shoulder.

"I see you have met Bishop de la Marchia," Alison said. "He is a distant relation of mine."

It occurred to Lizzie for the first time that Alison might already know about the signature on the tomb, and she hoped she had not dragged her here for nothing. It would be awful to disappoint her when the look on her face showed she was anticipating something wonderful.

"What have you found?" Alison asked.

Lizzie took her by the hand and walked with her around the tomb.

"Look here," she said, pointing at the monogram.

Alison leaned over, peering under the stone ear of the bishop.

"What is it?" she asked, not seeing it among the other scratches in the surface of the stone.

Stepping back, Lizzie waited for her to recognize the Weaver's mark. When she did, Alison straightened up and turned to Lizzie.

"Well that's odd," she said.

"So you haven't seen it before?"

"No." She was thoughtful for a moment. "What do you think it means?"

"My best guess is that she commissioned the monument, and this mark is similar to her marks appearing on the tapestry. She didn't actually make it, but she probably paid for it."

"He was her relation," Alison said, trying to remember everything she knew of Bishop de la Marchia.

"And she says in the journal that she made an offering here in his memory. Couldn't this be it?"

Alison thought about it and agreed it might be so. "She certainly had plenty of money."

She was leaning heavily on her cane and Lizzie directed her to the folding chair, then found another for herself and brought it to sit beside her.

"That's not all," Lizzie said, handing Alison the relevant photo and the magnifying lens. "In all the times we went over these photos in the last week we never noticed this, but her mark also appears on the image of this tomb on the tapestry." She pointed it out.

"Ah, I see it. I took that for shading."

"Me too. It's funny that we instantly saw the signature when it appeared in expected places, near the bottom or the edge of a panel, but she is using it here for another purpose. We weren't expecting that and we consequently missed it."

"What purpose?"

"I think to mark where she made a substantial offering."

"In the journal she mentions that she made an offering at almost every church along the way. I always just assumed she meant money."

"Wouldn't it be wonderful, though, if she was commissioning works of art along the way, and those were her offerings?" She pointed out the last vestiges of the fabric pattern in the stone pillow under the bishop's head. "Don't you think it is similar to the foliage pattern in the tapestry?"

Alison said she *might* see it, "but there really isn't enough left there to be conclusive."

"Of course," Lizzie agreed. "And it would have to be pretty distinctive to separate it from a whole range of similar patterns of that period, even if it was easier to read." She paused, then added that a good conservator might be able to bring out the image in the right kind of photograph. She saw the expression on Alison's face and smiled. "I have to admit that I like the idea that the Weaver might have done more than just pay for the thing, that she was involved in the design."

The two women stood and Alison took Lizzie's arm for support.

"Earlier I was thinking that she must have stood upon this same spot, our friend the Weaver, thinking about her cousin or uncle, or whoever the bishop was to her, and admiring this monument."

Alison squeezed her arm. "That's a lovely thought."

"I hope you don't mind that I called you to drive down here just to look at two letters scratched into an old piece of stone."

"Ah, but what letters! I'm very glad you called."

They walked across the grass in front of the Cathedral to where Alison's MG was parked on the street. Just across was a restaurant called the Swan and Alison asked Lizzie if she might treat her to lunch.

This was an opportunity for Lizzie to show Alison the similar small monogram that appeared on Glastonbury Abbey in the tapestry and as soon as lunch was ordered she took the photograph out of the envelope.

"Could she have made a similar offering there?" Lizzie asked hopefully. "Maybe she commissioned another work of art as a donation and the placement of the monogram indicates where we might find it."

Alison looked through the magnifying lens at the picture, and then raised her eyes to look at Lizzie. "Have you ever been to Glastonbury?"

"Not yet."

"Let's go there when we are finished," Alison said. "Before you speculate any more on what you might find there, you need to see it."

"What about the walk?"

"What route had you determined for today?

Lizzie pulled out the map, "the damned infernal map," she said, and told Alison that she had, in fact, seen some potential problems in the offing.

"The best thing about the route from Wells to Glastonbury is that it looks to be flat," she started. "But there are an awful lot of watery patches. Look at these moors," she said, pointing to places with names like "Queen's Sedge," "Splotts" and "Crannel." "They all seem to be connected and crisscrossed by canals, but there is no way across them but the A39, which is a road that I have already come to hate."

Alison took the map and folded it up. "Let's just drive there today," she said. "I'd like to see Glastonbury with you."

"You will not get an argument from me," Lizzie said quickly.

What would have been a long walk was a short drive, and by early afternoon the pair was in Glastonbury and approaching the site of what had been a glorious building in the age of Chaucer and the Weaver, but was now a ruin. Very little was left of the walls and any thought Lizzie had of finding evidence here of the Weaver's visit quickly evaporated.

As they came onto the grounds of the abbey she turned to Alison. "Ah," she said.

Alison was silent as they stood side by side and looked at the mirroring structures that must have flanked the original door of the abbey. The old stone was white in the afternoon sunlight and an arch in each of the pieces led into a grassy field that had once been the nave of the church.

"You know," Alison said quietly, "that before the murder of Becket at Canterbury, this was the most important pilgrimage site in England."

They had talked about Glastonbury several times in the last week as they researched each place along the path, and Lizzie had made a file of important sources. She pulled out the photograph of the tapestry and held it up in front of her.

"You can sort of see this archway in her image," she said turning it toward Alison, "but the place where she put her monogram is just gone. There is simply no building there anymore." They looked at the journal, which mentioned another offering, but Glastonbury had been rich with contributions. William of Malmesbury, who'd visited around 1125, had written about the wealth of relics in the church and Lizzie had transcribed one passage: "The stone pavement, the sides of the altar, and the altar itself are so loaded, above and below, with relics packed together that there is no path through the church, cemetery or cemetery chapel which is free."

"I'm sorry," Alison said, "but if the Weaver left anything here, it is long gone, swept away by those thugs of Henry the Eighth's at the time of the reformation." She described a particularly brutal devastation at Glastonbury. "Not only did they steal all the treasures, destroy the shrines and altars, and strip the roof off to expose the interior to the elements, but they executed the abbot and other influential churchmen." Without the roof, the walls deteriorated and local people removed the stones to build houses and pave roads.

There was a peacefulness about the place on a pleasant afternoon. The grass was meticulously tended and what remained of the walls was now clearly protected. The violence with which the building had been attacked in the name of the Church of England had disappeared with the centuries. Lizzie mentioned this to Alison, and was told that the same church had reconsecrated the site only a few years earlier.

When they reached the top of what had been the nave, a metal sign planted in the grass caught Lizzie's attention. "Site of King Arthur's Tomb," it read. "In the year 1191 the bodies of King Arthur and his Queen were said to have been found on the south side of the Lady Chapel. On 19th April 1278 their remains were removed in the presence of King Edward I and Queen Eleanor to a black marble tomb on this site. This tomb survived until the dissolution of the Abbey in 1539."

"How interesting," Lizzie said.

"What?" Alison asked suspiciously.

"That Henry VIII would not have had the tomb of Arthur protected. Didn't he, like Edward, try to make a link between himself and Arthur?"

"Perhaps he didn't really believe it was Arthur's tomb."

"Wasn't it?"

"Of course not!" Alison exclaimed. "I told you Arthur is

a literary character, not a historical figure." She thumbed through the guidebook they had picked up as they passed through the gift shop and read aloud, adding emphasis where she thought it was needed: "In this grave were laid bones *thought to be* those of King Arthur and his Queen, Guinevere. King Arthur was *probably* a chief who helped to defend this part of the country against the pagan Saxons. The stories of the Round Table came many years after his death."

"Not quite a declaration of belief!" Lizzie said with a laugh.

"They are waffling nicely," Alison said. "I like that they are so cautious; they don't try to prove the existence of a historical Arthur just because they happen to have his grave on their premises." She added that many historians over the years had allowed the vast Arthurian literature to influence them unreasonably.

"It's a compelling story," Lizzie argued. "Arthur had idealistic notions of government and was a wonderfully flawed human."

"Indeed," Alison said. "That is what makes him good literature. Accidental incest with his sister, his dysfunctional son, his ménage a trois with Guinevere and Launcelot, the Knights of the Round Table, it is great drama! It is not history, however. At the time the so-called corpses were found here, the Plantagenet Kings, who were of course Normans, were looking to link themselves to a Saxon-fighting royal lineage in Britain."

"I need to look more closely at your books on this topic when I get back to your house."

"I have been thinking about that," Alison said. "You might as well come home with me tonight and I will drive you to Castle Cary tomorrow, which is the next place mentioned in the Weaver's journal."

When Lizzie agreed, Alison said that there were a few more places they should visit in Glastonbury before returning to Bath. "Some people claim that the Holy Grail is here, you know."

"Because of the Arthurian connection?"

"No, interestingly enough, it is a coincidence that the

Knights of the Round Table were seeking it. Some people claim that Joseph of Arimathea, the man who provided the burial place for Jesus, brought the chalice of the last supper to England after the crucifixion." There was, she said, a well in town that was one of several locations claimed for the chalice.

As they walked to the car, Lizzie was struck by the number of shops that sold New Age paraphernalia, especially crystals, magic potions, Celtic jewelry, and prints of pre-Raphaelite paintings of Arthur's women. One store, located near the ancient market cross on the small square, was called "Archangel Michael's Soul Therapy Centre, Providing Tools for Personal and Planetary Ascension."

"It seems that there may be other reasons for a pilgrimage here today," she said, stopping to look in the window of the shop. A leaflet taped to the glass described Glastonbury as a global energy source, the chakra at the heart of the planet, a place of druids and goddesses, and then named them: the Morgans, the Merlins, Brigit the Swan Maiden, and Mikael the Sun Lord.

"The Arthur connection has attracted a whole range of knuckleheads," Alison said unsympathetically. "All this mystical nonsense!"

Lizzie could not help reminding her that there had been a strong mystical component to the medieval pilgrimage as well.

"Yes, but they had legitimate reasons to seek an escape from their lives in mysticism. The Weaver lived through the ravages of the Black Plague and the War of the Roses. The Catholic Church, which might have imparted some structure beyond the vagaries of patriotism or nationalism, was split under two different popes for half of her lifetime. There was little 'science' to speak of, the vast majority of the people were illiterate, and their lives were controlled by a grasping aristocracy." She realized she was ranting and took a breath. "It's no wonder they sought escape in a pilgrimage," she said finally.

"I would think for a woman like the Weaver it was also an opportunity for the adventure of travel."

"I think that was an important part of it."

"So what do you think the motives are of these New Age pilgrims?"

"They are embracing fantasy. I've been here many times; I've seen them in the shops and up at the well. The majority of these mystic seekers are solidly middle class. It is not hardship that drives them here—no plague or oppressive regime."

"Perhaps their burdens are more mundane. Misfortunes of love, failure at school, loss of health, or a job crisis can seem like huge burdens; perhaps those things lead them here."

Alison groaned. "To seek out the swan maidens and goddess sites and heart chakras and mythic nobles? Good lord!"

Lizzie didn't know if she should laugh or not. "It can't be an escape from technology," she said, "because I see their websites advertised on every building, and it appears that you can readily buy computer games here that are set in Arthurian landscapes on distant planets."

They reached the car. Lizzie wanted to offer to drive as Alison was looking so stiff, but the older woman went immediately to the driver's side and lowered herself in.

"Are you, as a historian, disturbed by the way history is used in support of this fantasy?" she asked, shifting the car into gear.

"Of course," Lizzie answered. "History is a process of interpreting evidence about the past, and that interpretation is always subject to question and criticism." She paused as she thought how best to express herself. "In each age, our interpretation changes because the questions that we ask about the past are influenced by events and ideas in our own time. In that way, history is always something of a tool to be used in the present."

"But you aren't saying that anyone can just use the past in any way they like," Alison demanded.

"No, of course not," Lizzie responded. "There were real events and ideas that we want to capture as best we can. The study of history provides us with a way of looking at human beings and how they respond to adversity, how they deal with each other, and how they fit into the natural world." She paused again and spoke slowly as she articulated things she had long thought about. "But if the people and events of the past are worth studying for what they tell us about the *present*, they are also intrinsically interesting, and it seems like we ought to have some responsibility to represent them fairly."

"That is what I hope we might achieve for the Weaver."

"I hope that too," Lizzie said. As she thought about the whole of the conversation, she wanted to add that religious folk from the Weaver's day to the present had always embraced a certain element of fantasy as part of their faith, but Alison looked exhausted from the outing, mentally and physically, and Lizzie thought there had been enough challenging discussion for the day.

As she entered Alison's house, the piles of books—which had once seemed like an impossibly disorganized mess—beckoned to her. One pile, Lizzie realized, was the one she herself had made to learn more about King Arthur. She settled into her customary chair with her now customary scotch and began to read.

Chapter 14

Two things that Alison said were of special interest to Lizzie, and they directed the course of her inquiry about King Arthur. The first was that he was a literary character and not a historical person, the second was that historians had notoriously misinformed the public about that fact.

She began with the grave at Glastonbury. Few modern historians doubted that the discovery of the bones was a medieval hoax, a way of bringing attention to the abbey at a time when its fortunes were at their lowest following a devastating fire; it was an age of relics and false relics. The Plantagenet Kings wanted to eliminate any question of their right to rule, and sought to link themselves to a character from English history. The fact that Arthur, like them, fought the Saxons, made him a brilliant choice. Henry II had died just two years earlier, Richard the Lionhearted was on the throne, and his nephew and potential heir was named Arthur, the Duke of Brittany.

The thirty-five-year reign of Henry II had solidified Norman rule in Britain, and Henry's marriage to Eleanor of Aquitaine had brought additional territory on the continent. Henry had been raised on the tale of Arthur, as penned in 1138 by Geoffrey of Monmouth.

Lizzie found the book beside her, the *Historia regum Britanniae* or "History of the Kings of Britain," and leafed through the translator's introduction. Geoffrey of Monmouth had incorporated a number of earlier historical sources into his book, but where the story bogged down, where it lacked romance, or where alteration could advance political motivations, Geoffrey filled in, and Arthur was born. Thus an Arthur was created who defeated all comers on the Continent, and whipped the Saxons, Irish, Scots, and Picts for good measure.

Henry II, according to other sources, liked the story of Arthur so much that he commissioned another version of it by a cleric named Wace, with even more drama, and positing that he himself, Henry II, was the legitimate heir of Arthur. When the monks at Glastonbury handily found the remains of Arthur and Guinevere, the legend gained legitimacy and began to be accepted as fact.

Henry's heirs took advantage of this and embraced their relationship with Arthur. His son Richard I, as Lizzie knew, was said to have presented Arthur's sword Excalibur to a foreign king while on a crusade to the Holy Land. Another Arthur would have succeeded Richard as king had he not been murdered by his uncle John, who took the throne himself. John's grandson, Edward I, brought a book of Arthurian romances with him on a crusade, sponsored "Round Table" feasts, and was the recipient of Arthur's crown when it was "found" in 1284. And when the Glastonbury bones were reinterred in a glorious black marble tomb in a rebuilt Abbey, Edward himself carried Arthur's coffin. His grandson Edward III is said to have been inspired by the Knights of the Round Table in the creation of the Order of the Garter.

Lizzie made notes as she looked at book after book, creating a time line of additional Arthur stories by French, English and Italian writers. Dozens of medieval authors contributed to the fanciful escapades of Arthur, including Rusticello, who had helped Marco Polo write his travel narrative, and Thomas Malory, whose *La Morte de Arthur* first appeared in 1460. Twenty-five years later, when Henry VII defeated Richard III in battle and claimed the English crown, Malory's book became important again. Richard was the last of the Plantagenets, Henry was the first of the Tudor kings, and he immediately linked himself to Arthur, christening his first son by that name in a ceremony at Winchester, the city Malory had identified as Camelot.

Much later, in the nineteenth century, Victoria and Albert found in Tennyson a writer who could do justice to the Arthur saga, and they too gave the name to one of their numerous children. Arthurian murals decorated the walls of their neo-medieval castle at Balmoral.

Lizzie pulled a big illustrated book from the pile and looked at the Balmoral murals, and at Arthurian scenes painted by the pre-Raphaelite brotherhood, artists who had picked up on the romantic theme of courtly love and explored every facet of the story in lush romantic paintings of red-haired Guineveres. Lizzie owned a painting by Dante Gabriel Rossetti, one of the founders of the pre-Raphaelite movement, given to her by George Hatton, and she was fond of the style.

She was looking closely at the details of one of Rossetti's paintings reproduced in the book when she heard Alison's footsteps behind her.

"I thought you had gone to bed," she said, turning.

"I've been thinking about finding the Weaver's mark on Bishop de la Marchia's tomb," Alison said.

Lizzie closed the book and put it back in the pile. "It's exciting, isn't it."

"Yes it is," she said. Alison moved to her own chair and sat. "I don't think I'm paying you enough, Lizzie. I can't believe that in such a short time you have seen so many things that I never observed."

Lizzie gave her a warm smile. "It's a good thing I'm not doing this job for the money. I live for these small thrills!"

"Really though, I am quite rich."

"So am I," Lizzie said with a laugh. "I own a Rossetti painting!" She explained to Alison how George had come to give her the painting, and a medieval triptych, which was worth even more. "I really am doing this because I love the work," she said, hoping to put an end to any further discussion of monetary compensation.

Alison took the hint and changed the subject. "What are you thinking now of Arthur?"

"That you are absolutely correct. He belongs in your literature class and not my history course."

"If you don't mind my being a Literature Professor for a moment, tell me what you think are the most important aspects of these legends, as you are going to write a footnote to the Weaver's visit to Glastonbury."

This took some thought to answer, but a few clear themes had occurred to Lizzie as the pile of books shifted from the floor beside her to the table in front of her, and back to the floor on the other side of her chair.

"I think the most interesting thing to me is how specifically the world described is that of the Plantagenet era, though any historical Arthur would have lived seven hundred years earlier, in the fifth or sixth century. All the details are of chivalrous armored knights, courtly love, quests, hunts, jousts, and revels at court, all from the twelfth or thirteenth century, when the first books were written. There is nothing in any of them that grounds them in an earlier time period." The idea became clearer as she articulated it. "It is really rather remarkable," she continued, "that this is true of Wace, who was basically describing his own world of the mid-twelfth century; of Malory, for whom these things would have been old-fashioned but not beyond the realm of the audience's memory; and continue all the way to Tennyson's "Idylls of the King" in the nineteenth century."

"So in the world described in these texts do you see any evidence of history?"

"Certainly no historical details that inform us about a real Arthur or that early age in which he might have lived, though in the earliest texts we get good information about how later medieval society worked. For our purposes, though, there are a lot of wonderful descriptions of the English countryside, and the pilgrimage path will take me right across a number of specific locations associated with Arthur."

"None more potently than Glastonbury, I think," Alison said.

"The discovery of a grave there was certainly put to very good use in supporting the legend. Bones are evidence of a person, and it seems that there have been a lot of people over the last nine hundred years who have been willing to believe that person was Arthur."

Alison picked up one of the books, *The Ruined Abbeys of Great Britain*, by Ralph Adams Cram. "Did you read this?" she asked.

"I skimmed it. He seems like a credible source until he

gets to Glastonbury, when he simply stopped being critical."

"Exactly! He was a well-respected architectural historian at the turn of the twentieth century, and he perfectly illustrates my point about how historians have allowed themselves to be taken in by the literature on this subject."

Lizzie opened the book to the description of Glastonbury. "He basically says that the fact that there was a grave proved that there was an Arthur. He relies on the account of Giraldus Cambrensis, who was an eye witness to the opening of the tomb."

Alison scoffed at that. "He was just as much a tool of the nobility as Geoffrey of Monmouth or Wace."

"Cram says that the description is 'concise, detailed, convincing, and full of internal evidences of perfect veracity.' He adds that if it is false it is 'a masterpiece of circumstantial evidence quite unimaginable in the twelfth century.'"

"Tosh!" Alison said, using an expletive reserved for English people of her class. "There is plenty of evidence that medieval confidence men were just as able to perpetuate scams as their modern counterparts, and Cram places a ridiculous amount of faith in so-called eyewitness testimony. There are many medieval narratives that begin with the claim that everything therein was witnessed by the author, and then go on to describe sheep growing on trees, bands of Cyclops, and sea monsters."

Lizzie added that it was also a period of false relics, into which category she would put the bones of Arthur. "At that time there were relics circulating around Europe that included the staff of Moses, samples of the manna from heaven, thorns from the crown of Jesus, and enough pieces of the true cross to build a boardwalk back to the Holy Land."

Alison smiled at the description. "The Pardoner in Canterbury Tales is an example of one such charlatan."

Lizzie had continued to scan down the page of the Cram book. "Here is the description of the opening of the tomb by Cambrensis: 'Between the two mysterious pyramids beside the chapel of the Blessed Virgin, seven feet below the surface, was found a large flat stone, in the under side of which was set a rude leaden cross, which, on being removed, revealed on its inner and unexposed surface the roughly fashioned inscription, "Hic jacet sepultus inclitus Rex Arthurius in Insula Avalonia." Nine feet below this lay an huge coffin of hollowed oak, wherein were found two cavities, the larger containing a man's bones of enormous size, the skull bearing ten sword wounds, the smaller the bones of a woman and a great tress of golden hair, that on exposure to air crumbled into dust.'"

"That last bit about the hair should have been enough to make people suspicious," Alison said. "But the fact that the lead cross could not subsequently be located was another clue to the charade. Surely such a treasure would have been preserved at least for a few years."

"I saw a picture of it, though," Lizzie said, pawing through the pile of books until she found the one she sought. "In 1607 a man named William Camden published a sketch of the cross, which he said he saw." She turned the page toward Alison and read the translation of the inscription: "Here lies buried the renowned King Arthur in the Isle of Avalon."

"Well Mr. Camden wanted to sell books too!"

Lizzie picked up another book. "This guy, Geoffrey Ashe, says that as he reads the cross as drawn by Camden, the lettering is too clumsy to have been made in the twelfth century, and the Latin is an old style."

"In this case you don't have to go back to the twelfth century. Camden might have made it up in the seventeenth century. And that book you're holding is a particularly silly one."

Turning it over to look at the back cover, Lizzie noted that the author had written eight books on King Arthur, which didn't make him any less silly in Alison's eyes.

"It's rather unfortunate too," Alison said. "Because much of the book is a competent exploration of various invasions of Romans, Saxons and Normans into Britain, and he has a good discussion of the early sources of the Arthur legend. But then he goes too far and argues that the literature was, in fact, based on an actual person, a local leader known as Riothamus."

"But you don't buy it?"

"No I do not. And I am sorry to see so much time devoted to trying to peg Arthur to one or another of the ancient kings—

nothing resembling the Arthur we know exists in the earliest texts that describe the history of England." Alison gave Lizzie a synopsis of the most important sources. "A monk named Gildas wrote a flaming condemnation of kings in the sixth century called *The Ruin of Britain*, and there is no Arthur there. The venerable Bede doesn't mention him in the eighth century, nor does another monk, Nenius, who wrote a history of Britain in the ninth century. Most importantly, the *Anglo Saxon Chronicle* goes back to the year 1, and you will not find any hint there of the man we now know as Arthur." She sighed loudly. "Of course you could take any of the names from around the right time period and say *this* is the one that was Arthur, and certainly that's what Ashe and others have done. But it doesn't matter if there was an early king named Arthur or Riothamus, because the stories we know don't describe his life." "

Lizzie turned to the appendix of the book. "Oh my God!" she exclaimed. "Here is an attempt to create a direct lineage from Arthur/Riothamus to your current heir to the throne, Prince William!" As she read it she narrated the plot to Alison: *If* Arthur was Riothamus, and *if* he had a wife before Guinevere, and *if* they had a child, then it *might* have been Cerdic who, according to the *Anglo-Saxon Chronicle* arrived from the Continent in 495. "Geoffrey of Monmouth would have been proud of this," Lizzie said. "The unknown wife, the fact that the *Anglo Saxon Chronicle* gives Cerdic a different father, and many other details are rationalized and explained away. And to top it off, Camden believes the tomb at Glastonbury was real, even though he says that Riothamus died on the continent."

She snapped the book shut. "I am reminded of a wonderfully goofy headline I once saw in a supermarket tabloid after Richard Burton died. It said 'Liz Can Still Have Burton's Baby!'—even though he was dead and Elizabeth Taylor was past menopause."

"Did they explain how that might be done?" Alison asked curiously.

"I believe they thought that if an egg could be harvested from Elizabeth Taylor and fertilized with a sperm bank donation that Burton might possibly have left behind, then a surrogate mother just might be able to bring the baby to term."

The two women simultaneously rolled their eyes and laughed.

"It's late," Alison said. "Almost midnight."

"I guess we've given Arthur his due this evening," Lizzie said, gathering the books together to return them to their shelf. "Perhaps the most intriguing thing to me is the intensity with which people desire a story like this to be true. It is not simply a *willingness* to believe, but a *wish* to believe. I wonder if the Weaver thought that Arthur and Guinevere were buried in that tomb."

"Luckily she does nothing more than mention seeing it in her journal, so we won't have to deal in this much depth in our remarks."

"Yes, but if we want to make the Chaucer connection, we will need to acknowledge that the Wife of Bath's tale begins with a knight in King Arthur's court who rapes a girl and is sent on a quest as punishment."

That reminded Alison of the Chaucer conference, which was now only a little more than a week away.

"Have you thought about what we should say there?" Lizzie asked.

Alison lifted her shoulders. "I think just the bare facts: there is a journal, there is a tapestry, and together they document a weaver's pilgrimage from Bath to Canterbury in the late fourteenth century."

"That seems good to me. It establishes you as the author of the project—and that much information alone will knock their socks off!"

"People will ask, of course, if we think our Weaver is Chaucer's Wife of Bath."

"Of course. Let us be sly in answering! It will give them something to look for in the work to come." Lizzie turned to go to her room, but Alison put a hand on her arm to hold her back.

"Lizzie," she said. "I am uncomfortable after all you've done in continuing to think of this as my project. It is clearly *our* work and I think you should refer to it in that way from now on."

Lizzie smiled broadly and could not resist putting her arms

around Alison and squeezing. "Thank you for that, dear Alison," she said. "I do think of it as our project—ours and the Weaver's!"

Chapter 15

In her journal, the Weaver described several towns through which she passed that were only minimally indicated on the tapestry or weren't there at all. As Alison drove Lizzie to one of them, Castle Cary, they talked about what the criteria might have been for making the distinction.

Lizzie had the typescript of the journal in her lap and read from it as they sped around curves at high speed. She was glad she was not walking along this road when Alison was at the wheel.

"This was apparently a textile center in the Weaver's day," Lizzie said as they entered the town. "She writes that she spoke here with spinners and dyers about specialty wools that she would pick up on her return trip."

"I'm afraid you'll find that there is not much to see here that is as old as her time."

"I assume from the name of the town that there must have been a castle here."

Alison pointed up a steep hill behind the town. "There are only a few stones from the fortifications left," she said. "You'll see them when you walk up there."

Lizzie looked up the hill. It was steeper than any she had climbed yet, but she felt much less reluctance at tackling it than she had the Mendips. After the first day of soreness she was convincing herself that she was getting stronger, and the expectation of what she might find at the top inspired her. It was clear from the Weaver's description in her journal that she had walked along the top of that ridge.

They parked the car in front of the Horse Pond Inn, where Alison said they might have an early lunch before Lizzie went on her way, but there was time to amble around the town for an hour before that. Across the street was the town market-place, a beautiful old building of warm yellow stone. Along one side, columns supported the building and provided a covered space for vendors to display their wares, protected from rain and sun. Lizzie was surprised that it was as new as the mid-nineteenth century. There was a museum in the building, but it wasn't open yet and the women agreed to return to it.

"I was here years ago," Alison said. "There is an oddity in this town, a wonderful old jail, though it is not old enough to have been seen by our Weaver."

A short walk took them to a round medieval lockup that was so small it looked like it could only hold one person. There were four stone stairs up to a solid nail-studded wooden door. There was no way to look inside and they continued up a small hill to the local church. In the yard that surrounded it was a tombstone that caught Lizzie's attention. It marked the grave of a long-dead 16-year-old girl, "Taken away from evil to come."

"That seems to me a very strange notion," Lizzie said to Alison.

"Aye, and to me too."

"Not having children I can't speak from experience, but it seems that of all the ways that one might justify the loss of a child—'it was God's will,' 'she's in a better place,' etc.— this would be the last one to memorialize forever on a tombstone."

They walked around the church, and then back down the hill to the main street of town. "Perhaps that girl had already exhibited some bad behavior," Alison said as they crossed the street to walk again around the tiny jail. There was not much traffic and they were deep in a conversation about the different expectations for girls and their behavior, both in comparison to boys and over time. They moved around the corner and back to the market building. Neither of them noticed the car that came toward them, slowly at first and then with increasing speed. There was a small plaza in front of the market, paved with stone, and set off from the street by black metal stanchions, and the car careened from the street, smashing over one of the stanchions. Lizzie looked up at the noise and saw the car barreling at them at top speed. She grabbed Alison by the arm and leapt and fell into the open area behind one of the columns as the car crashed full speed into its old stones.

The sound of smashing glass and metal was deafening, and there was a crack of stone as the column took the full impact of the car. Lizzie put her arms under Alison's shoulders and pulled her to the far end of the building, fearing that the column might break and bring the building down above them.

"Are you all right?" she asked with concern.

Alison nodded, but Lizzie could see that she was in pain.

A middle-aged woman rushed to them, dropping her shopping bags on the pavement, and knelt beside Alison. Several other Samaritans came to offer their assistance.

"That were a close one," an old gent said. "That car were aimed right for yer."

Lizzie acknowledged the truth of the statement. As Alison seemed in good hands, and as an ambulance had been called, she went to see the condition of the driver of the car. He was an elderly man, his white hair soaked with blood. There was a spider-web crack in the windshield in front of him where it had taken the impact of his head.

The front of the car was so smashed in the impact that it was impossible to open the driver's door, but his window was open and several people were trying to speak to him at once, asking him to describe his condition. His lips moved almost imperceptibly and Lizzie found herself at the side of the car, trying to understand what he was saying. For a moment he opened his eyes and looked at her. Blood dripped down his face from the wound on his head and he seemed to want to speak. Lizzie leaned her head in the window and heard him say one word, "Becket."

As police and firefighters moved in, Lizzie was pushed away from the car and she returned to Alison. A medic was with her, a young woman with a gentle and competent manner. Alison reached her hand out to Lizzie, who took it and crouched beside her.

"This nice girl thinks I may have broken my hip," Alison said.

Lizzie looked from her to the medic. "I'm sorry, I probably didn't help that by dragging you," she said apologetically.

Alison squeezed her hand. "Nonsense! You saved my life."

The square was rapidly filling with emergency vehicles. Several fire trucks and police cars were on the scene, and when an ambulance arrived for Alison, the police moved everyone out from under the covered area of the market until they could have an engineer assess the damage to the column and the building structure above it. The building was evacuated and there were soon several dozen people milling about. As Lizzie got into the ambulance with Alison, she saw firefighters working with hydraulic cutters to remove the door from the smashed up car. The driver was now covered with a sheet, but she couldn't tell if that was because he was dead, or to protect him from glass or metal fragments that might drop in the process of extracting him.

There was no hospital in Castle Cary, and as the ambulance drove the short distance to the next town, Lizzie called Edmund on her cell phone to tell him what had happened.

"Is she seriously injured?" he asked.

"Yes, I think so," Lizzie said carefully. Alison was clearly in terrible pain and she didn't want to express in her hearing how worried she was about her.

"Is she conscious?"

"Yes."

"Well that's always a good sign. Where are you headed?"

Lizzie asked the medic and repeated the information to Edmund. "Wincanton Community Hospital. Do you know it?"

Edmund answered that he did. "If I leave right now I can be there in an hour."

'Thank you, Edmund," she said with relief. She had hoped he would come, but had not wanted to ask, and was pleased he could arrange to leave his own practice so quickly.

When they arrived at the small hospital, Alison was wheeled away to an examination room and Lizzie sat in the hallway and called George to tell him what had happened. He also said he would leave immediately to join them, though it would take somewhat longer for him to arrive from Hengemont than for Edmund coming from Bristol.

As she turned off her phone, Lizzie leaned her head against the dull green wall of the hospital; it was a color that could induce sickness in the well. Feeling slightly dizzy, she leaned forward again and with her elbows on her knees held her head in her hands.

The doors of the ambulance bay opened and another stretcher was rolled in. The body on it was covered entirely with a sheet, one end of which was bloody from where the driver's skull had smashed against the windshield of his car. The young men who brought the corpse in wheeled the gurney into the hallway and left it opposite Lizzie.

Synthesized music played in the background, a circular non-melody that meandered around but never landed on a real tune; the automated rhythm track was unvarying. The combination of the music, the sickening green walls, and the corpse under the bloody sheet made Lizzie feel like she was in some weird drug-induced dream. Had that body, in its last minutes of life, actually said "Becket"? A policeman came in as she contemplated it.

A conversation between the policeman and the medics followed, and Lizzie saw herself being pointed to as a witness to the accident.

"You were at the marketplace in Castle Cary?" the officer asked. He was a young man, with close-cropped hair. When Lizzie answered that she had been there, he pulled a pen and a small tablet from the pocket of his uniform and began to ask her questions, beginning with her name.

"You're an American?" he asked.

She explained her relationship with Alison and described the accident, giving him details as he asked.

"Did you speak to the driver of the car?"

"I don't remember," she answered. "But he spoke to me."

"What did he say?"

"Just one word, 'Becket.'"

"Becket?" he asked, spelling the name out as he wrote it down. When he looked up, she nodded.

"Do you think he was intoxicated?"

"I don't know. I didn't smell alcohol on him, and he had a terrible head injury."

"Do you know what this 'Becket' means?"

Lizzie shrugged. "I may have misunderstood him, but I assumed it was St. Thomas Becket." She added that the saint was on her mind though, as she was following a pilgrimage to Canterbury. It didn't sound at all logical that a dying man would make a one-word reference to something she was already thinking about and she knew it.

"He's from Canterbury," the policeman said, nodding at the corpse, "so maybe there is something to it."

"Who was he?"

The policeman flipped back a few pages in his notes. "Bruce Hockwold was his name and he was ninety years old—which is too old to be driving, in my opinion." He lamented that it often wasn't possible to get the licenses away from elderly drivers before they became a danger on the road. "Since there was no other vehicle involved, it looks like he lost control of his car." He told Lizzie that he was sorry her friend had been hurt, and handed her a business card in case Alison needed a copy of the report.

When the door closed behind him, Lizzie was left alone with the body of Bruce Hockwold. She couldn't resist walking across the hallway and lifting the sheet to look again at his face. His eyes were open and she looked into them. Dead. The word was meaningful as she looked for something in the depths; there was nothing there of the man he had been just hours earlier. She wondered if she should close them, but he was sticky with blood and she wasn't sure that the eyelids would not already be stiffening from rigor mortis.

She heard a sound behind her and turned to find the medics returning with a nurse to claim the corpse. Lizzie dropped the sheet back into place and stepped away, embarrassed at the awkwardness of the situation.

She was saved from having to explain her morbid curiosity by the arrival of Edmund, who came bounding through the door at that moment and pulled her into a warm embrace.

"I'm so relieved you weren't hurt," he said. He stood back and looked at her. "You aren't hurt, are you?"

She assured him she wasn't injured and he kissed her on the cheek before turning to the nurse to ask about Alison's condition. He identified himself as a doctor and a friend, and asked if he could see the patient. Lizzie watched as he went into the inner sanctuary of the hospital, led by the nurse and followed by Bruce Hockwold and his two-medic escort. She sank again onto the molded plastic chair of the hospital hallway and pondered the strangeness of the day.

Chapter 16

Alison's broken hip required surgery and George and Edmund insisted that she be transported to Bristol to have the procedure done there. The patient was fully conscious when they loaded her again into the ambulance and she was adamant that Lizzie continue on the pilgrimage as planned.

"I think I should at least see you comfortably settled before I go on," Lizzie argued.

"Nonsense," Alison insisted. "Why should you spend time in a hospital waiting for me? Edmund can keep you up to date on my condition by phone."

George added that he would bring her to Hengemont for her recovery, and with that the doors of the ambulance closed and Alison was gone.

Lizzie turned to Edmund, who would follow them in his own car.

"I know this is all rather abrupt," he said, putting an arm around her shoulder. "That is the nature of accidents. Something happens that takes only moments, and then you spend days or months or years making adjustments to the unexpected changes."

"I feel like I should go be with her."

"Why? Because you were with her when it happened? That does not oblige you to nurse her through her recovery."

Lizzie tried to explain to him how close they had become in just a few weeks of working together.

"You certainly do go collecting friends and families on your research forays!" Edmund laughed. They walked to his car and he fished in his pocket for his keys. "It's a long walk from here to Canterbury," he said, "but you can drive it and be back in a few hours if necessary. I'll let you know if anything happens that requires your attendance."

There was good sense in what he said. Lizzie had been discomposed by the accident and now began to feel her equilibrium return.

"Do you want me to drive you back to Castle Cary?" Edmund asked.

"I don't want to delay your arrival at Bristol Hospital," she answered.

Edmund said it wouldn't be a problem. "Alison's own orthopedic surgeon is there. I'll check on her as soon as I get there, but she will be in very good hands."

As they began the drive back to Castle Cary, Edmund commented that his father would be a good nurse for Alison, and that the job would be a good distraction for him. "He has been too much on his own rambling around Hengemont," he said.

"Thank goodness he has the Jeffries to watch out for him," Lizzie added.

Edmund turned his eyes momentarily from the road and gave her a look of resigned condescension. When he spoke his voice had a measured patience. "However much you may want my father and Helen Jeffries to be friends," he said, "it simply will not be so. They are never going to eat a meal at the same table or sit by the fireside for a cozy chat." He paused. "I know you want all the class differences to disappear, but for that generation they are too deeply ingrained."

She looked at his profile as he drove; his forehead was creased and his mouth was drawn into a line which Lizzie read as displeasure at her comment.

"Oh for God's sake!" she said impatiently. "I only meant that Helen will make sure that he is eating and has clean clothes. I wish you would believe that I have learned something from all our past discussions on this topic!" She had not intended to be so snappish and instantly apologized. "I am more shaken by today's events than I thought," she said. "But I really did not mean to drag out once again a conversation we have had so many times."

Again he turned his eyes from the road for a moment and

smiled at her. "I'm sorry too," he said. "I don't know why, but you have made me so overly sensitive on this subject that I sometimes think everything you say casts aspersions on the aristocracy in one way or another. I shouldn't have read into your comment more than was there."

"Thank you for that," Lizzie said. "Of course," she added, grinning impishly, "it wouldn't hurt him to go eat in the kitchen once in a while! It's really quite nice there and the Jeffries are good companions."

Edmund rolled his eyes.

"I know, I know!" Lizzie added quickly. "None of them would feel comfortable crossing over those lines that proscribe their role in the ancient caste system in which they still operate!" She reached across and put two fingers on Edmund's lips as he turned his head toward her. "And that, my dear Edmund," she said with a flourish, "is the last thing you will ever hear me say on this subject!"

He looked ahead at the road and muttered, "Not bloody likely!"

She turned the conversation to Alison. "Will she make a complete recovery?"

"It is a pretty simple fracture of the hip and she was scheduled for a hip replacement anyway, so I think her doctor will probably just go ahead with that surgery. She'll be down for six weeks or so, but—as I almost hesitate to say again—Hengemont will be a good place for her to recuperate."

Edmund wanted to know more about the accident and how it had happened and Lizzie described to him the sequence of events.

"When did you see the car coming at you?" he asked.

Lizzie closed her eyes and concentrated. "I think I saw it first when it was across the square, but at that point it wasn't headed in our direction." In her mind's eye she could see the small red car on the far side of the Castle Cary thoroughfare. Did Bruce Hockwold actually look at them? She seemed to see his white-haired head turn and meet her eye, but too quickly that image was replaced by his dead eyes and his bloody head, first in the smashed up car and then on the hospital gurney. She put her hand up to her forehead.

"Are you alright?" Edmund asked, concerned.

"I'm just trying to get the sequence of events right," she said. "This is the first time I have actually turned my mind to it since it happened." She paused for a moment before she spoke again. "This will sound very strange," she said. "But I think he might have looked at us when he was traveling in a totally different direction."

"Are you saying he turned and drove at you purposefully?"

Lizzie grabbed at a piece of her hair and twirled it around her finger. "No, I'm sure that isn't possible. I think it might be because he spoke to me just before he died, and later that I saw his corpse. . . ."

"Memories are not like photographs. They don't actually capture events so much as interpret them sometimes. Maybe you are needing to process witnessing his death, and are doing it by picturing him alive."

"I'm sure that must be it," she answered, though she was more confused than she was admitting.

As they reached the center of Castle Cary they found that public works vehicles had replaced the fire trucks and ambulances at the accident scene. Cones and plastic tape defined spaces where the public was denied access around the market building.

"Where was he when you first saw him?" Edmund asked.

"Almost right where we are now," Lizzie answered, seeing again that red car in her mind, the image of Bruce Hockwold looking at her.

"And where was he when you next saw him?"

"Speeding toward us from that direction." Lizzie pointed up to the left as they made a right turn around the market.

"So he must have gone up and turned around if you were standing in front of the market." He pulled his car into the nearest space and got out. "Show me where you were," he said.

"Are you sure you have time for this?" she asked as she joined him on the sidewalk.

He took her by the arm. "Don't worry about it, Alison will be fine if I'm not there right away. Show me where you were."

They went as close to the market building as they could

before a barricade and a policeman stopped them. Lizzie pointed in a line that went from the road, across the space where the missing stanchion was obvious, and to the smashed up column, now being shored up with steel beams. "That is the route the car took, but I didn't see him until I heard him hit the stanchion."

"Well that must have slowed him down."

"It didn't seem to; he just came barreling on up here." She turned around and looked at the dark cavity under the overhang of the market. "I pushed Alison behind the column and jumped with her."

Edmund put his arm through hers. "You were both lucky," he said. "Thank God."

Lizzie acknowledged that they were. It was strange being at the scene again. It seemed like the whole thing had happened much longer ago than just a few hours.

"I see Alison's car," Edmund said, pointing to the black MG parked across the street. "Do you want me to take care of it so you can walk away?"

Lizzie had already decided to check into the Horse Pond Inn for the evening and leave Alison's car in their parking lot when she began her trek the next morning. "No need," she answered. "Alison won't be needing it for awhile, and if I need a car for anything in the next few weeks I can come back here and get it."

"I'm not sure I should leave you here alone."

"And I feel like I have already delayed your departure too long!"

She assured him she was fine, but when he drove away she felt a wave of loneliness. Turning one more time to look at the scene of the accident, Lizzie realized that she had forgotten to tell Edmund the most interesting thing of all—that Bruce Hockwold's last word was "Becket."

Chapter 17

The Horse Pond Inn was a comfortable place to recover from the events of the day. Lizzie got a room and called Martin in Newcastle to tell him what had happened to Alison, then retreated into a corner booth in the hotel's pub with a pint of cider. She brought her laptop to check email and found a message from Jackie with the tantalizing subject heading: "I'm here!"

"Dear Lizzie," it read, "I've decided to attend that Chaucer conference you mentioned in Oxford next week, and want to join you on your walk until then. Did you know that part of your path lies along something called the 'Leland Trail'? It's a pilgrimage for librarians! I will arrive in Glastonbury on the train this evening at 6:35. If I am following your passage correctly you should be there. Meet me if you can! Cheerio and all that, Jackie."

Lizzie looked at the clock on her computer. It was almost six o'clock; she could meet Jackie's train if she left right now. Alison's car was still at the curb in front of the hotel and she had the keys in her pocket, so she put her computer in her bag and headed for the car.

It was as strange to sit behind the steering wheel on the right side of the old MG as it had been to sit with *no* steering wheel on the left. It took several minutes for Lizzie to figure out how the gear shift worked, and it was an awkward left-hand procedure. She hadn't used a clutch in years and the gears ground ferociously as she worked her way out of the parking place, with a sound that made several pedestrians turn and stare at her. By the time she reached the train station in Glastonbury, she had mastered the car, and when

Jackie walked out the front door of the station she was able to give her a jaunty wave.

"Tally ho!" Lizzie called, bringing the car to a stop at the curb directly in front of her friend.

"Good God, Lizzie!" Jackie exclaimed. "You do rather get into the spirit of your work, don't you. Did you rent this?"

Lizzie sprang from the car and slapped a hand on Jackie's back. "Of course not, you foolish woman. This car is fifty years old! And a classic. You can't rent things like this."

"Where do we put my luggage?" Jackie asked, looking into the two seats of the car.

"In the boot, of course," Lizzie answered, though it quickly became apparent that she didn't know how to open it, and Jackie ended up holding one of her bags in her lap and squeezing the other in by her feet.

"I can't tell you how glad I am that you're here," Lizzie said, when they were finally settled in the car and on the road back to the Horse Pond Inn. She described the accident earlier that day and Alison's condition.

"So I won't get to meet the old girl?"

"Not unless we go visit her in the hospital, which I am inclined to do in the next few days."

"I'm even more interested in meeting her than I was before, now that I know she drives a car like this," Jackie said, running her hands across the polished wood of the dash. "Does she know you're driving it?"

"Not yet," Lizzie said with a laugh, "but I couldn't leave it just sitting on the street in Castle Cary while she is in the hospital—and she gave me a set of keys."

"I suppose this means that she won't be able to give the presentation at Oxford next week."

There hadn't been time to think about it since the accident, Lizzie said. "We've talked about it and the plan was to be fairly straightforward. I could certainly give the presentation, but I'm inclined to think it should be put off until Alison can do it herself. This journal is going to be the biggest project of her career."

"What journal?" Jackie asked in surprise. "You have not yet told me all I need to know."

"Sorry about that," Lizzie said, "Alison had previously sworn me to secrecy, but since I showed her that paper you wrote she has agreed to bring you into the coven of the Weaver. When we get back to the hotel I will tell you all, with illustrations that will surprise and amaze you!"

They had a light supper and then retreated to Lizzie's room, where she spread Alison's transcription of the journal and the photographs of the tapestry across the bed. Jackie's reaction to the material was exactly what Lizzie had expected: impressed, enthusiastic and knowledgeable.

"This is exciting!" she said as she compared back and forth between the images and the text. "Either of these things on their own would be considered a major find, but the combination of the two. . . ." She paused to look for the right word. "It's fucking awesome!!" she said finally.

"May I say again how pleased I am to have you here," Lizzie said, smiling at her friend.

"Fucking awesome!"

They spoke for another hour, until Jackie said her brain couldn't function anymore without sleep. As she prepared to go to her own room across the hall, she turned and told Lizzie that she simply had to present the material for Alison at the Chaucer conference. "It's too fucking awesome to keep to yourself," she said.

"Let's walk for a few days," Lizzie answered. "And then go see Alison in Bristol and talk about it."

Jackie gave a sleepy wave and agreed it was a good plan.

The next morning they took out the Ordnance Survey maps and looked at the path.

"Shaftesbury is just too far for one day's walk," Lizzie said, running her finger along the path.

"What about Wincanton as a halfway stop?" Jackie asked.

"I've been there already. It's where the ambulance brought Alison."

"Nice town?"

"I didn't really see much of it."

As it was just the right distance in the right direction, they decided to make it their destination for the day, and aim for Shaftesbury the following evening. Jackie showed Lizzie a brochure for the "Leland Trail," which she had picked up in the hotel lobby, and they agreed to incorporate as much of that as possible into their walk.

After making arrangements to leave the car and everything from Jackie's luggage that didn't seem essential for the next two days, the pair followed the sign that put them upon the "Leland Trail" and the "Public Footpath," which ran alongside one wall of the hotel. The first hundred feet or so was between the high stone walls of old buildings, but they quickly found themselves leaving the busy level ground of the town and working their way up an incline into farmland, and then up the steeper path to the top of the ridge. Here they stopped to catch their breath and found two stone benches sitting incongruously in a field, surrounded by cows.

"Clearly, we are on the right path for librarians," Jackie said, sinking onto one of the benches. "Who else would furnish the out-of-doors for the comfort of sedentary patrons?"

Lizzie fished the map out of her pack and began to orient herself. "I think we must be on the site of the castle for which this town was named," she said, looking around her for any sign of the old fortifications. "The Weaver would have come up this same path and around the castle."

"The Weaver?"

"Alison and I decided we needed a name for her."

"You may think about her if you like—I shall think that upon this path trod the velvet shoes of John Leland, bibliophile and librarian to His Majesty King Henry VIII."

They looked around them at the view of the village below, the fields dotted with sheep and cows and crisscrossed with short stone walls, and up the opposite side of the valley.

"That next big hill is called Cadbury," Lizzie said, pointing. "I wonder if it's where the chocolate comes from."

"According to John Leland, it's where King Arthur's court was."

"Camelot?"

"The very same." Jackie kicked at a stone with her shoe, and then stood up and tossed another down the long hill. "But I'm sorry to have to tell you that though he was a librarian, Mr. Leland was full of shit when he made that claim."

"I am all astonishment," Lizzie proclaimed facetiously. "What was he doing here anyway?"

Jackie pulled the brochure from her pocket. "According to the South Somerset Council," she read, "who has marked this path for our benefit, 'Leland traveled around England for five years collecting information for his book, *The Laborious Journey and Serche for Englandes Antiquities*'—spelled with many extra e's, as was the custom in those days."

"And where does the Arthurian part come in?"

"Apparently he misheard a local story about a ruin on Cadbury's summit and mushed it up with one of the Arthurian tales of Chretian de Troyes."

"You will not believe this, but two days ago I had that very book in my hand! I will say once more, dear Jackie, that I am very glad you are here, but this Leland guy does not seem like a model for us at all!"

"I know. He was really just an excuse. I was jealous that Kate was coming along on part of your walk and I wanted to get my oar into the enterprise."

Lizzie explained some of her conversations of the previous days with Alison about the persistence of the Arthurian legends. "And you should see Glastonbury!" she said with a hoot. "My God, it is King Arthur meets the Age of Aquarius! He is just as appealing to the New Age crowd as he has ever been."

"You will love this then. After John Leland identified Mount Cadbury as Camelot, a story developed that Arthur's secret burial is in a cavern on the hillside and every year he and his knights come thundering down the mountain to Glastonbury at midnight on Christmas Eve, or Midsummer Eve, or Midsummer Night, or Halloween, or maybe only every seven years, or some other bullshit."

"You and Alison will get along very well when you meet," Lizzie said, reflecting on the personalities of her old friend and her new friend.

They walked on companionably, discussing books and ideas, personal and professional lives, and the terrific journal and tapestry left by the Weaver. Though they had been colleagues and friends for many years, they had never spent so much time together so far from home. They passed a pretty little Norman church at Yarlington, and took the opportunity to step inside the cool darkness to break the heat of the sun. There was a monument there to the son of the "Lord of the Manor," killed at Ypres in 1916 at the age of twenty-three. It was a mosaic of an armored knight.

"The images of the aristocracy are everywhere!" Lizzie said in feigned disgust.

"You don't fool me, Lizzie Manning! You love this stuff!"

"Ha! I know an Englishman who will argue with you on that!"

Occasionally they pulled out the map to check their progress and they found several intriguing placenames. "Jack White's Gibbet" was especially interesting, but in trying to reach it, they ended up slogging through a calf-deep marsh that left them wet and soggy.

As the afternoon wore on they were eager to find a place for lunch or tea and decided to walk along the road for a time rather than stay on the footpaths. Their shoes and socks were soaked and squishy, and at one point Lizzie found that her knees were refusing to bend. A lovely old hotel, the Holbrook House, beckoned to them around a bend, with a sign out front advertising traditional English teas.

"That sign is like a bell and I am Pavlov's dog," Jackie said. "Bring on the food, I am salivating."

They entered the lobby and sank into low soft couches.

"I may not ever be able to rise from here," Lizzie said in a half-complaint. "I'd like to strip off these shoes and socks, but I don't think I can do it in a place so elegant."

Jackie leaned over and whispered. "It may have been elegant in its day, but that day is long past."

There were a few ancient relics sitting in chairs around the lobby. Like the place itself, they looked like they might have been elegant in their day.

"Maybe we should just stay here," Jackie suggested. "It will make tomorrow's walk a little longer to Shaftesbury, but I am beat."

Lizzie looked out the window and saw a field of buttercups, through which a small herd of cows sauntered. One of them strolled over and looked at her.

"All right," she said. "Let's see if they have rooms available."

Once they had changed and eaten, Jackie asked Lizzie to explain to her again the purpose of the pilgrimage. "It doesn't seem like the route is very exact, so how are you collecting evidence?"

"This isn't quite like any other research project I've ever undertaken," Lizzie started. "I know that you think I generally make things up as I go along—this time I really am."

It was so much the history and habit of their friendship to speak acerbically to each other, that Lizzie was almost surprised by the gentle tone with which Jackie responded.

"You know that you are my favorite scholar, Lizzie. You approach things with enthusiasm and you are open to changing your opinion if evidence goes in a different direction than you expect. I wouldn't quite say that is making things up as you go along."

"Why Jackie," Lizzie answered, touched by the remark. "That is positively sweet of you." She pulled the journal and the tapestry pictures from her bag. "In answer to your first question, I am confused about how to proceed, especially now that Alison is out of the picture at a particularly crucial moment." She gestured at the pile of papers and photos. "Will you help me?"

"Get the maps out too," Jackie answered. "You clearly know the major places to stop, as they are pictured on the tapestry map. But how are you determining the intermediate paths?"

Lizzie raised her shoulders in frustration. "Alison was never very clear on that, beyond that there are some paths that are clearly ancient and that the Weaver would almost certainly have traveled on them; the path up from Castle Cary today is a good example."

"Yes, but after a time there were too many options and we just sort of sloshed around. Her journal doesn't mention Wincanton or any other intermediate place?"

Lizzie shook her head.

"Then let us assume that unless a place is indicated in either the journal or the tapestry that it doesn't matter." Jackie began to line the journal entries up with the photographs. "So you have been to Bath, Glastonbury and Castle Cary, all mentioned in the journal. What did you find? Anything referring to our Weaver character?"

Lizzie pulled her camera from her bag and plugged it into her computer. She showed Jackie the picture she had taken in Wells Cathedral.

"Do you see this mark," she said, pointing to the AW monogram carved into the stone. "This is her signature."

"Was she a stone carver?"

Lizzie explained that she thought the Weaver might have commissioned a stone carving, in the same way she had commissioned Flemish weavers to make the tapestry.

"So her monogram is on the tapestry?" Jackie asked.

"Yes," Lizzie answered, "in several places." She drew one of the pictures from the pile. "It is on the edge of each of the panels. Here, for instance, you see it near Canterbury Cathedral, and here near London." She explained that she had also seen it in the cartouche of Wells Cathedral on the tapestry, but only after she had found the signature on the stone. "And here it is on Glastonbury Abbey," she said, the disappointment in her voice obvious. "If her mark means that she left some evidence there in the form of a donation, there is now no way to find out what it might have been. The whole place is a ruin."

Jackie arched one eyebrow and gave Lizzie her best imitation of a penetrating look. "Ha! No way to find out? Please Lizzie, it is our job to find things that seem *not* to be there."

Lizzie shook her head. "You are my favorite librarian, Jackie, because you are a font of knowledge on such an arcane range of subjects, but I don't see how even you can pull an object out of the wreckage of Glastonbury Abbey five hundred years after it was destroyed."

Jackie knocked twice on Lizzie's head. "Hello?" she said. "The Abbey was destroyed, but what about the stuff?"

"What stuff?"

"The contents! The marauders sent out to destroy the various religious houses carted the valuable contents back to London. And I would be surprised if our friend John Leland didn't have something to say about that. Those guys kept excellent records; there is probably a list somewhere of everything they stole."

This had not occurred to Lizzie. "Where would such a list be kept?" she asked dubiously.

"Don't know yet," Jackie answered, "but give me an hour on the Internet."

Lizzie began to feel excited at the possibility. "But how would we ever be able to know what *she* might have given from a list of thousands of articles?"

"If that distinctive monogram appears on anything, then it will likely be mentioned in a catalogue description if the piece still exists. You know that." Jackie opened her computer and began to search. "My guess is that records like this are at the Public Records Office." She spoke as she typed, "Reign of Henry VIII, Glastonbury Abbey, and oh my God, look at this!"

Lizzie sat beside her and looked at the computer screen.

"They actually have the records of an outfit called 'The Royal Commission for the Destruction of Shrines.' No attempt whatsoever to disguise the crime by a euphemistic name." She scrolled through page after page of manuscripts that had been scanned and downloaded. "There may be a searchable transcription of this list," she said, "and we certainly aren't going to be able to get through it tonight, but now you know that all is not lost, Lizzie. We may yet find out what your friend the Weaver gave to Glastonbury Abbey."

"You are an absolute genius!" Lizzie gushed. "Thank you, thank you, thank you! I wish Alison was well enough for me to tell her." She grabbed her cell phone. "I will call Edmund instead, and find out how she is doing after her surgery."

The news was good. Alison was resting comfortably and was expected to make a full recovery. She would stay in the hospital at Bristol for three or four days and then go to Hengemont with George. Lizzie told Edmund that Jackie was with her and that they would trek to Shaftesbury the following day. "Will Alison be ready to receive visitors the day after tomorrow?"

"I know she'd love to see you. She was babbling a bit about

some conference coming up next week, and wanted me to tell you that you must still go."

"I'll let her get her full faculties back before we make that decision," Lizzie said, "but please tell her I am thinking about her."

When she turned off her phone Jackie was looking at her. "Edmund?"

"Yes, and why are you saying it with that look on your face?"

"Is Martin jealous?"

"Of course not," Lizzie insisted, "and just to prove it I will call him as soon as you go to your own room."

As Jackie packed up her things they talked about the next day's walk. "It's going to be a climb," she said. "Steeper than today. The desk clerk told me that Shaftesbury is on a hill higher than the spire of Salisbury Cathedral."

"What a wonderful way to measure it!"

"Such an optimist," Jackie said with a laugh. "My first thought was Ugh!"

"Thanks again for coming, Jackie. Your timing was perfect!"

Chapter 18

The weather was cool the next morning, comfortable for walking. Both women felt strong and refreshed and they made good time along well-marked footpaths. The day was so quiet that they could hear the munching of cows as they passed along the side of a pasture. Their first goal was a nature reserve called Duncliffe Wood, and as they approached it, Lizzie told Jackie that this was the sort of path she had dreamed about when she accepted Alison's offer. It was a straight path of hard-packed dirt; a high canopy of trees overhead blocked the brightest rays of the sun, but allowed pale beams to pick their way through and move about the path like small spotlights, as the trees bent and moved with the wind.

The path gained elevation as the woods became thicker. At one point a ruddy brown deer stepped onto the path before them and Lizzie and Jackie instantly stopped, holding their breath to keep from startling it, but it seemed unconcerned about their presence and moved on at its own pace.

They were silent for much of the time, though Jackie occasionally recited lines from poetry as the surroundings inspired her.

"I know I should probably quote from Shelley or Byron," she said at one point, "this being England and all, but when it comes to describing woods I don't think any of them can compare to our own Robert Frost. These woods *are* lovely, dark and deep."

"And we have miles to go before we sleep."

"Okay, that too, but I was going to go on to that other great Frost poem about woods, because I think it speaks to your pilgrimage route planning:

Two roads diverged in a yellow wood,
And sorry I could not travel both
And be one traveler, long I stood
And looked down one as far as I could
To where it bent in the undergrowth.
Then took the other, as just as fair."

"You know that Alison teaches the British Romantic poets?" Lizzie broke in.

"Of course. You remember that I looked up her entire career as soon as you said you were going to be working for her."

"Oft I had heard of Lucy Gray," Lizzie quoted, trying on Jackie the Wordsworth poem that had failed to impress Alison. "And when I crossed the wild, I chanced to see at break of day, the solitary child."

Jackie gave her an unimpressed look.

"What?" Lizzie whined. "Didn't you think those little footprints disappearing in the snow were creepy?"

Her friend ignored her. "Didn't Alison write a book on Coleridge that has some Captain Cook references? Right up your alley I'd say."

"I read it and it's not bad."

"So how is it, working for her?"

"I am really loving this project. And I've come to love her too. She's smart and straightforward. I think you'll like her."

"Will we go see her tomorrow?"

"That's my plan. If I am going to give a presentation at the Chaucer conference, I need to check in with her."

As they left the woods and progressed to the back roads into Shaftesbury, the climb got steeper. At one point the hill was so steep that they could take only five or ten steps before they had to rest. They walked alongside an old stone wall which they learned at the top defined the perimeter of Shaftesbury Abbey. On the other side of the road were thatch-roofed cottages and beyond them a deep valley. It was a dramatic view.

Shaftesbury Abbey was in even more of a ruinous state than Glastonbury. No part of it that had been above ground survived, and only an excavated foundation showed where the outline of the buildings had been. Here too, the Weaver had made a donation of some kind, described with frustrating terseness in the journal, and here she had put her mark on the tapestry.

Jackie attempted to be encouraging when she saw the disappointed look on Lizzie's face. "At least we now know that when the Commission for the Destruction of Shrines rampaged through here they left some records. We'll just add this place to the search when we look at the Glastonbury material."

Lizzie nodded and thanked her. "What a terribly destructive business that was," she said with a sigh. "To wreck centuries of art and architecture in the name of God."

"I don't think God had anything to do with it. Henry VIII was not exactly a paragon of religiosity." She asked how this site compared to Glastonbury.

Lizzie answered that the site was much smaller, and the destruction much greater. "Time and neglect seem to have finished the work here that Henry started."

"It's a nice garden, though," Jackie said. She picked up a brochure at the gate. "They have reconstructed an Anglo-Saxon herb garden."

They wandered through the garden and read about the site in the brochure.

"When Alison and I were in Glastonbury," Lizzie said, "we spent almost the whole time talking about people with only a mythic relationship to the place, King Arthur and Joseph of Arimathea, but here the historical record is really substantial. It was founded by Alfred the Great, who we know was an actual Saxon king."

Jackie was still reading the brochure. "I'm interested in the story here of Edward the Martyr. Apparently his corpse was the important one in terms of drawing people here for a pilgrimage."

"Who was he?"

"In a nutshell, he was the son of a Saxon King, Edgar, and his first wife Ethelfleda the Fair. Young Edward succeeded his father to the throne in 975, but was murdered four years later by his father's second wife Elfrida, who wanted her own son, Ethelred, to rule."

"How does that make him a martyr? Don't you have to die for God?"

"I think kings have a fast pass to martyrdom if they are murdered." Jackie responded before continuing the story. "Anyway, Edward's remains were placed here in Shaftesbury Abbey and started to perform miracles and attract pilgrims. Ethelred, who was called 'the Unready' for the rest of his life, was deposed by Vikings in 1013. His son also became a saint, Edward the Confessor."

"I wonder what happened to his corpse," Lizzie mused. "Here was another former king, whose remains were apparently just swept away when the abbey was destroyed. Don't you think that is strange?"

Jackie shrugged. "I don't know. Who cares?"

"Obviously not you."

"I don't care about kings *or* saints! In fact the whole idea of relics is just fucking weird!"

As they walked back through the gate and onto the main street of Shaftesbury, Lizzie asked the gatekeeper what had become of the relics of Edward the Martyr.

"They were hidden at the time of the destruction of the Abbey," he explained, "and buried elsewhere on the grounds." He leaned over to whisper to her. "They found them again when the site was excavated in 1931, and his majesty was sold to a Russian Orthodox Church in Woking that needed relics."

"What?" Lizzie said, shocked by the information. "The remains of a king and saint were simply sold?"

The man nodded. "They were. This land then was owned by the Claridge family of hotel fame, and they sold them relics to the Russians. There are those who hope they will be sent back some day." He pointed to a large square stone in the middle of the site. "You see that altar? That is where they hope to lay him when he returns."

Lizzie thanked the man and walked away. Jackie whispered, "What did I tell you? The whole thing is fucking weird."

Out on the street Jackie laughed until Lizzie could not help but join her. The sky was beginning to darken and they stepped into a small restaurant called The King Alfred Tea Shop to eat.

"You must admit this is a strange business, this pilgrimage, what with the body parts and all," Jackie insisted.

"Absolutely it is," Lizzie admitted without hesitation. "But don't you find the macabre bits fascinating? You just learned about the sale of the bones of a tenth-century murdered king, a thousand years later, to a Russian Orthodox Church in some place called Woking! Tell me this isn't a great way to spend your vacation!"

"You know, of course, why Woking is particularly funny?" Jackie asked, wiping tears of laughter. When Lizzie said that she didn't, Jackie answered the question. "It's where the Martians landed in H.G. Wells' *War of the Worlds*! I wish we were going there," she added. "That's a place for a pilgrimage—dead kings and aliens! But I must admit that you do know how to show me a good time."

They discussed where to stay for the evening and decided to get a cab to take them back to the Horse Pond Inn in Castle Cary, and to drive from there the next morning to Bristol to visit Alison.

"And now to end the perfect day, we drive for one hour to get back to where we started walking two days ago!" Lizzie said as they settled into the back seat of the cab.

"You do see my point about the other road being just as fair, whatever road it happens to be."

"I do. I amble a bit, I get lost, I wade through pig shit, I cross electric fences and barbed wire, I find myths about the bones of an ancient king accepted as reality, and an actual story about the bones of another one so fucking weird that nobody in their right mind would believe it. I see deer and sheep and cows and birds, and my dear friend joins me for a couple of days and we ride in a taxi halfway across England. This, Jackie, is the modern pilgrimage and we are on it!"

Chapter 19

Alison was in excellent spirits when Lizzie and Jackie arrived at the hospital, and was thrilled to meet Jackie. "I read that paper you wrote on the Wife of Bath," she said, "obviously you are one of us."

"The coven of the Weaver?"

"Is that what Lizzie called us?" Alison asked with delight.

"I was thinking of some other descriptors as we walked to Shaftesbury yesterday," Jackie said.

Alison asked what they were and Jackie answered "Amasaxons! Big women. Strong, smart, hearty-laughing women. Women who walk all day singing, then drink a pint of hard cider and sleep well."

Lizzie had known that Alison and Jackie would like each other, but she was especially pleased at how amusing Jackie was being for the benefit of the old woman, who was laughing heartily at the colorful description of their walk. Each of them had a crotchety side, but neither was displaying it today.

"Is there any chance that we can put you in a wheelchair and roll you to the Chaucer conference?" Lizzie asked hopefully when there was a break in the banter.

"I just don't think so," Alison said resignedly.

George entered the room, and hearing the last part of the conversation repeated Alison's answer. "There is no way that she will be able to attend any conference for at least several weeks."

He greeted Lizzie with a kiss on the cheek, and then was introduced to Jackie, who was quite curious about him, and even more so about his son, who followed a few minutes later. Jackie knew most of the story of Lizzie's relationship with the

Hattons as a researcher, and that they had become friends in the course of the work she did for George at his house, but Lizzie had not told her about her familial relationship with them.

Lizzie brought them all up to date on the progress of the walk, including the information that Jackie had located a list of the artifacts looted from Glastonbury and Shaftesbury Abbeys, in which they might find a record of donations made by the Weaver.

Alison was excited by the news. "Will you be able to look at the list before the Chaucer conference?"

Lizzie said that she wouldn't. "I was thinking, Alison, that since you can't be there you should withdraw your name from the program and wait for another opportunity to make an announcement about the work."

"Nonsense!" Alison said determinedly. "You can make the announcement. You know everything I do, and I trust you to make a decision about what should be made public."

"I just don't feel right about it," Lizzie argued, but everybody in the room urged her to do the job.

"Having put even the title of the presentation into the conference program, you have raised a lot of interest about your sources," Jackie said. "The best way for you to control how the information gets out is to present it right away. This conference is definitely the right venue for that."

The arguments were convincing and Lizzie agreed to do it.

Alison seemed pleased and asked Lizzie to come sit beside her. "This is the right decision," she said. "You will need to take good notes for me about who is there and what questions they ask."

"I'll have Jackie with me," Lizzie said. "She can be our spy!"

Alison liked the idea.

Taking Lizzie's hand she asked if she was suffering any after effects of the accident. "You weren't hurt, were you?" she asked with concern.

Lizzie assured her that she was fine.

"You and I were both very lucky," Alison said. "I've seen that car coming at us over and over in flashbacks. We could have been killed." She asked about the driver.

"I'm sorry to say he died at the scene," Lizzie said softly. She thought about whether she should tell Alison about his last word and finally decided she would. "It was so strange," she said. "And now I'm not sure what I really heard, but I could swear he said 'Becket' to me."

"Becket?" Alison, Edmund and Jackie repeated the word in unison.

When Lizzie nodded, Alison asked if she had any idea who the man was.

"His name was Bruce Hockwold, and he was from Canterbury," Lizzie answered.

"Bruce Hockwold?" Alison asked.

"That's what the policeman told me. And he was from Canterbury, which I thought was a very strange coincidence."

Alison sat up in the bed. "His name isn't Bruce Hockwold," she said, her voice trembling in confusion. "His name is Hockwold Bruce, Hocky they call him. He was a friend of my father's."

"What?" George said from across the room. "Impossible! Are you saying that you knew the man who almost killed you?"

"I haven't seen him in years, but he was frequently at my house, visiting with my father before he died."

"What are the chances of that?" George demanded. "That you would know the man."

"Very small, I should think," Edmund answered. He gave his father a sign not to pursue the subject any more in Alison's presence, and when a nurse came in to check her dressing, used it as an excuse to move the rest of the party out to the hallway.

"Lizzie, you told me that this man, Bruce Hockwold or Hockwold Bruce, looked at you before he tried to run you down. Is it possible that he did this on purpose to hurt or kill Alison?"

"It's so hard to believe," Lizzie answered. "The guy was ninety years old." The image of his red car across the square, his face turning to look at them. "But yes, I think he might have intended to hit us."

There was a stunned silence as the four of them tried to process the implications of this information.

"I have two questions that need answering," Edmund said. "The first is whether Hockwold Bruce's death means there is no longer a threat to Alison." He turned and looked at Lizzie as he finished. "And Lizzie, whatever this threat is or was, does it extend to you?"

The question was completely unexpected.

"How could a dead old man possibly be a threat to me?" she asked.

"I'm not sure," Edmund answered, "but you said he intended to hit *us*?"

"But I only meant because I was standing beside Alison. There is a chance she is mistaken about this. His name might actually be Bruce Hockwold; he may be an entirely different person."

She shook her head and thought again of the accident scene. Her thoughts then moved to the man lying dead on the gurney. She had been in a hospital corridor not unlike this one, the same green walls, the same soft non-music in the background.

"And even if he was the same man and saw me with her, he never had time to convey that information to anyone else. From the first time he saw me until the moment his car hit the market building was only a few minutes." She looked from Edmund to George and back. "No, whatever this is, I don't think it has anything to do with me."

"What does it mean, that he said 'Becket?'" Jackie asked.

Lizzie shook her head. "I have no idea. I mean the Weaver's pilgrimage ended in Canterbury at Becket's shrine, but the shrine itself is long gone—destroyed almost five hundred years ago by the same guys who leveled Glastonbury and Shaftesbury." She thought of the Becket reliquary. Alison had told her that her father had a secret that he meant to share with her, but never did. She had only mentioned it one time.

"Can we sit down somewhere?" she asked.

Edmund knew of a small waiting room nearby and directed them there.

"I'm not sure how relevant this is," Lizzie began when they were all seated, "but Alison has a Becket reliquary—that's where she found the Weaver's manuscript."

George asked if it was worth killing for.

"It's enormously valuable," Lizzie said. "And there is an early edition in it of *Canterbury Tales* that is also worth a fortune."

"Anything else?" Edmund asked.

"Two relics that are probably Becket's—a finger bone and a blood-soaked piece of cloth—and two lenses from a telescope."

"When you say 'enormously valuable,'" Jackie asked, "how much are you talking about?"

"Millions," Lizzie answered. "For the reliquary and the Chaucer, I think a few million pounds."

George stood and walked to the window. "If this were just about stealing these things, there would be no reason to kill Alison. If she were in her house when robbers arrived, that would be one thing, but she was hit by a car far from home."

Edmund leaned forward in his chair, resting his elbows on his legs and touching the fingertips of one hand to those of the other. "If Hockwold Bruce knew Alison's father," he said slowly, "he might have known those things were in the house all along." He turned to Lizzie. "Has anything changed that might have brought them to his attention again?"

"The Chaucer conference," Jackie answered. "The announcement that Alison has found the Weaver's journal means that she has found the reliquary."

This seemed important to Lizzie, but she just could not see how anything in the reliquary would have led an old friend of Alison's father to try to kill her. "Alison's father had a secret," she told the others, hoping the combined efforts of the group might clarify the situation. "He was supposed to share it with her, but he got Alzheimer's and never did."

"Perhaps he shared it with this Bruce character," Jackie posited.

"But why would he try to kill her?" George asked. "If Alison was supposed to know the secret anyway, why wouldn't he just tell her? I think he might have been senile or deranged. With him gone, that is probably the end of this."

His son disagreed. "We have to explore the possibility that there is more going on than we currently know. Alison needs security, and I'd like to go have a look at her house to see if we can find anything else. At the very least we should remove the reliquary to a safer location."

"What should we tell Alison?" Lizzie asked.

"As little as possible at this juncture," Edmund answered. "She needs to recover from her surgery before she starts worrying."

"Too late for that, I think," Lizzie said. "The worrying has begun."

Chapter 20

"Oh my God, the place has been ransacked," Edmund said when they entered Alison's house.

"No it hasn't," Lizzie said calmly. "This is how she keeps it."

"Well, this is a kind of security system, I guess. Good luck to the robber who can find anything here." Edmund asked Lizzie if she knew where the reliquary was, and she took them through to the library.

"I don't know if we could find anything in here if we didn't already know what we were looking for," he said.

"It's not quite so disorganized as it seems," Lizzie responded. "Having worked here for a few weeks I am getting to know the structure of the place."

Jackie had been silent through the conversation, but now she turned to her companions. "You are such neophytes when it comes to serious book collecting!" she said. "I've seen places with ten times the number of books in this amount of space."

"Jackie put herself through library school working for a book auctioneer," Lizzie said to Edmund in a loud whisper.

"I'm just saying that there is a system for moving efficiently through a room like this. First show us the reliquary."

Lizzie pointed out the collection of Chaucer editions on the shelf behind the desk and then the smaller shelves, which served as a door to the space behind. She pulled out the reliquary and put it on the desk.

Jackie gave a gasp of excitement. "It is fabulous!" she said.

"Thank you for using an appropriate 'f' word in front of my friend," Lizzie said. She opened the box and laid the contents on the wood of the desktop.

Jackie could not resist picking up the small book. "You're certainly right about the value of these things Lizzie. This is one of the early Caxton editions of *Canterbury Tales*, the second edition maybe?"

"That's what Alison told me."

"I think there are maybe only a dozen or so of these that survive."

"What about the rest of these?" Edmund asked, indicating the other copies of the book on the shelves, maybe fifty in all.

"It's a really extraordinary collection," Jackie said. "Few libraries can boast anything like it for the number of early editions. It would be almost impossible to assemble it today by purchasing the individual volumes—most of them are found only in libraries." She asked Lizzie who made the collection.

"I think Alison might have said it was her father, but as I think about it, this collection in itself might be an interesting clue to the relationship between the Weaver and Chaucer. What if *she* purchased the earliest edition and put her own journal in it?" She felt a thrill as she said it. "I assumed, and I think Alison did as well, that some later descendent saw the similarity between the Weaver's journal and *Canterbury Tales*, but what if *she* is the one who made the connection?"

"Sorry Lizzie," Jackie said. "Unless she lived a lot longer than a hundred years that just isn't possible. I think the first published edition of *Canterbury Tales* was 1477 or thereabouts. And, very importantly, didn't the Weaver make her pilgrimage in the late thirteenth century—before the printing press?"

"Damn!" Lizzie said. "It was such a great idea, but of course you are right."

"I see where your thoughts are heading, though," Edmund said. "You are thinking that these early editions of *Canterbury Tales* might have been purchased by Alison's various ancestors as each volume came on the market."

"That is not what I was thinking, but it is a brilliant thought, simply brilliant!" Lizzie said enthusiastically. "The collection was made over generations by people interested in the book because of the Weaver's connection to it."

"If there was any way that you could prove *that*," Jackie

said, "it would be the story of the century in the library world."

"Thank you Jackie, but is that a world we want to be in?"

"It is a lovely world, as you well know," Jackie answered, mimicking Lizzie's sarcastic tone.

Edmund had picked up the bone from the table and was studying it.

"Alison is pretty sure that is a human finger bone." Lizzie said. "Is she right?"

He said that she was.

Lizzie handed him the scrap of cloth. "And this might be covered with the blood and/or brains of Thomas Becket."

"Hard to tell after all this time," he said turning it over in his hand. "I suppose we could send it to the lab to see if they could get any DNA off it."

Jackie made a joke about cloning the saint, but the others ignored her.

Edmund had moved on to the lenses. "Any idea what these are for?"

"I think a telescope," Lizzie answered, "but Alison and I went through all the ones her father had here in the house and it doesn't seem to be for any of them."

"All right then," Edmund said briskly. "What do we need to do here, beyond removing the reliquary and its contents to a safer location?"

"I suppose we should look to see if Alison's father left any clue to the secret he was supposed to tell her."

"Any suggestions on how to do that?"

Lizzie said that Alison thought if there was a clue it was probably in or among the books. "But I don't think she has ever undertaken any sort of systematic search. She found the reliquary only when she went searching for a reading copy of Chaucer."

"How many books do you think there are in this house?" he asked with a sigh.

Jackie estimated over ten thousand, and Edmund sighed again.

"I think if there is anything to find, it would most likely be here," Lizzie said. "This was her father's room and Alison told me that she did not often come in here after he died. I think she regularly moves things around in the rest of the house, and she told me she has found unimportant things that her father stashed in books, but this is the place where she would be least likely to have stumbled on something by accident."

"So only when she was looking for something specific, like the Chaucer," Jackie added.

Lizzie agreed. She asked Edmund if he wanted to stay and work with them on searching the room. He answered that he had the rest of the day and evening available and was willing to help.

As Jackie was the most knowledgeable about books and editions, it was decided that she should quickly examine each volume. Lizzie wanted to start with the Chaucer collection, but Jackie told her that it was better to develop a system and stick to it. They should start with the shelves nearest the door and work their way, shelf by shelf, around the room. She asked Lizzie to clear the desk and then instructed her to empty the first section of shelving, bring the books to her, and then examine the empty shelf to make sure that nothing was hidden there.

Jackie looked at each volume, set it aside if it deserved further scrutiny, and made a pile to be returned to the shelf, which Edmund did. In this way they worked quickly around the room, processing almost a hundred books an hour for three hours. Jackie called out to Lizzie when she found a copy of John Leland's *Laborious Journey and Serche for Englandes Antiquities,* and occasionally made a comment about a particularly rare or important volume. When they reached the Chaucer collection, they took their first break of the day.

"Before we go any further, I need a cup of coffee," Lizzie declared.

"I could use something stronger," Jackie said, "and I think I saw some pretty good scotch on the sideboard in the other room."

"Alison's specialty," Lizzie said. "It has lubricated all our work." She offered to fix them all something to eat, and realized when she got to the kitchen that if Alison was not going to be returning home for several weeks she should get rid of the perishables and empty the trash. Their lunch consequently consisted of sandwiches made from cheese, apples and onions, accompanied by a salad of squash, beets and nuts. She made a pot of coffee, and found that Jackie and Edmund had perfectly replicated Alison's scotch and soda recipe.

As the three sat around the desk to eat, Jackie casually pulled books from the pile she had set aside. "A number of these," she said, "used to be very valuable, until someone cut a hole in them." She opened one to show a cavity cut into the pages, into which was stuffed a roll of bills.

Edmund took the bills and unrolled them. "It's the old currency," he said, "before we converted to the decimal system."

"And before bill sizes became standardized," Jackie said. "Look at the size of some of those! How did you ever fit them into a wallet?"

"Our wallets were so big we had to drag them behind us in wagons," Edmund answered with a straight face.

Lizzie asked how much money was in the wad and if it still had any value.

Edmund quickly counted it. "Two thousand and some pounds," he said. "It was a substantial amount when it was hidden here. Today, the bills aren't worth anything like their face value. You can buy them online for a few pounds."

Other books held additional money, some in modern currency, which Lizzie pulled out and put aside for Alison.

"These books have papers tucked into them," Jackie said, turning to the next small pile. "This book on astronomy, for instance, has a manuscript page of calculations."

"Alison's father was an amateur astronomer," Lizzie said.

"Should we leave it in the book or take it out?"

"Let me have it," Lizzie said, "and I will make a note of where it was."

There were other papers that had lists of sums or dates, and three had incomplete family trees, and Lizzie took them as well.

When the lunch plates were cleared and another round of scotches poured, they began on the Chaucer collection. Before they began to remove any of them from the shelves Jackie took a quick inventory.

"Right now they are more or less organized by height," she said. "That puts the earliest ones somewhat together as they tend to be small, but if we really want to understand how this collection was assembled, I think it might be useful if we organized them by date."

The whole collection was consequently brought to the desk and separated into piles, first quickly by centuries, as Jackie glanced at each one. The nineteenth- and twentieth-century copies were then returned to the shelf and Jackie sorted what was left into a careful chronology of editions.

"It is a testimonial to the staying power of the book that it looks to have been published in almost every generation since Chaucer wrote it," Edmund said, and both women agreed.

As Jackie leafed through one of them, a piece of paper fell out. It was a receipt from a bookseller: "Peter Quince, on London Bridge, Anno 1595."

Lizzie picked it up and held it silently up to Jackie, then both exploded in a shout of excitement.

"What is it?" Edmund asked.

"It is a receipt for this book," Lizzie said.

"Dated the year it was printed," Jackie added. "If there are others like this, your brilliant idea can be supported."

A quick search of the rest of the books located three other receipts, which was disappointing to Lizzie, but Jackie was still very excited. As she went back to processing the books, she found a copy from 1540 with a spidery brown signature on the flyleaf: "William Kent, his book." Between books with signatures of owners, and receipts for books purchased, nine of the books prior to 1800 could be associated with a member of the Kent family.

"This would be a great paper at the Chaucer conference!" Jackie said as the evidence was assembled.

"Maybe next year," Lizzie said, "when we have been able to put the whole story together."

An examination of the modern editions revealed only one hidden treasure. In an edition of 1945, a cavity had been carved out that contained two folded pages. One had calculations similar to those they had found in the astronomy book; the second was a list of names, three to a line. "William Kent, Thomas Bokland, Dunstan Hockewold" were at the top of the list. The same surnames were repeated in line after line, though "Bokland" became "Buckland" and eventually was replaced by "Wickersham." "Hockwald" was replaced by "Bruce" near the end of the list.

"Hockwold," Lizzie said, pointing at the name. "And here it is again, and again." She moved her finger down the list. "What the hell?"

Her companions looked on silently as Lizzie studied the page.

"The top line is much older than the last," Jackie said, reaching out to take the piece of paper. "The inks and signature styles are all different." She rubbed the page between her finger and thumb and then sniffed the paper. "The compounds in some inks have a distinctive smell," she said in response to the puzzled look Edmund gave her. She handed him the page. "This list has been kept over a very long time," she said.

"Obviously it shows a relationship between the Kent and Hockwold families," he said. He read the last line: "William Kent, Hockwold Bruce, Frederick Wickersham."

"Is it a family tree of some kind?" Jackie asked.

Lizzie shook her head. "There are only men's names on the list." She took the paper back from Edmund. "This might have something to do with the secret that Alison's father meant to share with her." She paused to ponder this. "What information would be important enough to be passed from generation to generation in three families? And yet would still have to be kept secret after what, a few hundred years?"

"At least," Jackie said. "How many lines are there?"

Lizzie quickly counted. "Fifteen lines."

"Say thirty years or so to a generation, with some being substantially longer and war and plague taking their toll. . . ."

"Four hundred and fifty years," Edmund said.

"At least."

"What secret that old could possibly be worth killing for today?" Edmund looked at Lizzie as he asked the question, but she couldn't think of an answer.

"This can't possibly be about the Weaver's journal," she said. "It is a straightforward description of a pilgrimage."

"You've only read a translated transcript," Jackie said. "Is it possible there is something there that Alison missed? Or that she kept from you?"

Lizzie defended Alison. "She might have missed something, but I'm certain she isn't deceiving me in any way about what is in the Weaver's journal."

"Do you mind if I have a look at it?"

Lizzie took the manuscript from the reliquary and gave it to Jackie. "I'm pretty sure the secret can't be based on this though. It is from the late fourteenth century and this list of names starts when, a hundred and fifty years later?"

The mystery occupied another fifteen minutes of their time until Edmund, looking at the clock, said that he would need to be starting home soon. "Do you want to try to process the rest of this room?" he asked.

It was with some difficulty that they turned their attention back to the task, but they once again got into a working rhythm and began to process books even more quickly than before. On the last shelves, as they came around the room and back to the other side of the doorway, were a number of tall volumes, lying on their sides rather than standing up, as the shelves were too short to accommodate them. Among these were several atlases.

"Here is something of interest for you, Lizzie," Jackie said, leafing quickly through a sixteenth-century atlas of England. "It seems to have someone's path marked on it from Bath to Canterbury."

Lizzie put down the pile of books she was carrying and went to look at it.

"It is almost your pilgrimage trail," Jackie said. "In fact, it seems to be two different, but almost identical paths." She leaned in to examine it more closely, then gestured to Lizzie. "The first line was put on in iron gall ink, so that could be quite old. The second one is India ink, which is more recent in European use."

Lizzie took the book from her and looked at several of the smaller area maps that had been annotated. "I think I'll take this with me," she said, "and look more closely at it."

It was now almost ten o'clock and Edmund announced that he needed to get back to Bristol.

"What should we do about the reliquary?" Lizzie asked.

"I think a safe deposit box is the best answer, especially while Alison is away from home. I'll take care of it."

Jackie suggested that he take a few of the Chaucers. "They are really valuable," she said. "Once Lizzie makes her presentation at the conference, it might draw attention to the collection, and as you say, with Alison gone. . . ."

Edmund agreed to take them. "But I'm not so sure Lizzie should make the presentation at the conference," he said as he placed the reliquary and the books into a box.

"Why not?" Lizzie asked.

He put his arm around her. "I'm just not convinced it's safe," he said. "We aren't sure what set off Hockwold Bruce, and he may not be the only one with an interest in what you have to say about the journal and the tapestry."

Jackie had an entirely different opinion. "This information is too important not to make it public, and Lizzie needs to protect Alison's work, and her own, by declaring their ownership of it. Besides," she added, "the best way to protect yourself from a secret is to reveal it.

"It might still be dangerous," he said with concern.

"Danger from whom? Chaucer scholars? What are they going to do, write something bad? They'll do that anyway."

Lizzie felt caught between the oppositional opinions of her friends. "I really have to make this presentation for Alison," she said to Edmund. "One of her colleagues already knows she has the journal, and a librarian at Oxford knows the tapestry is a map of the trip. If they spill the beans before Alison or I can announce it, then someone else could scoop her on the work and that would be terrible."

Jackie had been thinking about Edmund's concerns. "If there is still any danger related to a secret shared by Hockwold Bruce and Alison's father, then it would probably come from the last person named on the list." She picked up the paper again and read the name: "Frederick Wickersham." She looked from Alison to Edmund. "I will Google him," she said. "Then we can find out where he is located and Lizzie can avoid him."

Edmund was clearly not convinced, but he could see that there was no way to keep Lizzie from going to Oxford for the conference.

Chapter 21

The Chaucer meeting was held in the conference center at St. Hugh's College, so Lizzie was able to show Jackie the tapestry before she gave her presentation. They had spent the last three days visiting with Alison every morning, and working their way through her books in the afternoons and evenings, but hadn't found anything more that might reveal the secret that Alison's father had inadvertently kept from her.

Jackie, who was conversant with Middle English, had searched the Weaver's journal for additional clues but hadn't found anything that wasn't represented well by Alison in her transcription. She spent several hours plodding through scans of the documents of the Commission for the Destruction of Shrines, but she had as yet found no artifacts mentioned that bore the Weaver's monogram. She had also searched for information on Frederick Wickersham. The most likely candidate to match the name on the list was a solicitor who had recently died at the age of 88. His son of the same name was already dead, and there was a grandson, also named Frederick Wickersham, who was a graduate student at Oxford. It seemed unlikely to both Jackie and Lizzie that this Frederick Wickersham could be a threat.

As they sat on the couch opposite the tapestry, Jackie read to Lizzie from the conference program. "There is someone named Dante Zettler giving a paper on the sources of the Wife of Bath's tale."

"He is Alison's nemesis," Lizzie explained. "A junior colleague in her department who once tried to copy the Weaver's journal without her permission."

"We don't like him then?"

"We don't know him yet, but we do not expect or intend to like him."

"He is on for an hour this morning. I see that you have twenty minutes in the 'Announcements of New Work' section this afternoon. There are a couple of slots left open in that panel for late signups. Are you sure I can't just make a mention of the Kent family's generations-long collecting of *Canterbury Tales* editions?"

"No, I forbid you to speak about it until Alison has a chance to look at all the material. That will have to wait for next year."

They were approached by Michael Moberley and Lizzie introduced the two librarians to one another. "I'm so sorry to hear about Professor Kent's accident," he said. "But am very glad that you are able to step in for her. She called me this morning to assure me that you are a full collaborator in her project."

Lizzie gave a nod of acknowledgement. Alison's call, and Michael mentioning it, seemed an unnecessary formality to her.

"Oh, here is Professor Zettler," Michael said, pulling a young man aside and introducing them. "This is Professor Manning from America. She'll be reading the paper for Professor Kent."

Dante Zettler was about thirty years old and fastidious about his appearance. His expensive suit was perfectly tailored, and the blue-patterned tie he wore picked up the color of his eyes, which seemed too obvious to be an accident.

"So sorry to hear about dear Alison," he said, taking Lizzie by the hand. "I hope you didn't come all the way from America for this; I would have been happy to read Alison's paper for her; we're colleagues you know."

"It's not exactly a paper yet," Lizzie said. "It is an announcement, and I will simply describe the work in progress."

"Can I assume then that you and she are collaborating on the work?" He smiled throughout their conversation, but Lizzie couldn't help feeling that he was fishing for information and nervous about what she might know.

"Yes, you can assume that," she said. She pulled Jackie

forward and introduced them. "We were just talking about your paper on the sources of the Wife of Bath's tale," Lizzie said. "It is a topic in which we are keenly interested."

Dante Zettler raised an eyebrow. "Indeed?"

"Yes," Jackie echoed, "very interested. We look forward to hearing your lecture."

Jackie had a smile on her face that reminded Lizzie of one of the Rockettes in a Christmas show. From behind Dante's back she gave her friend a look to tone it down.

"Perhaps we could have lunch together?" Dante asked. "I'd like to get your critique of my ideas after you have heard them."

"I still have preparations to make to my own presentation," Lizzie answered, "but could we sit with you at the banquet tonight?" She wanted to wait until he had heard a full description of the Weaver's journal before she talked to him.

"I think the seating chart has been arranged," he said, "but let me speak to the proctor and see if I can be moved to join you. It would be delightful," he said, before leaving them.

"He's a bit weasily, I think," Jackie said as he walked away. "No wonder we don't like him."

"You don't mind having dinner with him, do you?"

Jackie gave Lizzie a wink and a sly smile. "Of course not! I assume we are feasting with him in order to taunt him."

"Absolutely."

"Then let the games begin! Let's go hear what he has to say about the Wife of Bath."

The lecture that Dante Zettler gave on the sources of the Wife of Bath's tale was torturously dense, even to Lizzie and Jackie, who really had been interested in the subject when he started speaking. While he attempted the occasional grand flourish or humorous aside, they mostly went unacknowledged by his audience.

"Geoffrey Chaucer did not so much *write* the story told by the character described by Russell Chamberlain in his 1986 book, *The Idea of England*, as—and I quote—'the broad-beamed, ineradicably vulgar, indestructible Wife of Bath'— end quote, so much as he *crafted* it from multiple sources. Let us examine them." His stress of certain words and simpering accent made the prospect of the next hour exceedingly dreadful.

Jackie not only yawned, but leaned over to Lizzie and said "Yawn."

"In Chaucer's own time," Dante continued, "this story might have been recognized by his audience as a familiar text, but in the twenty-first century we are forced to dig into and ponder multiple literary works seeking its roots."

"I hate that Chamberlain quote," Lizzie whispered to Jackie, still thinking about Dante's first sentence long after he had gone on. "Why 'ineradicably vulgar'?"

Jackie responded with a mock snore.

"Like many of the Arthurian legends," Dante droned, "this story began in ancient Ireland, travelled from there to Wales and then via balladeers to Brittany. When the Normans invaded England, William the Conqueror was followed by the balladeers, whose stories came with them."

"That Irish bit is something new," Jackie said.

"To me too," Lizzie said. "And I've just read a pile of books on the Arthurian legends."

Dante divided his examination of the story into three main elements: the hag (whom he called "the Loathly Lady"), the rape, and the quest for the answer to the question about the thing most desired by women.

"The story of the Loathly Lady begins in ancient Ireland where, according to myth, the goddess Ériu married Lugh, the sun. Ériu was a beautiful young woman in the spring, but aged through the year until in the winter she became an old hag. Over time, Ériu came to be seen as a personification, first of the landscape changing its face with the seasons, and later as a symbol of the nation itself, and was called the 'Sovereignty of Ireland;' sometimes she would even symbolically marry the king."

Dante paused to take a drink of water and then looked up. Lizzie thought he was looking right at her when he said, "The connection between sovereignty over a nation and sovereignty over one's husband are, I think, too obvious to require explication."

She turned to Jackie. "Huh? I don't see that link at all."

"At dinner you can ask him to explicate."

"As to the rape in the story, the roots there are not so charming," Dante continued. "In every potential source incident, a man of high rank rapes a woman who is—at least in his judgment at the time—of a lower class than himself. His power over her is more than just physical strength, it is political, and he consequently believes that she can demand no justice. Except that things then turn around. Maybe she isn't of such low class at all, maybe she is a princess in disguise, and if that is so then he will have to be punished to the full extent of chivalrous law."

Jackie nudged Lizzie with her elbow. "That means he had to marry her."

Lizzie was silent and a moment later Jackie nudged her again. "You know I'm not kidding," she said.

Lizzie nodded.

Dante gave a couple of potential literary sources for the rape, including the medieval *Life of St. Cuthbert.* "This interesting story of a seventh-century bishop—later saint—was written in Latin in the twelfth century and translated into English in the fifteenth. There is some evidence that Chaucer had a copy of the Latin text and took from it the scene in which a king rapes a maiden."

A number of examples of what he referred to as "the politics of rape" were then given from English ballads collected by Francis J. Child in the nineteenth century. "Many of these song texts had survived, as we all know, for many centuries in the folk culture of rural Britain." He then quoted from Child:

A knight met a shepherd's daughter in a secluded place and raped her. Then, in nine of the versions, the girl asked the knight for his name. In ten versions he gave it. Then he rode back to court, and she followed on foot. There the girl complained to the king in eight versions and to the queen in four, and the knight was ordered, under penalty of death, to marry the girl. The knight, who was the queen's brother in seven versions, the king's brother in one, a squire's son in one, and a blacksmith's son in one terribly garbled version, attempted in ten versions to avoid marriage by offering the girl gold. Nevertheless there was a wedding, described in two versions as big or gay. That night the knight turned his face from the bride in two of the versions. Surprisingly, the girl who had been believed to be a shepherd's daughter turned out to be the daughter of a person of high rank who was variously described as an unnamed duke, the King of France, the Earl of Stockford, the King of Scotland, the King of Gosford, the Earl Marshall, the Earl of Stampford, an unnamed king, or the Earl of Hertford. As her rank was equal to or better than his, they lived happily ever after.

"Ah, what a wonderfully romantic tale," Jackie sniped. "The rapist and the princess living happily ever after."

"What would have happened had she actually been the daughter of a shepherd?" Lizzie asked.

"Who was the rapist in this story?" Dante asked his audience before answering the question for them. "Sigmund Eisner believes it was Gawain, one of the best known of Arthur's knights. Certainly Gawain is associated with the story of the quest for the answer to the question of what women desire, but not as punishment for rape. He is, rather, saving Arthur from a threatening black knight who had been the first to ask the impossible question, and Gawain is consequently a hero."

In the last twenty minutes of his carefully timed speech, Dante turned to the quest, saying that it was generally accepted that Chaucer's primary source for this part of the story was the *Tale of Florent,* written by his friend John Gower. In Gower's version, the hero Florent, the nephew of an emperor, killed a knight in battle and was then captured by the father of his victim, who would have murdered him in retribution. The dead man's grandmother intervened, however, to send Florent off to find the answer to the question of the age: What do women most desire?

"There is no rape here," Dante said, "but it is significant that the hero is the nephew of the emperor—it links Chaucer's story to an *oeuvre* built around the nephew or son of a duke, king or emperor. Gawain is Arthur's nephew in two English Arthurian loathly lady tales," he explained. "It is possible that in a story known to Chaucer and Gower, Gawain was indeed guilty of rape, but Chaucer did not wish to name him and possibly distract his readers from the thesis of the Wife of Bath: female marital autocracy."

"What bullshit!" Lizzie whispered. "If that was really her theme, why does she tell that story at all?"

There was polite applause as Dante Zettler finished his discourse.

"Nothing new here at all," Jackie said. "Almost everything he's got was already published by Eisner in the fifties."

When questions were asked for, she raised her hand. "Do you think Chaucer's own history as a rapist may have played into the way he handles the theme here?"

There were several groans and hisses from the crowd. This was a contentious theme in Chaucer circles, as the circumstances of the crime were so sketchy.

"I'm glad you asked that," Dante said uncomfortably. "That document of 1380, in which Chaucer is said to have paid ten pounds to be released from the charge of *raptus* against Cecilia Chaumpaigne, is by no means clear." He turned immediately to the semantics of the argument. "In the *Life of St. Cuthbert,* the assailant is said to have *rauyst* the woman. Of course in the Wife of Bath's Tale there is no question, the knight, 'By verray force, he rafte hire maydenhed.'"

Jackie reiterated. "Ten pounds was an enormous sum at the time."

"Yes," Dante said, "it was about equal to what he earned in a year working at the custom house."

"Doesn't that seem to imply guilt?"

"I don't know," Dante said simply.

Jackie felt sorry for him and ceased her harangue. It was no fun if the opponent had no information and was not willing to defend a point of view.

When Lizzie's turn at the podium came, she gave the facts with very little interpretation. She announced that a journal had been discovered describing a pilgrimage to Canterbury in 1387, that the author was a weaver from Bath named Alison, and that her signature was also on a tapestry strip map of the journey that had been woven in Flanders around the same time. Lizzie showed images from the tapestry as she read from Alison's transcription of the journal, clearly making the link between the text and the pictures. She mentioned that when the tapestry was restored the panels had been placed in the wrong order, and she urged the audience to see it in the lobby of this building.

While she didn't make any attempt to link the Weaver directly to Chaucer, the possibility that this journal was by a woman who might have inspired the character of the Wife of Bath was clear. When she finished speaking hands shot up all around the room.

"Is it possible this is a forgery?" someone asked. "Have you submitted it to forensic examination or had it authenticated?"

"Not at this time," she said, "though the owner plans to do that very soon."

When asked who the owner was, she answered that it was Professor Alison Kent of Bath University, who was sadly unable to join them. Most of the people in the room knew that Alison was a reputable scholar; they had also heard she had been injured in a car accident.

"Can you describe the circumstances under which it was found?"

"Not at this time, but that information will be described when the manuscript is published." Alison had particularly instructed Lizzie not to mention the reliquary until they knew more about its history.

There were many questions about Alison's plans for publication. Lizzie said that the project was still in its early stages, but that a facsimile of the manuscript would be published with an annotated transcription in modern English, and that images of the tapestry would illustrate it.

"Is this a source for the Wife of Bath?" someone asked.

Lizzie looked to where Dante Zettler had been sitting, but his seat was empty. "We are not prepared to make that connection at this time," she answered, "but of course we are exploring the possibility."

The presentation created an enormous buzz of interest and

Lizzie found herself surrounded by Chaucerians peppering her with questions as she walked back to her seat.

"I knew this would be the hit of the show," Jackie whispered as they walked to the lobby with a few dozen people to look at the tapestry. "Excellent job!"

"I am just so sorry that Alison isn't here to see the interest," she said. "She deserves all this."

A number of people asked Lizzie very direct, even rude questions about the authenticity of the manuscript, demanding that she produce it for inspection. Several asked for a report on Alison's condition, and three publishers slipped business cards into her hand and said that she or Alison should call to discuss details on how the book might be published. One of them was a friendly young man who worked for a library in Canterbury which was, he said, interested in anything having to do with medieval pilgrimages there.

He introduced himself as Tyler Brown as he gave her his card. "I'm the archivist and librarian at the Canterbury Catholic History Society. We might be interested in publishing your book when it is ready." He seemed a little apologetic when he added that they didn't have the money that a large press might have to offer. "But I promise you we would produce a very handsome volume. We would take care to ensure that the illustrations from the textile were first rate."

Lizzie took his card and smiled at him. "Thank you, I'll pass this along to Professor Kent."

"It would be essential for us to know the origin of the journal of course."

"Of course," Lizzie said, nodding. "When Alison makes a final decision about publishing, she will share that."

"Can you tell me anything now that I might be able to use to interest my board of directors?"

Lizzie said that unfortunately she couldn't.

"Was it found in her house?"

Lizzie shook her head. "Sorry, I'm not at liberty to say."

"Because if it is part of a family collection, that makes it even more interesting."

"I'm sorry, Mr. Brown, I simply cannot tell you anything more at this point."

"Just this then, was anything else found with it?"

When Lizzie didn't answer, he smiled and said in an off-hand way, "As I said, we are interested in all things having to do with Canterbury pilgrimages, and often the discovery of one source leads to others."

There were several other people waiting to talk to her and eventually Lizzie told Tyler Brown that she looked forward to talking more about this when she actually had more to tell. She saw Dante Zettler and went to confirm their dinner date.

The conference banquet was in the dining hall of the college, a traditional Oxford eating room with long tables down the length of the room and a "high table" across the top where the dignitaries sat. There were name cards at each place, which Jackie thought exerted a bit too much control over an academic crowd. Dante Zettler had arranged it so that he was sitting next to Lizzie, and Jackie's place was on her other side.

"This won't do," Jackie said to Lizzie when she saw the arrangement. "I was looking forward to some friendly banter and I don't want to have to talk around you." She switched Lizzie's card with Dante's, so that he would be between them.

"I knew Alison had a journal," Dante said when they sat down to eat, "but I didn't know it was as close to the Wife of Bath as you describe. The date is, of course, the same year that Chaucer is thought to have made his own Canterbury pilgrimage, and the coincidence of her name, occupation, and origin in Bath are very compelling."

Lizzie felt a little sorry for him. His paper had been entirely overlooked in the excitement over hers. It must be difficult to be the average son of a brilliant father, she thought. He would have been wise to choose a different career than the one that made his father famous.

"Alison told me that it was your interest that first alerted her to the potential of the journal," she said. She meant to be kind, but she realized after she spoke that it would almost certainly be taken in the wrong way. Dante must now know that Lizzie knew the history of his relationship with Alison and the journal, including that he had attempted to copy it without her permission.

He seemed a little flustered and she turned the conversation to his work. Even Jackie seemed sympathetic and joined in.

"I am very interested in the link you have made to the Irish material," Lizzie started.

"I too," Jackie said. "The story of Ériu is not one I would ever have linked to the tale of the Wife of Bath."

"On the face of it, the connection is not always clear," Dante said, clearing his throat, "but of course ancient people, lacking what we would call a scientific perspective, attempted to explain natural phenomena by anthropomorphizing them. Once you have put the name of a supernatural being on an element of nature, you can explain it, worship it, pay it off, make sacrifices to it, whatever it takes to make you feel like you have some control over it. Keep Ériu happy and the cold dark winter will eventually be warmed by the sun of spring."

"Ah," said Jackie, "The ground thaws, the crops grow, and the worn out old hag returns as a beautiful young virgin, ready to be fertilized and bear fruit again."

Dante seemed pleased by the description.

Jackie smiled sweetly. Lizzie could see that Jackie's sympathetic moment had worn off and poor Dante Zettler was about to be made into intellectual mincemeat.

"It's the leap from there to women being the masters of men that I don't get," Jackie said.

"I don't think I understand your question," Dante said innocently.

"Take the knight in the Wife of Bath's story as an example," Jackie explained. "When he lets his wife make the decision he gets a reward for it—instead of being an ugly old hag, she will be a beautiful girl."

He nodded.

"But why should he get the girl of his dreams? He is still a rapist. What about the innocent maiden he raped? If I remember correctly she is introduced and disappears from the story in four lines of verse."

"Perhaps his punishment is that he now has a wife who will be his master."

Jackie gasped. "Are you saying that is equivalent to being executed?"

Dante laughed uncomfortably.

Lizzie stepped in to rescue him. "Do you have an opinion on whether or not the tale that we associate with the Wife of Bath is the one that Chaucer intended her to tell?"

He seemed relieved. "Now that is an interesting question," he said. "When one puts together all the fragments of manuscripts, it seems that she might have been meant to tell the story that is currently associated with the shipman."

Lizzie asked him to remind her what that story was, but Jackie stepped in first.

"It's the one about the woman who has an active sex life with both her husband and his best friend, a monk." Jackie held up her glass of wine. "Now that's a story she could have told with pride!"

Dante wiped his mouth on his napkin and told Lizzie what a pleasure it had been to spend the time with her. "And you too," he said, turning to Jackie. "But I am afraid I must go. I have another appointment."

"That was abrupt!" Jackie said when he had left them. "We haven't even had dessert."

Lizzie scolded her for picking on someone who was clearly not her equal.

"I couldn't help myself," Jackie answered. "For some reason I just felt compelled to master him."

Chapter 22

Dante Zettler died that night at Oxford Hospital.

Lizzie left Oxford early the next morning to take Jackie to Heathrow Airport and did not learn of it until late in the day, when she drove to Hengemont to visit Alison.

"What terrible news," Lizzie said when she heard. "I had dinner with him just last night."

"Did he seem ill?" Alison asked.

"It's hard to tell," Lizzie answered. "Jackie was giving him a rather hard time about his theories on the Wife of Bath and he was clearly uncomfortable. Beyond that, I would have to say I didn't notice anything."

"Several people called to tell me about it," Alison said, "and also to report on what a splendid job you did on your presentation. You got very high marks from some of the most critical people I know."

"I wish you had been there," Lizzie said.

They spoke for several minutes about details of the conference, and about Dante Zettler's work, which had, lamentably, plowed no new ground in the field of Chaucer scholarship.

"I'm sorry he's dead," Alison said, "but since I have already told you that I didn't like him, it would be hypocritical to spend a lot of time mourning his passing."

Lizzie acknowledged the sentiment, but felt a sense of disquiet as they moved on to other topics.

"There were some publishers interested in the Weaver's journal," she said, handing Alison the business cards she had received in Oxford. "And enthusiastic interest." She explained that there were also questions about the authenticity of the manuscript. "You will need to get it vetted soon," she added. "There were several people there who really want to examine it."

"I have been thinking about that," Alison said. She laid the business cards on the table without looking at them. "As soon as I am up and around I'll take care of it. I've had several calls from Tyler Brown in Canterbury, did you meet him?"

"One of his cards is in that pile," Lizzie answered.

"He seems like a good sort," Alison continued. "And very knowledgeable about Canterbury pilgrimages."

"He's from a historical society, though, and not likely to have the clout for publicity and distribution that a big press would give you. The book has attracted enough interest from serious publishers to warrant pursuing one."

Alison was now comfortably set up in Hengemont, and far enough along in her recovery that Lizzie could talk to her about the things they had found in her house.

"This is the most interesting and important, I think," Lizzie said, handing Alison the list of names. "Hockwold Bruce is on this list, along with your father and fourteen other men named Kent." Lizzie had called the policeman in Castle Cary and confirmed that the driver of the car was the very same Hockwold Bruce who had known Alison's father.

Alison studied the list intently. "Many of these names are familiar, of course, starting with my father and grandfather, but I also knew Frederick Wickersham." She paused to think. "I knew two men by that name, in fact, father and son. Freddie and I were great friends as children. He died of a heart attack about twenty years ago. Very sad, he left a young family."

"And his son is also Frederick Wickersham."

"So he is. How did you know?"

"Jackie Googled him."

Alison smiled at that.

"Is there any reason why one of them might want to hurt you?" Lizzie said seriously.

"Who? The Wickershams? Certainly not! I've known them all my life!"

"What about Hockwold Bruce?"

"Hocky? I've known him all my life too." She shook her

head in disbelief as she remembered the accident. "I have to think that it was just a coincidence that he was there. Otherwise, Hocky would have to have become senile with Alzheimer's or some other kind of dementia."

"Could this have anything to do with the secret your father said he would tell you?"

Alison seemed startled by the question, and after a first small gasp of surprise, was silent for several minutes. She picked up the list again and scrutinized it.

"How old is this?" she asked. "Do you have any idea?"

"We thought that the oldest part of it might have been started 450-500 years ago, given the number of generations represented—if those are generations."

"If they are, then the last one is missing," Alison said. "I wonder if I was supposed to be on the list—and Freddy Wickersham."

"You would be the first woman on it," Lizzie said. "Would Hockwold Bruce have been threatened by that?"

Alison couldn't believe that was possible.

"Did he have any children?"

"No. He never married. In fact, for a long time he considered becoming a priest."

"Anglican or Catholic?"

"Catholic, of course! All these families are good Catholics, long-standing Catholic families like mine."

"If he didn't become a priest, what did he do?"

"He ran some sort of society in Canterbury. A Catholic society as a matter of fact. They have kept the faith there ever since we lost the Cathedral to Henry VIII and his barbarians. That was a story my father told me often enough."

Lizzie took this all in, but didn't quite know what to make of it.

"There are some other things that I took from your father's study," she said, opening a folder of the loose papers they had collected at Alison's house. "These things were tucked into various books." She laid out the family trees and the two pages of astronomical calculations.

"This is familiar," Alison said picking up one of the pages with the family tree, "and I have other versions of it. Let me keep these and I will compare them with what I know." She put her hand on the other papers. "I told you that my father was an amateur astronomer. So were Frederick Wickersham and Hocky Bruce, by the way, but I have no idea what these are or if they are important."

The fact that the atlas had the route of the pilgrimage drawn on it was interesting, but she didn't know who had marked it in the book, or if it was meaningful. The most thrilling discoveries to her were the receipts and inscriptions in the early Chaucer volumes.

"That was Edmund's idea and Jackie's discovery," Lizzie said. "We can have a note about it in the book, but Jackie might like to write about it separately as well, for a library publication."

Alison said she was welcome to it. "I like your friend very much," she said.

"She did a lot of work for us while she was here," Lizzie said. "She found a list of articles raided by the Commission for the Destruction of Shrines, and will continue to look at it now that she is back in Boston."

"What is your next step?"

"Literally my next step is along the ridge pathway between Shaftesbury and Salisbury. I have to get back to the walk, and another of my friends, Kate Wentworth, will be joining me in two days for that part of the path."

"Is she as saucy as Jackie?"

"No," Lizzie laughed, "no one is as saucy as Jackie. You'll like Kate though. She's a sea captain and has had many interesting adventures."

Lizzie stayed that night at Hengemont, in the corner room that she had been so comfortable in on previous visits. After having been so anxious for so long about the walk, she found she was now very anxious to get back to it.

Chapter 23

Lizzie and Kate had chosen their rendezvous location six weeks earlier, sitting at the table of Lizzie's kitchen in South Boston. At that time neither had any first-hand knowledge of this part of England, so they relied on the Ordnance Survey map and the Internet, and eventually chose a B&B because they liked the name: Peas Full Farm. It was in a village called Broad Chalke, named for the chalk ridge that defined the region. On top of that ridge had run one of the main thoroughfares across medieval England; it was now a footpath and Lizzie's plan was to walk on it to Salisbury, the next great cathedral town along the route.

The days spent searching Alison's house had put Lizzie behind schedule, and she could no longer make the walk from Shaftesbury to Broad Chalk unless she missed her rendezvous with Kate, which she was unwilling to do. She found herself on a bus instead, rolling up and down the hills of the Salisbury Plain through towns with picturesque names like Ebbesbourne Wake. Around her on the bus, the other passengers might have been the cast for *Canterbury Tales*, traveling to a production of the play on the road. Across the aisle sat a woman of indeterminable age, probably about fifteen or twenty years older than Lizzie, who had her blond hair swept up off her neck and face and rolled into a crown of hair on the top of her head. If she added a veil, Lizzie thought she could be the Weaver or the Wife of Bath.

Kate Wentworth's broad grin was a tonic when she saw her, and the two friends greeted each other with a hearty hug when they met at the Peas Full Farmhouse. As they stood in the yard, Kate pointed to a clear path that ran straight up alongside blooming yellow fields and up to the top of the ridge behind the farm.

"That's our path," Kate said. "It's very clear on the map."

The certainty with which she made this declaration gave Lizzie confidence. There would be no more confusion over where she was now that Kate was here. She thought about the difference between her two friends and the value of each as a companion on this adventure. Jackie knew books, their contents as well as their value. Not only had she been indispensible in tackling Alison's library, but she had a vast knowledge of literature and had frequently amused and impressed Lizzie by her ability to quote from various authors. Kate's skills were more practical. When she read a map she pulled out a compass; she had an application on her cell phone that allowed her to measure the angle of the sun above the horizon. She had sailed tens of thousands of miles, travelled by dogsled across Baffin Island, and Lizzie had once heard her describe eating raw seal liver. She had that indefinable but recognizable quality possessed by sea captains, a confidence that inspired confidence in others.

As it was early in the afternoon and there was time for a stroll around the village, they wandered and caught up on each other's affairs. There was a lovely old church in town and they admired a carved stone Saxon cross and other statuary, including a wonderful band of angels playing the flute, harp, bagpipe, lute, and fiddle. As they finished their tour, Lizzie picked up a brief handout on local history in the vestibule of the church and was astonished to read that "the legend that Sir Gawain—the most famous hero of Arthurian romance—is buried at the top of Howgare Hill is possibly true."

"Look at this," she said to Kate. "I am being haunted by the Knights of the Round Table. Alison has absolutely convinced me that they are literary characters, and yet they are persistently described as historical."

"It does say *possibly* true."

"Yes, but it is *not* true, so how does the legend start?"

Kate had already pulled out the Ordnance Survey map and was looking for Howgare Hill. "I don't see the place," she said. "Maybe it's a legend too!"

"The extent to which those stories have seeped into the local lore of the English countryside is really wonderful." Lizzie took out her cell phone. "I'm going to send Jackie a text about this, she will love it!"

"There are a number of prehistoric mounds in this region," Kate said, continuing to study the map. She pulled out a pen and began to circle them. "They are called *tumuli* in the key and we should pass a couple of them tomorrow."

"If I were inclined to imagine any of the Arthurian knights sleeping under one of them, it would be Gawain, because he is the one sometimes associated with the Wife of Bath's tale." She thought for a moment of Dante Zettler and his description of Gawain's encounter with the "Loathly Lady." "In one version of the story, Gawain went on a quest to discover what women really want."

"What is with that question anyway?" Kate asked. "If ever there was a silly question to pursue, that has to be it—and only a man would think of it."

"I heard a lecture on it just a few days ago, and the guy who gave it died that same night."

"Was he very old?"

Lizzie put her hand out and touched the stone of the church wall. She could feel where it had been cut with some ancient tool. "He wasn't old," she said softly. "He was younger than we are."

"How did he die?"

"I don't know," Lizzie said, shaking her head. "Jackie and I had dinner with him and a few hours later he was dead."

"Is it possible that Jackie talked him to death?"

It was impossible not to smile, as much as Lizzie felt the gravity of the subject.

"She did give him a pretty good earful of feminist diatribe, after which he looked kind of sick and left."

"Who knows how many corpses are in her wake."

Lizzie's cell phone made a tone to indicate there was a text message.

"It's from Jackie," she said. "She must have known we were talking about her."

"What does it say?"

"It says 'read your email.'"

Lizzie went back into the nave of the church and sat down in a pew to open her email on her phone. There was a message from Jackie regarding the burial of Gawain.

"No other source refers to this location as the burial place of Gawain," Lizzie said, reading aloud to Kate. "Thomas Malory says that Gawain died in battle at Dover and was buried at Dover Castle where 'yet all may see the skull of him.' William of Malmesbury, who wrote so extensively of Glastonbury in the twelfth century, says that Gawain is buried in Pembrokeshire. A chapel on the coast of Wales called St. Govan's is said by some to be the resting place of both a saint of that name and Sir Gawain, though the similarity of names alone would be enough to warrant the claim by fervent Arthurians. Neil Fairburn's comprehensive list of Arthurian sites in his *Traveller's Guide to the Kingdoms of Arthur* doesn't mention Howgare Hill or Broad Chalke."

"There you have it. Jackie speaks and we listen." She wrote a quick note of thanks back and added a line about the death of Dante Zettler.

They had a comfortable night at Peas Full Farm and left early the next morning up the lane between the fields to pick up the path across the top of the chalk ridge into Salisbury. Variously called the "Herepath," the "Old Shaftesbury Drove," and the "Coach Road to Bath" over the last several centuries, this might have been a route for the Weaver on her way to Shaftesbury and Salisbury en route to London. In the age of the motor car the main road moved from the top of the ridge to the bottom of it, and the oldest roads in the region could no longer be traveled by car.

The ridges, known as "downs," spread across the south of England like the fingers of a hand stretched out from London. The paths on their crests were among the most popular footpaths in present-day England, Lizzie knew. Unlike the paths that so confounded her on her first day, these were not merely ancient rights-of-way indicated on the map, but real paths used by many walkers, and there was no question about their superiority over the road. Where the roads were bounded by antique hedges that confine them to a narrowness completely anachronistic to the vehicles and drivers currently upon them, the path up the down was perfect. The views from the tops of the ridges went for miles across the landscape, while the view from the road was often only the hedge.

The path was hard and clear for almost the entire distance that Lizzie and Kate traveled that morning, and while there were some uneven surfaces and a steep hill to climb at the beginning and to descend at the end, it was altogether a good walk. Lizzie found Kate an excellent companion, good humored, interesting and extremely observant. She spotted a weasel and a pheasant in the brush near them. Lizzie tried to argue that a small bird they saw was a chickadee and was informed that "chickadee" was the first word Kate spoke as a child, and consequently was a bird she knew better than Lizzie.

Descending from the top of the down, they passed an ornate and elaborate set of gates, mounted with stone statues, through which could be seen not a house, but a collection of old trailers and cars. On the other side of the wall a dog was howling and growling, and seemingly throwing himself against the side of a cage. It was a ferocious sound that was followed a few moments later by the sound of movement in the grass beyond the gate. As the two women prepared to meet their doom in the jaws of a mad dog, a tiny little mutt came yipping its way out of the mysterious compound, a Yorkshire terrier-sized terror.

"The Hound of the Toonervilles," Lizzie said to Kate.

Several miles outside of Salisbury, they began to see the spire of Salisbury Cathedral in the distance, a beckoning white needle.

"What are we hoping to find there?" Kate asked.

"I'm not certain," Lizzie said. "The Weaver wrote in her journal that she presented something to the Cathedral, though unfortunately she didn't say what. I wrote to the librarian there, Nora Stanley, whom I met when I was here last year working for George Hatton, and asked her if they have a record of anything in their collection that is marked with an old-style AW monogram."

"Have you heard back from her?"

"I got a message that she is expecting us tomorrow, but she hadn't yet found anything."

They approached Salisbury via a bridge named after the painter John Constable, who produced the most famous views of the great church. Near a medieval mill, gigantic swans and a herd of cows provided the foreground for changing views of the cathedral as they walked along. At one point they stopped to eat the pears that had been given to them by the owners of the B&B, but as there were no options for a place to eat along the path, they weren't able to get a real meal until they arrived in Salisbury in the afternoon.

As they walked across the vast expanse of lawn toward the great west face of Salisbury Cathedral with its carvings of saints and bishops, Lizzie was overcome with memories of the last time she had been there. On that strange evening, the heart of the crusader knight John d'Hautain had been taken from a small grave along the aisle of the cathedral to be returned to Hengemont. At that time she had only known that he was the ancestor of George and Edmund Hatton; now she knew that he was her ancestor as well.

She had not told anyone but Martin about the discovery of that relationship, but now she told Kate, as they stood in front of the cathedral looking straight up the massive front wall. Lizzie's eyes worked back and forth across the carvings and then up to where the steeple pierced the sky.

"Why didn't you say anything about this before?" Kate asked.

"It changes my notion of my self in a strange way."

"I'm not sure I understand."

"Just think what Jackie would say if she knew I had such an aristocratic pedigree!"

Kate smiled. "Ah, I see what you mean. She can barely stand that I have an English name!"

"Those things shouldn't matter, but they do, not only in how others place us into preconceived categories, but how we position ourselves in relationship to other people. The Irish immigrant identity has a rather large component of hating the English aristocracy, so it was a bit of a jolt to suddenly find myself living in both camps."

"Do you find that you identify with them now?"

"It wasn't at all difficult to believe that Edmund Hatton and I are related. He was a soul mate from early on, but I have no emotional attachment to the rest of it."

They continued the conversation as they went into the church, where a number of the memorial monuments honored the wealthy dead by recommending them to God and posterity in doting terms.

"You see that there isn't much recognition here of the eye-of-the-needle idea," Lizzie said.

She led Kate to the left aisle and pointed out the small carving that had covered the heart of John d'Hautain. "This was his comrade in the Crusades," she said, indicating the carved effigy adjacent to it. "William Longespèe the Younger. They both died in Egypt."

Like Wells Cathedral, which had so impressed Lizzie with its elegant simplicity, Salisbury Cathedral was open from one end to the other. All of the principal features, including the main body of the church and the carving-covered west front, were built in the thirteenth century, with the fabulous steeple being completed in the first decade of the fourteenth. All of it was there when the Weaver made her pilgrimage.

"I wonder what she left here?" Lizzie said, almost to herself.

"Is there any way to know after such a long time?" Kate asked.

"Only if someone has spotted her mark, I think."

She had not yet showed the pictures of the tapestry to Kate and now she pulled them out of their envelope and handed them to her one by one.

"Here is how she depicted Salisbury Cathedral," she said as she gave her the appropriate photo.

Kate studied it for a moment and then looked up and around the church. The late afternoon sun was streaming through the windows in slanted rays.

"Look at how the sun enters here," Kate said, nudging Lizzie.

"I know, it's beautiful," she said. "Such an ethereal quality."

"Yes, but that's not what I mean. In the picture you just gave me, the church has stained glass windows." She handed the picture back to Lizzie. "Are you sure this picture is of Salisbury Cathedral and not one of the other churches along the route? Because I only see one stained glass window in this building, and it looks very modern."

There was a tiny woven banner that declared 'Salisbury' under the image on the tapestry, and Lizzie pointed it out to Kate. "This is definitely Salisbury."

"Well then either the artist made a mistake, or the windows have been replaced since this picture was made."

"How interesting," Lizzie said, puzzling over it. "I know that there have been a lot of alterations here over the centuries. Certainly the stained glass is emphasized in this illustration in a way that makes it distinctive from the other places on the tapestry, and there is the Weaver's mark," she said, putting her finger under the tiny monogram.

None of the guidebooks available in the cathedral answered their question about the stained glass, and so it had to wait until the next day and their appointment with Nora Stanley.

Chapter 24

In 1789 the architect James Wyatt undertook a three-year project to improve Salisbury Cathedral. He tore down a separate belfry that had stood beside the cathedral for five hundred years, as well as two small chapels that had been added later; he lined up all the graves inside the church on a "plinth" to define the side aisles up the nave; he removed all of the exterior grave stones to drain the marshy area around the cathedral and create the expansive lawns that now surround it; and he replaced the surviving thirteenth-century stained glass with clear panes.

Nora Stanley told all this to Lizzie and Kate as they sat on uncomfortable chairs in her cramped office. Lizzie had shown her the picture of Salisbury Cathedral as it appeared on the tapestry strip map and she instantly recognized the features that had been changed, including the stained glass.

"You've hit on something here, Lizzie," Nora said. "Since you contacted me a few weeks ago I have been looking through our records for references to an AW monogram and I found one."

"A stained glass window?"

"Yes, in fact it is."

Lizzie clapped her hands with pleasure. "I knew it! As soon as you pointed out the colored windows on the tapestry, Kate, I knew that had to be it! Can we see it?"

Nora looked at her patiently. "Those windows are, I'm sorry to say, long gone."

The disappointment on Lizzie's face was obvious.

"I can show you a drawing of them, though," Nora added. "Fortunately, there was someone here when the windows were removed who had the foresight to think of this moment."

She pushed a large folder across the desk and Lizzie opened it carefully.

On large sheets of stiff paper, the arch-topped outlines of dozens of windows were drawn in pen. Each of them was divided into panes and in each pane the lines where lead had been used to bind together cut pieces of colored glass were carefully delineated. Small notations along the side of each window indicated what the colors were. Lizzie scanned each page and turned it over onto Nora's desk.

"The pages are numbered in the upper right corner," Nora said. "You are looking for page five."

When she turned over that page, Lizzie saw a window that depicted the martyrdom of Thomas Becket. At the top was Becket as archbishop, sitting on his throne with all the regalia of his office. Below it was an image not unlike the one on the reliquary in which the Weaver's journal had been found. Four knights with raised swords were captured at the moment of murdering Becket. He was shown kneeling at the altar of Canterbury Cathedral, his hands lifted in prayer. One of the swords was imbedded in his head, slicing through the crown and severing that part where his tonsure was shaved. In the next panel down, Becket was being lowered into a tomb, and below that was an interesting image that Lizzie had never seen before. She asked Nora if she knew what it was.

"That is the great shrine of Thomas Becket. It was built when his bones were translated from the original grave some fifty years after his death, and it was destroyed at the time of the Reformation. There are only a few images of it that survive." She handed Lizzie a photocopy of an article. "The reason I was able to locate the signature monograph you asked about is because it appears on that window and there have been Becket scholars who have written about it. This is a good article, and I have written a link to another on the top of it. "

The fact that the Weaver's signature appeared on a stained glass window depicting the life, death and reburial of Thomas Becket was incredibly exciting to Lizzie. She looked for the monogram and saw where it appeared in the drawing. It had a prominent place in the center of the bottom edge of the window, the flat-topped A clearly drawn over the lines of the W.

Lizzie breathed deeply. "This is simply unbelievable," she said. "I never expected anything so wonderful."

"It must have been pretty expensive to have a window like that made," Kate said as she moved to see the image on the page more clearly.

"Yes indeed," Nora said. "I think that there might be information about that in the article."

"Can I get a picture of this?" Lizzie asked.

"I anticipated that question," Nora said, handing her the last folder on the desk. "These are copies of the photographs that were taken to be included in one of the articles."

· · · · ·

That night at their hotel, Lizzie called Alison to tell her about the window, and then called Martin to ask about progress on the mural and tell him her discovery. He was especially interested in the nature of the Weaver's gifts to churches along her track.

"So she commissioned tapestry weavers, a stone carver, and a stained glass maker to create these various offerings that she made?"

"She must have."

"I think that is very interesting. She could have just donated one of her own weavings to each place; the fact that she didn't means she wanted to be a patron of other artists."

"I hadn't thought of that, but you must be right," Lizzie said, delighted at the thought. "Weaving and widowhood had obviously made her very rich. I'm not sure about the stone carving, but the tapestry and stained glass window were probably done by a workshop of artisans under a master and very expensive."

"Maybe she traded her work for theirs. From what you say she was a talented designer as well as being an expert weaver."

"I'm reminded of the times you have commissioned work from other artists, including the bronze plaque at the Hengement church, which is your design but made by someone who works in a different medium."

"I suspect that has been a practice among artists and artisans for centuries. These works of art she commissioned— were they all made as gifts for churches?"

Lizzie said she wasn't sure for whom the tapestry was intended. "It was still in the family when Alison's father was a kid, so I think not that one. But I'm beginning to suspect that she had something made for each of the cathedrals along the path of her pilgrimage. I found the ones at Wells and Salisbury; Glastonbury and Shaftesbury are total ruins, but Jackie is looking to see if anything can be located that was taken at the time of Henry VIII's destruction of the shrines. That leaves Winchester, Westminster and Canterbury, and I'll be at all three soon."

Martin reported that his mural was going to be completed on schedule and the dedication would be at the end of the following week. Lizzie promised that nothing would keep her from being there.

When she hung up the phone, she shared Martin's idea about the Weaver as an art patron with Kate.

"You are very lucky in your friends and relations, Lizzie," Kate responded. "You have a librarian on hand when you need expertise on books, and when you want to know how an artist thinks, you just call the one you happen to be married to." She lamented that her area of expertise was unlikely to come into play on a long walk.

Her comment reminded Lizzie of the two pages of astronomical calculations that had been tucked into the books at Alison's house.

"On the contrary, dear friend!" she said, going to her file to retrieve them. "I have a puzzle that requires the knowledge of a navigator." She put the papers on the desk and asked Kate what they were.

"These are notes on the declination of the sun on two different days of the year," Kate said after a quick glance at the first lines of the top page. "It is probably copied directly out of a nautical almanac." She spoke as if this was no mystery at all. "And someone has calculated the arithmetical mean to determine local apparent noon."

"Why would someone want to know that?"

Kate shook her head. "Not sure. There are two latitudes here, and something else, which seems to be calculations to adjust for altitude at the first location—544 feet, and then adds twelve feet above that."

"And why would someone do that?"

"Well, if this person was using a nautical almanac, the tables are set up for observations from sea level; on a vessel we calculate it when we shoot the sun at noon. On my ship, *St. Brendan's Curragh,* if I don't consider the height of my eye above the surface as I stand on the deck, I can throw off my fix by 3.4 miles."

She pulled out the map of England and using the side of an envelope, drew two straight lines. "These latitudes are close together and not far from where we are now. They are both 51 degrees north; one is at 13 minutes and the other at 16 minutes." She ran a finger along the first line. "It's kind of close to Wells, where I remember you said you were, and it runs just south of some place called Guildford."

"What about the other one?"

"Smack on Canterbury, and there really isn't any other major town on that line. Bath is slightly further north, London is well north, Salisbury and Winchester are south.

"What about the dates?" Lizzie asked. "Are they important?"

"I'm sure they were important to someone," Kate said pragmatically, "or they wouldn't have bothered."

Lizzie pulled the paper back toward herself. "July 7 and December 29. What could they mean?"

Again Kate said that they could be anything.

"Canterbury," Lizzie said. "Of course that's the destination of the pilgrimage."

"Yours or hers?"

"Both. Well, mine because of hers."

"And on July seventh we know the declination of the sun there will be 22 degrees and 45 minutes north."

"And then what?"

"I have no idea."

Chapter 25

Thomas Becket was born in London in 1118 and went to work for the Archbishop of Canterbury when he was twenty-one years old. He subsequently studied law and theology on the continent and when he returned to England was appointed archdeacon of Canterbury. A tall and charismatic individual, Becket clearly stood out among the men of his age. When Henry II was crowned in 1154, the Archbishop recommended Becket to the young king and he was made chancellor, in which position he became Henry's ally and friend. When Henry tangled with the pope over control of church affairs in England, Becket stood strongly with the king. In 1162 Henry thought that he could gain the reins of the church in England if he had Thomas Becket named Archbishop of Canterbury. If Becket was both archbishop and chancellor, the powers of church and state would be consolidated, and Henry would be able to stand up to the pope. Becket did not seek the position and vainly attempted to persuade Henry to choose another candidate.

Once he was appointed, Thomas Becket had something of a conversion experience. He became a zealous defender of the Catholic Church, resigned his position as chancellor, and devoted his considerable energy and talent to fighting the king over who would control the church in England. Many of the stands that Becket took were petty; he would not agree that minor clerks in the church should stand trial in the civil courts for crimes committed among the populace. Henry was also petty, eventually even accusing Becket of having embezzled funds during his chancellorship.

They were the two most powerful men in England, not

only by virtue of their offices, but by the strength of their personalities; they were former confidantes, they were also highly visible celebrities. When Henry ordered Becket to appear in court, not as the Archbishop of Canterbury, but in a civil action, Becket refused, left England and headed to Rome for papal support. Such support was a long time coming and then only in name. Becket remained in exile in France for six years while he and Henry blasted away at each other from either side of the Channel. Henry persecuted Becket's family; Becket excommunicated half of England just for speaking to Henry.

In 1170 the king had his oldest son, Henry, crowned by the Archbishop of York, to secure the succession. Becket was furious and excommunicated the Archbishop of York and the Bishop of London for having participated. (English kings, by tradition, were always crowned by the Archbishop of Canterbury.) Henry and Becket finally met in France in July of that year, each made some concessions, and Becket returned to England on the first of December. The public acclaim at his return was compared (after his death) to that given to Christ on his entry into Jerusalem on Palm Sunday.

Henry was still in France and fed up with the whole business. In the presence of several members of his court he muttered the immortal words: "Will no one rid me of this troublesome priest?" Four knights immediately crossed the channel and made their way to Canterbury: Reginald Fitzurse, Hugh de Moreville, William de Tracy, and Richard le Breton. Becket was warned but would not hide. On December 29, 1170, he went from his dinner to the church for the vespers service and was followed by the knights.

It was five o'clock in the evening when the knights rushed into the church. There were a number of monks there for the service, and a small crowd, having heard the commotion, followed the king's men into the nave. Becket violently resisted their attempts to take him prisoner; he swore at the knights, not just as the Archbishop of Canterbury but as their social superior. Tracy swung at him with his sword but Edward Grim, one of the monks of the Cathedral, deflected the blow from Becket by taking the force of it on his arm. Becket's scalp was grazed and began to bleed. When he saw the blood Becket said, "Into thy hands, O Lord, I commend my spirit." Another sword blow brought him to his knees and from there prostrate to the floor. Richard le Breton then delivered a blow to Becket's head so forceful that it severed the cap of his skull, instantly killing him and breaking the blade of the sword on the pavement.

Hugh of Horsea, a fifth knight who had joined the party as they came into the cathedral, then put his foot upon the neck of Becket's corpse and put the tip of his sword into the exposed brain matter, scattering it out onto the pavement. "Let us go, let us go," he said as he finished, "The traitor is dead; he will rise no more."

After the knights clattered out of the cathedral there must have been profound silence, though there were numbers of witnesses. Finally Osbert, Becket's servant, went to his master and bound the severed piece of his head back on with a strip of his shirt. Others began to come out of the darkness. The floor was soaked with brains and blood and the people in the church began to soak them up with pieces of cloth; some are said to have dipped their fingers in the blood and smeared it on their faces. Becket's body was carried to the high altar and bowls were placed beneath it to catch his blood. They knew he was a martyr. They knew he would be a saint. The collecting of his relics began instantly upon his death. The blood was put into small bottles called ampullae or phials. It would work miracles for centuries.

Becket was an arrogant man but he also tried to be a holy one. When the monks of Canterbury prepared his body for burial they found that under his vestments he wore a lice-infested hair shirt. It was meant to make him suffer constantly in a small way. He apparently took it off only to be scourged or whipped on the back, a greater suffering to which he had submitted himself that very morning. Fearing the return of the knights, the body was buried quickly in the crypt of the church—though some of the monks reported that there was a short delay while they waited for it to rise and make the sign of the cross over them before lying down again.

The miracles began immediately. A blind man, who didn't

know about the murder, came to the cathedral that day and was cured. A paralyzed woman drank some water into which drops of blood were dripped and she walked again. The pilgrimages began.

For the next fifty years pilgrims made a point of venerating three places in the church: the scene of the crime, called "The Martyrdom," where an altar had been constructed called "The Altar of the Sword's Point"; the high altar where Becket's body had lain overnight; and the crypt where he was buried. The tip of the sword that killed him was saved and exhibited as a relic; the blood-stained stone on which he died was cut out of the floor and sent to Rome. Eventually the makeshift grave was replaced by a masonry tomb. Two large openings in each side allowed the faithful to be closer to the saint by sticking their heads or hands inside to touch the coffin.

A fire in the cathedral five years after Becket's death damaged much of the area above the tomb and when rebuilding began it was decided to expand the Trinity Chapel above Becket's grave and to build there a new shrine. On a summer day in 1220, fifty years after the murder, the new shrine was dedicated and, with great pomp and circumstance, Becket's remains—his "relics" since he was a saint—went into it. This "translation" of the corpse, as they called the exhumation and movement of the body of a saint from one place to another, would thereafter be venerated each year on July 7.

Since Becket had not been embalmed in any way, all that was left to move into the new shrine were bones, and at least some of them did not get translated into the new shrine. The head and the severed cap of the skull were each kept in separate jeweled reliquaries. At least some bones went to Rome and to other shrines, and for years one could see various parts of Becket around Europe. (A tooth, for instance, was in Verona.) Weirdest of all, there were at least three arms attributed to him, in Florence and Lisbon.

Two monks from Canterbury went on to positions at other monasteries and brought relics of Becket with them. Benedict, the Abbot of Peterborough, arrived at his new post in 1179 with two bottles of blood, clothes that had belonged to the Archbishop, and stones from the floor where Becket fell. Roger, the Abbot of St. Augustine's monastery, just around the corner from the cathedral in Canterbury, received his new post by agreeing to their request to bring with him a portion of the skull of the saint.

Thus the flesh and bones and blood and brains that made Thomas Becket such an impressive man when he was alive were transformed by the circumstances of his murder into the relics of a saint.

The article that Nora Stanley gave to Lizzie had an excellent outline of the life and death of Thomas Becket, and an account of all the known sources that described the shrine that had held his bones. There were a number of good descriptions in medieval journals, but only a few surviving images. A stained glass window in Canterbury Cathedral had, by some good fortune, escaped the ravagers who destroyed the shrine that it depicted. There was a manuscript drawing that had, unfortunately, been damaged, destroying the lower part of the image. There were a few pewter pilgrim badges in the shape of the shrine, one of which, from the collection of the Metropolitan Museum, was illustrated in the article. And there was the stained glass window that had been commissioned by the Weaver for Salisbury Cathedral and now survived only in the ink drawing made of it in 1789, when the stained glass was replaced with clear panes.

Between the time it was dedicated in 1220 and its total destruction in 1538, the shrine had dominated Canterbury Cathedral and been the focus of every pilgrim's visit. As Lizzie read the various descriptions of it, she examined the details of the images, especially the one that had been on the stained glass window that was, presumably, originally drawn by the Weaver.

There were four parts to the shrine: a six-foot-high base made of pink marble; a bejeweled and gold-plated wooden ark that held the feretrum, the box that contained the bones; a gold mesh covering onto which particularly rich pilgrims had attached jewels and other precious and valuable offerings; and a painted wooden cover that could be lowered over the top to protect the valuables and raised again by a rope and pulleys.

On the pilgrim badge in the Metropolitan collection, a tiny figure with a stick pointed out the most valuable jewels on the mesh. Below him the saint was laid out full length in his vestments and mitre, his hands clasped in prayer. The Weaver had created more of an x-ray image, showing not an effigy of the saint, but rather his bones, visible through all the containers that surrounded them. The long bones of the legs and arms were wrapped in a decorated piece of fabric, though the details of the design on it had not been captured by the artist who replicated the window. The skull was placed at the top of the bundle.

"I absolutely love the Weaver!" Lizzie announced to Kate when she finished reading the article. "It is amazing how well you can come to know someone who lived six hundred years ago."

"You always say that about the people you study."

"I know, but this is special, maybe because she's a woman and my subject matter usually steers me to the stories of men."

Kate was, as usual, studying their collection of maps, looking at the route for the next two days, which would take them to Winchester.

"I asked about the path at the tourist information office," Kate said. "There is a path between Salisbury and Winchester that is well marked and you'll love this, the logo is a bishop's hat. It looks from the pictures here that there might be one on every stile."

"Every *damned* stile, if you don't mind," Lizzie said, cursing the ubiquitous fence-crossing ladders of the public footpaths. "Please give them their correct name."

"Stiles may not be the worst of it for the next few days," Kate continued. "The woman there told me we need to be careful of adders."

"Adders!" Lizzie exclaimed. "Good Lord! I hope you are kidding."

When Kate's expression made it clear that she was completely serious, Lizzie began to worry about snakes, and the next morning when they set out for the top of the ridge and a continuation of their journey she jumped in fear at a large earthworm, a bent stick, and a piece of red twine.

Their path was called the Clarendon Way and, as promised, there were markers with a bishop's mitre on every stile. Lizzie and Kate turned frequently in the first hour to see the steeple of Salisbury Cathedral shrink in the distance. It was a lovely Sunday and the path was filled with walkers, more than Lizzie had seen at any point along the way. There was great color, many flowers, fields of yellow blooms and fragrant pea blossoms. All along the way pheasants popped their heads up above the tall grass, and then ducked down again. Bees buzzed in the blossoms and beetles were in profusion. Lurking beneath the beauty, Lizzie imagined adders, slithering among the stalks and stems.

They had a full Sunday lunch of roast lamb at the Silver Plow in Pitton and asked about the path to Winterslow.

"I'm sorry," their young waitress answered. "I'm not from around here."

When pressed further, it turned out that she was a native of a place about four miles distant, but in the other direction.

"Gadzooks!" Kate said as they left the restaurant. "I just don't understand people who are so disinterested in their surroundings!"

Between West Winterslow and Middle Winterslow they encountered a stile that was barricaded, with a notice attached saying that the footpath was no longer a public right-of-way, and that those who wished to argue this fact should appear at the office of an official in a town that couldn't be found on the map by a date that was now some three weeks past.

To backtrack and find another path would mean a great loss of time. They pondered the situation, discussed it for several minutes and finally decided that three weeks wasn't such a long time and they would simply cross the stile and push on. At the far end of the illegal field was a much more menacing sight, black long-horned cows.

"Are those bulls?" Lizzie asked.

"How would I know," Kate answered, "I'm from Boston and I spend half my time at sea."

"That Wainwright book you gave me has somewhat freaked

me out on this topic," Lizzie told her friend. "He was really afraid of bullocks, as he called them. He had this theory that you could look the thing in the eye and tell whether or not the animal was a bullock or something else—some surgically altered alternative, I believe—though he never was quite specific about this."

"It seems to me if *that* is what you want to know, you should probably look someplace other than his eye!"

"Can you see the other place on these animals?"

"Nope."

"Would you recognize the surgical alteration if you saw it?"

"Nope."

"I think giving a bull a sympathetic look in the eye to see if he has been castrated must be a guy thing."

"I have to agree with you there. One thing I can say with certainty is that these animals have no udders."

"Most of them are lying down and they look pretty peaceful."

They agreed to walk softly along the fence and be ready to jettison their packs and dive under it if it became necessary. In this way they got to the far corner of the field and a hedge-bound road. They looked across the low hedge, well-trimmed but thick and brambly; climbing over it was out of the question. The next stile was on the far side of the livestock, which were presenting themselves in a dramatic tableau at the opposite side of the field.

"We can go back or we can go forward," Kate whispered. "Which is it?"

Lizzie gripped the sturdy walking stick that she carried. While striking a bull with it had not seemed out of the question when she was back in Massachusetts, it was clearly not a desirable option here. The cattle were much bigger than she expected. Nonetheless, she could not bear the thought of turning around.

"Let's do it!" she whispered. "Though if one of them stands up, I am going to wet my pants!"

They walked quickly but softly through the herd. Except for the occasional flick of a tail to ward off a fly, there was no movement made by any of the cows. The stile was crossed and they were once more on their way.

"I hate Wainwright," Lizzie said. "Not only was he really a sexist creep, but he made me afraid of cows! And I'm no fan of the woman at the information center either," she added. "Between my fears of cows and adders I'm a nervous wreck."

"Don't talk about it so much and it won't be so bad."

"What? Are you saying you weren't just as afraid of those cows?"

"I'm not saying," Kate said. "That's the point."

"Is this some captain thing?"

Kate nodded sagely.

They reached their lodging for the night at Broughton, an inn said to have been frequented by Charles Dickens, and threw down their packs. They each took a long bath and re-treated to the pub for a meal and a pint of cider, which had become their drink of choice.

"Here's to our mastery of the herd of bulls," Lizzie said raising her glass.

The publican smiled at them. "Now there's one I 'aven't 'eard afore," he said. "Are you in finance?"

Lizzie laughed. "No, I meant it literally. We actually walked through a field filled with bulls," she said proudly.

Now the barman laughed. "Well now, that's not very likely," he said, trying to maintain a polite expression. "You never find more than one bull in a field."

Lizzie put down her glass. "What are those menacing things that you sometimes find gathered in a field?"

"If they weren't cows, they were steers." He looked at the blank looks on the faces of the American women. "They've been castrated and are no more dangerous than lambs."

Simultaneously, the two women picked up their pints and drained them.

"Damn Wainwright!" Lizzie said as she put her glass back on the bar.

Chapter 26

The day was hot and the sun was bright as they continued the next morning from the inn, through the local churchyard and onto the path. Lizzie put on a straw hat that Martin had given her, with two silver scallop shells attached to the ribbon, signs of the pilgrim in ancient times. It was a bank holiday in England and once again the path was a popular place to be. They passed families and solo walkers, bike-riders, people on horseback, dogs, and even a woman pushing a baby in a stroller along the packed dirt of the path.

Not far out of Broughton they found themselves in very dry and dusty fields. There was none of the waving grasses or cool forest of the previous day. Here the agriculture was all low to the ground and baking in the hot sun. Up and down hills they tramped. Lizzie taught Kate the words to the William Blake poem that had been set to the hymn tune "Jerusalem."

"And did those feet in ancient times, walk upon England's mountains green," they sang.

"Is this going to be our theme song?" Kate said.

"If I recall, when we spoke about this last, you said you wanted to choose a Beatles song."

"My choice is the song 'In My Life,'" Kate said. She made a stab at singling about places she remembered and how much she loved them despite their having changed, but gave up the effort when her memory of the lyrics failed her, and turned the conversation to their plans for the day.

It amused Lizzie that Kate always referred to their walk as a "voyage" and she mentioned this to her.

"I have variously thought of it as a project, plan, journey, adventure, or error of judgment, but I like the notion of a voyage. It imparts structure to this amorphous thing that at times seems to have neither conscious beginning nor foreseeable conclusion."

"That is because you are interested in the *process*, Lizzie, where I like to have a *plan*."

They crossed the Test River and at the village of King's Samborne lunched at the John of Gaunt Inn. Lizzie told Kate that John of Gaunt had been Chaucer's chief patron, and through him Chaucer was connected to three kings: Edward III, Richard II, and Henry IV. When Kate asked for more information, Lizzie pulled out her notebook and constructed a narrative of the facts.

Chaucer's father bought a position for him as a page in the court of Edward III, probably in the household of the Earl of Ulster. The Earl's daughter was married to Lionel, the second son of Edward III, and from them came the House of York. John of Gaunt was Lionel's brother, the father of Henry IV, and the founder of the House of Lancaster. These were the feuding families whose conflict was the War of the Roses.

"John of Gaunt apparently took a liking to young Geoff and sponsored his rapid rise at court," Lizzie said. "He even became related to Chaucer when he married Katherine Swynford, the sister of Chaucer's wife—this was John of Gaunt's third marriage, though, so Chaucer was not the uncle of Henry IV."

Lizzie's feet were tired and she enjoyed drinking cider, and she pulled out a guide to *The Royal Line of Succession* for details of the story she was telling to prolong their departure. It was with regret that she put her shoes back on to return to the road, and with relief two hours later that she saw the B&B they had booked in Winchester.

As they unpacked their bags, Kate handed Lizzie a small package. "After the great Wainwright disaster I almost fear to give you this," she said. "But I think you'll like this guy better."

In the package was a copy of a book called *The Old Road*, written by Hilaire Belloc in 1911.

"You might know him from some of his essays on nautical themes," Kate continued. "I have always liked his writing. I saved it until Winchester because it describes a pilgrimage from here to Canterbury."

"Thank you," Lizzie said warmly. "It was on my reading list early on, but I never got myself a copy. I'll start it tonight."

They still had time to visit the Cathedral before dusk, and decided to walk there as the afternoon cooled. By chance they passed the simple yellow-painted house where Jane Austen died. Though a private residence, it had a plaque acknowledging her life and death. It was just a few steps more to one of the passages through the wall that surrounded the cathedral.

"Strange to think Jane Austen must have walked these very steps when she was able," Lizzie said. "I've been thinking so much about the Weaver since I started, but Alison and I noticed when we planned the trip that much of the path could have been planned as a Jane Austen pilgrimage. We'll go by her house at Chawton in a few days."

The interior of Winchester Cathedral was vast and remarkably cool. The two friends went immediately to Jane Austen's grave.

"There is the stone that covers the relics of my favorite author," Lizzie said.

Kate read the inscription: "The benevolence of her heart, the sweetness of her temper, and the extraordinary endowments of her mind obtained the regard of all who knew her, and the warmest love of her intimate connections. Their grief is in proportion to their affection, they know their loss to be irreparable."

Over the years a brass plaque and a stained glass window had been added, to acknowledge her genius as a writer. The stained glass window was disappointing in every way except the choice of the main text: "In the beginning was the Word."

"That's fitting for Jane Austen," Lizzie said. "I think when the stone was carved they had no idea what a lasting impact her writing would have."

"Why do you love her books so much?" Kate asked.

"She's smart and funny," Lizzie answered. "And so are her characters. Sometimes she is so sarcastic that I completely misread her the first time around. When I first got *Pride and Prejudice* from my mom for my thirteenth birthday I instantly related to Elizabeth Bennet. It would have taken a dozen Nancy Drews to compete with her."

"I liked Nancy's friend George, though," Kate interjected.

Lizzie continued with her rhapsody, discussing Jane Austen's insightful social commentary. "Mostly though," she said, finishing, "she's fun. I approach rereading her novels as I approach visiting with much-loved friends, and I am sorry each and every time I turn the final page."

"That ought to be on her tombstone!" Kate said. "And I really did think George should have been the star of the Nancy Drew Books."

They turned to look at the rest of the church. Winchester Cathedral had neither the elegant simple grandeur of Salisbury, nor the stylistic purity of Wells, but it was crammed with interesting stuff and there was a lot to look at. The first church on the site, which came to be known as "Old Minster," was built in 648. In 971 the remains of St. Swithun, a local bishop who died in 862, were transferred into it.

By all accounts Swithun was a humble man who had requested a humble grave in the churchyard; the violent midsummer storm that accompanied the transfer of his relics into the more opulent resting place was seen as a sign of his displeasure. The notoriety gained from the storm, which lasted for forty days, and the miracles that began to occur at his new tomb, created a powerful magnet for pilgrims.

The movement of Swithun's relics from one place to another defined subsequent building projects around Winchester Cathedral. After the Norman Invasion, a new and grander church was laid out, and in 1079 construction began so close to Old Minster that the building of the new church and the demolition of the old occurred almost simultaneously. Major additions were made in each of the next five centuries, the most dramatic being the total transformation of the nave between 1350 and 1410, during the period when the Weaver made her pilgrimage there.

In 1476 a grand new shrine was built to hold the relics of St. Swithun, and for sixty-two years it occupied the central place in the town of Winchester, until the raiders from the Commission for the Destruction of Shrines swooped in to destroy it.

"Those guys did a hell of a lot of damage, didn't they?" Kate said, reading from the guidebook she had purchased when they entered the church.

"Our particular venture seems almost designed to highlight that," Lizzie said in response. "All the things the Weaver traveled to see were swept away by those same guys. It is very hard not to think of them as just a band of violent criminals."

When they reached the place where the old shrine had stood, they saw that a simple new shrine had been constructed in 1962, eleven hundred years after Swithun's death.

"No bones, of course," Lizzie said.

"Not here," Kate said, "but there are some other very interesting bones left in the Cathedral."

She led Lizzie to an area behind the choir of the Cathedral, where an elaborate wrought-iron screen enclosed an area referred to in the guide as the presbytery.

"Look up," Kate said.

Around the top of the screen were a number of elaborate chests, carved in wood and covered with gilding. Each had a shield and crown carved on the lid.

"Those are the bones of the Anglo-Saxon kings and queens," Kate whispered. "Apparently, Winchester was the capital of the Anglo Saxon kingdom of Wessex, and many of the Anglo-Saxon kings and queens, as well as the Danish invader Canute and his wife Emma, are deposited here."

"When were those put up there?" Lizzie asked.

Kate looked in the guide. "1525."

"So they were here when St. Swithun's shrine was destroyed. I wonder how they escaped being vandalized?"

"Maybe the vandals couldn't reach them," Kate said logically. She continued to read from the guidebook. "Emma was the queen to two kings. The first was the Anglo-Saxon Ethelred the Unready, who had apparently murdered his brother to take the throne from him."

Lizzie interrupted to tell her that she knew of the victim, Edward the Martyr, whose gravesite she had visited at the ruins of Shaftesbury Abbey.

"Her second husband was the Viking Canute, whose bones

are in one of those boxes. *His* father apparently booted Ethelred off the throne for a year or so in 1013. Ethelred managed to be king again for another couple of years only to have Canute succeed him to both the crown and his wife."

"I wonder if she was just the pawn of the men, or if she had any choice in all this?" Lizzie mused. "The theme of the importance of marrying to maintain position is so persistent we still find it in Jane Austen."

"Don't kid yourself Lizzie, we still find it today."

"Goodness gracious Kate! You are channeling Jackie!"

"Well I have learned some things in the years I've spent with the two of you."

"Anything else I should know about Emma before we go outside and sing a verse of 'Winchester Cathedral You're Bringing Me Down?'"

"She had a son with Ethelred, called Edward the Confessor—though I'm just going to assume that that last part got added some time after infancy. He was the last English monarch crowned here. He is the one who moved the government to London and he built his own church, Westminster Abbey, where all subsequent coronations have taken place."

"I'm pretty sure he's still buried there," Lizzie said.

Out on the vast lawn they found bricks that marked the outline of the "Old Minster," and Lizzie burst into song.

> *Winchester Cathedral, start ringing your bell,*
> *I did something awful, dum dum I'm in hell.*

"Those aren't the words!" Kate said.

"It's a long time since I've sung the Herman's Hermits repertoire," Lizzie said defensively

"I don't think that was Herman's Hermits," Kate said. She began to sing "I'm Henry the Eighth I Am," but like Lizzie, could only remember the words of the chorus and half a verse.

"Oh that's much more effective," Lizzie said. "Can we agree to end our musical tribute to Winchester?"

They stopped into a nearby pub to order their end-of-the-day cider. Lizzie checked her phone and found a text message from Jackie.

"I have news," it said. "Call me instantly!"

Lizzie stepped outside to call and Jackie answered before the first ring was completed.

"Where are you?" she demanded.

"Winchester," Lizzie answered.

"Good," Jackie said. "I hoped you'd still be there. I have made an appointment for you tomorrow morning at nine o'clock to meet with the librarian at Winchester Cathedral. Her name is Jenny Carroll." She paused for a moment. "Lizzie, they have a manuscript!"

"What kind of manuscript?"

"An illuminated manuscript," Jackie said. The excitement in her voice popped through Lizzie's cell phone. "An illuminated hagiography of Thomas Becket, given to Winchester Cathedral by the Weaver!"

"It survived?"

"Yes!" Jackie practically shouted. "The library there was somehow left intact when everything else was destroyed."

In her excitement, Lizzie couldn't think of anything to say.

"Is that not fucking awesome?" Jackie screamed.

"Yes it is! It is fucking awesome!" Lizzie repeated. "Sometimes your descriptive powers are completely right."

"Some profuse thanks are in order," Jackie said.

"I wish you were here so that I could deliver them in person."

"Me too. Are you and Kate having a great time?"

"We are."

"Is she as much fun as I am?"

"Of course not. You know you are my favorite friend!"

"Hey!" Kate said at her side. She had come out to see what Jackie had to report.

Lizzie winked at her.

"There's another thing," Jackie said, "but I haven't completely tracked it down yet. There might have been a chalice of some sort at Shaftesbury that had the Weaver's mark on it, but the inventory isn't clear."

"Any way to know for sure?"

"I'm hoping that if it survives in some collection it can be traced by the mark, but I'm still working on it."

"You are absolutely the best!" Lizzie said. "And I owe you

something wonderful for this."

"Convince Alison to let me write about that collection of Chaucer editions."

"Already done. You can get started on it at any time."

Lizzie decided to wait until she had seen the manuscript to tell Alison about it, but felt almost a dizziness from the excitement of Jackie's discoveries: two more gifts to add to the Weaver's legacy!

The next morning they found Jenny Carroll waiting for them with a manuscript box.

"Your friend, Ms. Harrigan, is very persuasive," she said. "She tracked me down at home on the holiday and convinced me to come here early this morning to get this manuscript ready for you."

"We understand completely," Kate said sympathetically. "We run our lives at her command."

Lizzie found that her hands were trembling with excitement as she put on a pair of latex gloves and reached for the box.

"May I?" she asked.

"Of course," Jenny said, nodding.

The book had a vellum binding, mottled yellow and curling at the edges. Inside were about twenty additional sheets of vellum, covered with a Latin script in black ink. At the beginning of each page the capital letter was filled with a tiny picture, and decorative leaves and vines ran down the left edge of the pages. Lizzie instantly recognized the pattern from the tapestry; it was the same design she thought might be on the carved stone pillow of the Bishop de la Marchia monument in Wells.

She struggled through the old Latin, but the story of Becket's life and death was clear. On the last page was a picture of the shrine, very similar to the one that had been in the stained glass window in Salisbury, but vibrantly colored. Reds and blues were still brilliant after six centuries, and details had been highlighted with real gold, pressed onto the page. Beneath the shrine, in a handwriting different from the text, was inscribed, "Thys ys my gyffte," followed by the familiar AW monogram.

"I can't tell you how exciting this is," Lizzie said, looking up at Jenny Carroll. "I know who commissioned this work to be given to the Cathedral. This last line is in her hand, and this is her mark." She explained the project to Jenny, describing the journal and bringing out the pictures of the tapestry, and of the window in Salisbury that she had received from Nora Stanley.

When the images of the shrine from the manuscript before her and the drawing of the window that had been in Salisbury were compared, the resemblance was clear.

"I'm surprised the researchers working on the Becket shrine didn't use this manuscript," Kate said. "It's really better than the others for showing details of the shrine."

"I'm sorry to have to admit that this manuscript was not cataloged very well," Jenny explained. "They wouldn't have found it through a standard search. We recently had our catalog cards from the 1950s digitized and put online, but there were no details about these illustrations. The most prominent feature mentioned was the AW monogram—which is how your friend found it."

Lizzie studied the side-by-side images of the shrine. "Look at this," she pointed out to her companions. "Though these are in three different media and by three different artists, if we count this manuscript, the stained glass window, and the reproduction of the window in the pen drawing, it is obvious that the original source was the same. The details and proportions are identical in every way." She talked as she observed, going back and forth from one image to the other and from the top of the shrine to the bottom.

"You can actually see individual gifts placed upon the shrine cover," Jenny said, pointing to the tiny gilt jewels painted with remarkable detail.

"And details of the fabric. . . ." Lizzie stopped talking when she realized that the pattern of the fabric that wrapped the bones of Becket was made up of alternating mitres and monograms in gold against a brilliant scarlet background.

"Ha ha!" she said eagerly, almost shouting with enthusiasm. "Look at this. She has designed a fabric specifically for the purpose of wrapping the bones and it has her monogram incorporated into the design!"

"What is that other thing?" Jenny asked.

"It's the bishop's hat," Kate said, "just like on the stiles of the Clarendon Way."

"Indeed it is," Lizzie said elatedly. "It's the mitre of the archbishop. Oh dear Lord, I can't believe how fucking awesome this is!" She immediately turned to Jenny Carroll and apologized for her language, but the librarian, caught up in the excitement of the discovery, simply waved her hand to indicate it wasn't a problem.

"I must call Alison and Jackie," Lizzie said to Kate, "and I must get some pictures, if that's okay." She turned to Jenny.

"As long as you don't plan to publish them," Jenny answered.

"We will definitely want to include this manuscript in our upcoming book, but we can arrange for permissions and for a professional photographer to take the pictures at a later time. For now, I just want some reference shots."

With Jenny's permission, Lizzie used the camera on her cell phone to take a photograph of each page of the manuscript, with several showing the details of the shrine and the fabric that wrapped the bones.

When they had thanked Jenny and left the archive Lizzie was practically skipping with delight. "Could anything possibly top that?" she said happily.

"Well I understand that the Round Table is also here in Winchester," Kate said, "in case you still need a King Arthur fix." She had procured a guide to the town and was reading from it.

"What else?"

"Hyde Abbey, the place where the Saxon King Alfred the Great was buried, though his bones were destroyed by those same marauders who smashed up everything else."

"He wasn't a saint. Why did they need to bust up his remains?"

"According to this, Thomas Wriothesley, who was in charge of the abbey's dissolution, wrote to Henry VIII that he intended to 'sweep away all the rotten bones that be called relics; which we may not omit, lest it be thought that we came more for the treasure than for the avoiding of the abomination of idolatry.' They also destroyed the head of St. Valentine, which had been given to the Abbey by Queen Emma."

"I am still astonished that kings and saints both came to the same end," Lizzie said. "But I'm glad that this Thomas Wriothesley was able to prove by rifling through the bones of Alfred the Great that he wasn't just in the business of looting churches for their treasure!"

"The road then?"

"The Old Road! I read most of the Belloc book last night, by the way, and it will be a good guide for us in the next few days. Thanks for it; he is the antithesis of Wainwright!"

"Alfred the not-so-great Wainwright?"

"Yes, perfect! Let us leave him behind in Winchester too!"

Chapter 27

Hilaire Belloc's *The Old Road* was a perfect guide for the two friends, interested as they were in history and technology. When Belloc set off on his pilgrimage in the first decade of the twentieth century, he had a theory about roads that he wanted to test. His reasoning on how to find the oldest road—the pilgrim's trail—was largely common sense: sharp corners on the path were to him suspicious, one should pass through the most ancient villages, and no one of sense would choose to walk through marshy ground.

He made a distinction between two kinds of ancient path: those built upon the chalk ridge, like the one Kate and Lizzie had been traveling on since Broad Chalke, and those built by the Romans which, because labor was cheap, ran arrow-straight up and down hills and across streams, never seeking the easy route or the natural ford. Many of the modern motorways followed those Roman roads.

Even before Belloc, nineteenth-century antiquarians in England had been interested in some sort of a "Pilgrim's Way" between Winchester and Canterbury, and over time it even came to be included on the Ordnance Survey maps.

"There are, of course, more than these options," Kate said as they compared Belloc's path to the one marked on the map.

Lizzie agreed. "If we were going directly from Winchester to Canterbury, I would absolutely follow Belloc, because I like his theory of the road, but the Weaver went to London, and both of these paths bypass it." She studied the map. "We have to head north someplace near Guildford, and from London I want to follow the path described by Chaucer, which follows the ancient Roman road from the coast."

214 • Mary Malloy

"This pilgrim's path on the map looks nicer to walk," Kate said. "It is along something called the 'North Down Way,' which looks to be very rural, while the coastal route follows the major motorway through a built-up area."

"I'm sure you don't regret that you will have left me by then."

"I will regret it when I have left, but I am prepared to enjoy the time we still have," Kate said philosophically. "Belloc gives us two choices to leave Winchester, the main road or the 'Nun's Walk.'"

"Well that is no choice at all," Lizzie said. "The Nun's Walk!"

The path went along the Itchen River and through a landscape that the English called a water meadow. The stream was filled with watercress and the water barely moved, except where it was stirred by enormous swans. Nesting coots were visible in the grasses along the riverbed, and baby ducks lazed through the water behind their mothers.

At Kings Worthy, the two women stopped at the local pub, the Coach and Horses, for lunch and cider and pondered the path to the next village, Martyr Worthy.

"This is all very English," Lizzie said to Kate, "with Kings and worthys, swans and watercress, cider and churches."

"Rah-ther," Kate answered, trying her best to mimic an English accent.

They had arrived in Jane Austen country and Lizzie recounted every episode she could remember where Austen described a walk through the countryside—and it seemed there was at least one in every novel.

They walked along the edge of Chawton Woods, grounds inherited by Jane Austen's brother from a wealthy childless relation who adopted him in order to have an heir. He remained close to his family, however, and set up his mother and two sisters in a comfortable house in Chawton where Jane Austen lived from 1809 until she went as an invalid to Winchester in 1817 and died. It was here that she wrote *Persuasion,* and here she lived when all of her books were published. She saw the first copy of *Pride and Prejudice* there. "I want to tell you that I have got my own darling child from London," she wrote upon receiving it.

Lizzie and Kate walked around Austen's house and sat in her garden. It had been a moving experience for Lizzie to stand upon the stone under which her bones rested in Winchester Cathedral. "But this is the real relic for me," she said to Kate as they stood in Jane Austen's room. "She sat at that small table in front of this window and wrote *Mansfield Park, Emma* and *Persuasion.* As powerful as it was to ponder her tomb, it is doubly so to ponder that table."

As there was no one nearby and no physical barrier to keep her from touching it, Lizzie stepped forward and laid her hand upon the wood and felt the power of the artifact.

"If I were a real pilgrim, and not a hired one," she said, "this is what I'd come for."

Kate gave a great sigh. "Good grief, Lizzie! Don't be such a dramatic dope! You are here, so if this is what you *would* come for, simply make it what you *did* come for. And anyway, you have totally bought into Alison's project. If she stopped paying you, you'd still finish it, and you know it."

Lizzie looked at her friend and laughed. "You're absolutely right, of course. That was a bit too much drama."

"I marked something in the Belloc book that reminded me of you." Kate took off her pack and retrieved the book. "Speaking of medieval pilgrims, he commented on the 'peculiar association of antiquity and religion' and the 'mingling of the two ideas almost into one.'"

"Are you saying that I've made a religion out of history?"

"Something like that."

There was a sound of voices on the stairs and they were joined soon after by three women wearing saris.

"Are there Jane Austen fans in India or Pakistan?" Lizzie whispered to Kate as they left the house.

"You might as well ask me what women most desire," Kate answered.

"Is it the same in every culture and across time?"

"Of course not."

"It is a truth universally acknowledged, that a single man in possession of a good fortune, must be in want of a wife," Lizzie said, quoting the opening line of *Pride and Prejudice.* "The converse expectation is that all single women are in want of a husband, but that clearly was not true in Jane Austen's case. She received an offer of marriage, accepted it, and then after thinking about it for one night, declined. Elizabeth Bennet refused the proposal of the odious Mr. Collins only to find that her friend Charlotte accepted him."

"And Mr. Darcy was rich, handsome and loved her more than she loved him," said Kate. "That one was easy! Haven't we had this conversation like a dozen times before?"

"Yes, but each time it's different."

"No it's not."

"But this time we're actually standing in Jane Austen's house!"

Kate agreed that there was a certain novelty in the situation, but Lizzie didn't need to be hit on the head with a brick to know it was time to move on. She wanted to call Jackie anyway, and find out if there was more information on the chalice at Shaftesbury.

"I'm calling from Jane Austen's garden," she said when Jackie answered the phone.

"Poor Kate! I'm thinking that by now you're in heaven and she's in hell."

"Pretty much. Do you have good news?"

"Astonishing news. The Ashmolean Museum has a chalice with the Weaver's mark on it."

"Is there a provenance of where it came from?" Lizzie asked excitedly.

"I'm still working on that," Jackie answered, "but I think I am going to be able to make a plausible, though not necessarily positive link to Shaftesbury Abbey."

Lizzie could not wait to convey the news to Martin and called him immediately. "I haven't even told Alison yet," she told him after explaining about the chalice.

"So this makes a stone carving, stained glass, an illuminated manuscript, and metal work. Your weaver hired an artist in every medium."

"And with the tapestry, she added weaving as well."

Martin thought about that. "Yes, but I wouldn't be surprised if she made some absolutely remarkable example of her own work to give to the most important place on the list."

"That would be Canterbury."

"That's what I would do." Martin asked her to remind him of her itinerary.

"We'll be in Guildford tomorrow, then transit to London the next day, where Kate will fly home, then four days to Canterbury."

"I'm sure you'll miss Kate's company."

"It has been so great to have her and Jackie along." She lowered her voice. "I miss you. I'm really looking forward to seeing you next week in Newcastle, and I can't wait to see the mural."

"I have to admit, it is looking great. I'm very pleased."

By the time Lizzie finished calling Martin and then Alison, Kate was standing beside her in the yard and they said their good-byes to Jane Austen's house. They had booked a B&B in Alton, where they would spend the night and then move on to Guildford in the morning.

As they came back onto the main road out of Chawton they saw a lone bull on the opposite hillside. It was the snorting bullock of Lizzie's nightmares. There was no mistake. Wainwright was right, he had a certain expression on his face that looked mad. Even from a distance, across a good-sized highway, he was scary. Lizzie thought she saw him stroke his hoof along the ground as he eyed them, like bulls do in cartoons. His eyes were fiery, smoke seemed to come from his flared nostrils. Lizzie and Kate stood rooted to the spot, the hair on their necks standing straight up.

"Could he," she asked Kate, "with the advantage of the hill, race down, leap the fence, and be across the road in an instant?"

Kate said he wouldn't dare, and even shouted at him from a distance to taunt him as they walked nervously on.

The next day in Guildford would be their last day walking before they moved north to London and Kate returned home. Lizzie asked her friend how this adventure compared to others. Kate was a treasure trove of esoteric travel tidbits. She spoke about being in the Antarctic and seeing there a Japanese researcher who had a three-legged pair of long underwear. He first wore his legs through two holes for a day, then moved each leg over one hole and back each day. This was supposed to keep them from having to be washed as often as regular underwear, but both women were skeptical.

Belloc's old road had long ago been paved and become the major motorway between London and Southampton, and it was more difficult than before to find a good path. At one point they had to cross the four-lane highway by racing across it through traffic. On the far side they found themselves on a narrow path leading through a field of bright yellow flowers up to their shoulders. They had learned from the farmer in Broad Chalke that this plant was called "rape," though he said he preferred "oil-seed rape" to lessen the impact of the word. It was oily and sweet-smelling, the basis of canola oil.

"A terrible name for such a lovely plant," Kate said as they walked through it, touching the plants on either side with their shoulders. She sometimes got far enough ahead that Lizzie could just see her head bobbing above the blossoms.

"It is strange sometimes how powerful words are," she said at her friend's back. "The same word describes both this flower, and the violent act that propels the narrative of the Wife of Bath's Tale."

Kate turned around and smiled at her. "I think it is just amazing that you can connect everything to either Jane Austen or your project."

Lizzie smiled back. "It is wonderful, isn't it."

"I'm only surprised that you couldn't get a knight of the Round Table into that thought."

"Oh but I did! The rapist was one of Arthur's knights."

They passed through a small and pretty village called Wyck. Beyond it in marshy ground they encountered their first snake and their first nettles, which considerably dampened Lizzie's spirits. Between Farnham and Guildford the A31 motorway ran along the ridge top known as the "Hog's Back," and they could find no good options for footpaths. A double decker bus happened to stop in front of them as they studied the map, so they boarded it and rode to Puttenham, a village mentioned by Belloc as having had a "pilgrim's market" in ancient times.

When they found the path again, there was a small house

on it with a sign saying "Pilgrim's Way Cottage." It had a weathervane that showed a classic pilgrim with pack, hat, and staff. There was also another snake along the path, small and flat and a silvery black color.

"I don't think that is an adder," Lizzie said. "But then I don't think I would recognize one anyway."

"It hardly matters now," Kate responded. "We are now on the 'North Downs Way,' one of the most popular long-distance walks in England. I'm pretty sure it is safe."

The path was hard-packed earth and well defined.

"I fear neither snake nor bull!" Lizzie declared as she marched briskly along.

They crossed under the A31 and looked up to see two large wooden crosses mounted on either side of the highway above them, official markers of the "Pilgrim's Way," and a reminder to the occupants of the trucks and cars whizzing along the motorway that an ancient path passed beneath them.

"I like that," Lizzie said. "Not for its religious overtones, but for its acknowledgement of history."

As they neared Guildford they came for the first time onto the official "Pilgrims Way" as acknowledged on the Ordnance Survey map.

"You know those papers you showed me with the noon calculations of the sun's declination?" Kate asked, referring to the documents Lizzie had removed from books at Alison's house. "We are about to cross the first latitude indicated on it."

Lizzie stood beside her and looked at the two red lines Kate had drawn on the map as her friend checked their position on her cell phone's GPS.

"Fifty-one degrees, thirteen minutes north," she said. "Of course that line of latitude goes all the way around the world; without longitude, latitude doesn't mean much."

"What would you do with just latitude?" Lizzie asked.

"I've been thinking about that since you showed me those papers. It might be used to set up a sundial, for instance, but I can't think why else you wouldn't mark a place with both coordinates."

"We'll be in Guildford soon, but surely that latitude alone won't be very meaningful there."

"This line is slightly south of Guildford, however, and the place mentioned is 544 feet, plus twelve feet, above sea level."

"I hope you will be able to recognize something that is 544 feet high, because I certainly won't."

Kate told her that the tallest mast on her ship was 110 feet high. "And the mainmast of the *Constitution,* which you can see from the window of your office in Charlestown, is twice that."

As they spoke, the stone tower of a square Norman castle came into view and Kate wondered aloud if that might be the place. "I don't think that is five hundred feet high, but we are so close to the latitude mentioned."

"But then what? Do you think that we will see something that will make sense in some context that we aren't yet expecting?"

"I don't know. We may never understand it. It might just be someone's doodling through a problem solved long ago."

The castle was surrounded by a park and they made their way through it to the base of the tower, but could find no way in. Kate took out her binoculars and walked around the structure, scanning the top of all four sides.

"I just don't see anything there," she said. "And I don't know what we might observe if came back at noon on December 29."

"So should we go to Guildford? Or continue along this line of latitude?"

"I'd just as soon push on," Kate said.

The path climbed and became more woodsy, with a dry piney smell. At the top of the hill a vista opened to the south. Several villages were visible, as well as a patchwork of farmland, hedges and roads, and small groves of trees. A stream broadened into a lake where it had been dammed between two mills.

"This valley is called 'The Vale of the Chilworth,'" Kate said, looking at the map.

"It's beautiful," Lizzie said. "It brings to mind all those words that English poets used to describe their countryside: wold and copse and weald and grange."

There was a chapel at the crest of the hill, St. Martha's,

and they went inside. A map for sale in the vestibule described the "Probable Course Near Guildford" of the "Pilgrims Way, 1171-1538," which they took, along with a history of the church.

A talkative old gent greeted them. He was a volunteer and would be happy, he said, to give them a tour of the church, the only one in the world known to be dedicated to St. Martha.

"In the corner is a statue carved by a girl of nineteen in the 1940s, which just shows you what youth can accomplish when they put their minds to it," he started. There was little in the church that was more than a few hundred years old, though the guide said that it had been an important pilgrimage site for many centuries. The Norman church that was on the site was destroyed in the explosion of a nearby gunpowder factory.

When another couple arrived at the door of the chapel, the guide left to greet them and Lizzie and Kate sat down in one of the pews.

"I think Belloc might have said something about this place," Kate said, retrieving the book. She found the passage, one of many she had marked with a sticky tab. "Belloc says that the original dedication of this church was not to St. Martha but to the *Saint and Martyr*, meaning Thomas Becket.

"I saw right away that there is a Becket window," Lizzie said in response, "though it is not as well done as the one designed by the Weaver."

As they spoke, Lizzie's gaze moved around the chapel from one window to the next. She couldn't believe her eyes when they landed on the familiar AW monogram of the Weaver, set prominently into a leaded glass window.

"What the hell?" she exclaimed. "That is not possible."

"What?" Kate asked.

"Look at that," Lizzie said, rising from her seat and pointing. She walked over to the window. "How is this possible? This window can't be more than a hundred years old. It certainly isn't from the fourteenth century."

"It was installed in 1948," Kate said. "It says so right on the glass."

Lizzie read the inscription: "In loving memory of Stephen

Buckland, who died in London on 26 January 1941, and John Hockwold, who died at Antwerp on 21 December 1944, by their friend William Kent. 29 December 1948." She thought about this before she spoke again. These names were all on the list they had found in Alison's house. She turned to look at Kate. "Alison's father gave this window to the church," she said. "But why?"

Kate was looking at the GPS on her cell phone. "We are now at the exact latitude written on that sheet of paper. Is it possible that he wrote it?"

"Absolutely," Lizzie answered. "It was in his library."

"The hill we are on could certainly be 544 feet above sea level. Is there anything in that window that is twelve feet above the floor of the church?"

They stood side by side and looked up at the window.

"The Weaver's monogram is about that height, but what does it mean?" Lizzie asked.

"What happens at noon on December 29?" Kate said softly, mentally working through the possibilities. "The sun is due south, the direction this window faces, we are just past the winter solstice . . . the angle of the rays is . . . at noon it would come . . . right through that hole!" She pointed to a hole in the wall of the stone window casing, which went upward at an oblique angle. "It's a pointer of some sort," Kate said excitedly.

"Is there any way to know what it points at?"

Kate looked around her at the floor of the church, which was set with dozens of memorial stones. "I want to go outside and see what is on the exterior of the wall at that point."

While Kate was outside, Lizzie was approached again by the volunteer guide. "Can I answer any questions?" he asked. The other couple had wandered away.

"Do you know anything about this window?" she asked.

"I know that it was installed just after the war, when some repairs were made to the church. The first man mentioned on it was, I think, killed in one of the German bombing raids on London, the other fellow was killed at the Battle of the Bulge in Belgium. "

When Kate returned, she asked the man about the hole in the window casing.

"It is designed to catch the sun on the winter solstice," he said.

"And do what with it?" Kate asked.

He didn't understand her question.

"Does it illuminate some spot in the church?"

"Some specific spot?" he mused. "No, it just casts a sort of glow."

Kate pulled Lizzie outside and showed her the exterior end of the long hole that had been bored through the stone of the window casing. "There is a piece of glass there," she said. "If that is a lens, and you could put another lens at the other end of the hole, and if the focal length was calculated correctly between them, you could aim the beam onto a specific spot."

Lizzie thought about the two lenses in the Becket reliquary. "There is a lens," she said. "William Kent, Alison's father, left two lenses in his house." She tried to remember what had been inscribed on them, but couldn't. "We need to go to Bath and get them," she said eagerly.

"And come back here on December 29?" Kate said. "No, there must be another way to figure out where the beam would point."

They went back into the church and studied the window again. There was a tomb in front of it with a carved marble back panel that stood against the wall of the church. "I could climb up to the hole on that," Kate whispered to Lizzie, gesturing at the tomb. "There are just enough places to grab onto."

"And then what?" Lizzie said. "You could reach it, but you couldn't look through it in the right direction."

The two women were silent until Kate turned to Lizzie with a look of excitement. "I think I have a star laser pointer in my pack! I don't think I took it out after my last trip on the ship."

Lizzie had gone several times with Kate and her students to study constellations and knew the tool she was talking about, a green laser pointer with a beam strong enough to point at stars.

"If I can secure it in the hole somehow," Kate said, thinking aloud. "The diameter of the hole is bigger than the shaft of the pointer, and that is going to make it inexact, but at least we should be able to narrow the possibilities on the floor to a few of the memorial stones."

"That guy is not going to let you climb up on that tomb," Lizzie whispered, nodding at the guide.

"He will need to be distracted," Kate whispered back.

The other couple in the church were now in the vestibule.

"Get your laser," Lizzie said to Kate, moving toward the door of the chapel. She told the guide that she would like to know more about the explosion in the gunpowder factory, and asked him if he would show her where the factory had been. The other couple, hearing the question, followed them outside. As soon as the guide began to expound on the Vale of the Chilworth, Lizzie slipped away.

Kate was already climbing the tomb when Lizzie returned to the scene. With one foot balanced on the head of an angel she put her hand up to the hole. "There's a ridge up here where you could put a lens in," she said as she turned on the beam of her laser pointer and pushed it into the shaft of the hole. She gently rolled the pointer back and forth inside the tunnel in the stone, and the green beam made an arc on the floor of the church at the edge of the center aisle.

Lizzie ran to the spot. There were four stones intersecting within the arc. They all looked to have been carved at about the same time. Three of them had death dates in the 1940s, but the fourth was completely anomalous:

Brother Osbert Giffard
Monk of Canterbury
1167-1538

Kate climbed down from the tomb and joined Lizzie at the stone. "That can't be right," she said, pointing at the inscription with her toe. "He'd have to be, what, three hundred seventy-one years old."

"Obviously, this is a clue to something," Lizzie said, the frustration clear in her tone. "But I have no idea what. Could this possibly have anything to do with the Weaver and her pilgrimage?"

She took a picture of the stone and of the window with the camera of her cell phone, and then dialed Alison's number. There was no chance to tell Alison any of what she had learned, however.

"The police from Oxford are looking for you," Alison said as soon as she knew it was Lizzie on the line. "Dante Zettler's death has been ruled a homicide. He was poisoned."

Chapter 28

The news of Dante Zettler's murder had already reached Boston. Soon after Lizzie ended her conversation with Alison, Jackie called to tell her that she had been contacted by the Oxford police department, who wanted to conduct an interview with her by video conference at Boston Police Headquarters.

"Apparently the poison that killed him has a pretty specific time line. They think he ingested it at the dinner we ate together or in a cocktail immediately preceding it."

"Is there any chance that it was accidental?"

"The guy that spoke to me didn't seem to think so." At the other end of the line, Jackie cleared her throat. "I hope you don't mind, but I gave them this number. They told me they wanted to contact you."

"Of course I don't mind," Lizzie responded. "It's not like I'm a suspect. I don't even see how I can help them."

"You don't think anyone overheard me giving him the business about the rapist in the Wife of Bath do you?"

"Oh Jackie!" Lizzie said, suppressing a laugh. "Even if they did, his being stupid did not give you a motive to kill him."

"In my experience that is one of the best motives there is!"

Lizzie reassured her friend. "I'm sure they just need to talk to everyone who had contact with him that night."

· · · · ·

Lizzie and Kate walked into Guildford and rented a car to drive to London. Kate's flight was the next morning and they booked a hotel near Heathrow Airport. The Oxford Police called and asked Lizzie when she could come in to make a statement, and she made an appointment for the following afternoon.

"Is this the end of the pilgrimage?" Kate asked as they stashed their backpacks in the car.

"I hope not," Lizzie answered. "It certainly isn't the end of the project. We have found so much new material! The tapestry, the offerings to the churches, it's all really astonishing stuff."

"How much is left to do?"

"Well, I will need to visit Westminster Abbey in London and see if I can find anything there, and then the road to Canterbury as described by Chaucer, and the Cathedral there."

"What about the clue we found at St. Martha's?"

"The first thing is to describe it all to Alison and see if she can help us figure out what it means. I'll go to Hengemont from Oxford to talk it over with her."

It was a sad parting for both women the next morning.

"I hate to be leaving just as things are heating up," Kate said as Lizzie dropped her at the airport curb. "Do you want me to stay and go with you to the police interview?"

"No, but thanks. Edmund called late last night to tell me that he will meet me there, and he insists on bringing along a friend who is a solicitor—which seems completely unnecessary to me." Lizzie gave her friend a hug. "You might like to go hold Jackie's hand, though. She is likely to start ranting, and she'll have a captive audience of police officers on both sides of the Atlantic."

"I'll see if I can't keep her from getting herself charged with murder." She handed Lizzie an envelope. "Here, I don't want you to think Jackie is the only one who can find just the right literary passage for a special occasion. Think of me when you are next on the road."

Lizzie missed her friend as soon as the door to the terminal closed behind her. She drove directly to Oxford from the airport and was there in plenty of time to park and find the restaurant Edmund had suggested for lunch. She was about twenty minutes early for their rendezvous and she opened the envelope Kate had given her. Inside was a poem by Tennyson and message: "You will be missed by your friends, who are jealous that you walk on without us!"

I climb the hill: from end to end
Of all the landscape underneath,
I find no place that does not breathe
Some gracious memory of my friend;

No gray old grange, or lonely fold,
Or low morass and whispering reed,
Or simple stile from mead to mead,
Or sheepwalk up the windy wold;

"Perfect!" she said softly. She missed both of her friends, and wondered if any part of the week to come would match the pleasures of the last two.

Edmund and his friend were right on time. The solicitor seemed to feel, as Lizzie did, that his participation was superfluous and kept a low profile both during lunch and the interview that followed.

The first questions were very straightforward: when had she arrived in Oxford? when did she meet Dante Zettler? how well did she know him? what was her perception of him? There were only a few questions of how their work overlapped, and though the Oxford police seemed very conversant with the competitive nature of the academic world, they had already deduced that Dante's work on Chaucer was probably not worth killing for.

"We understand from several sources that your work was likely to eclipse his," a sergeant said to Lizzie. "Is that so?"

Lizzie explained that it wasn't her own work, that she was employed as a researcher and collaborator with Alison Kent, but yes, the project they were working on would definitely eclipse the work of Dante Zettler.

They then asked about the seating arrangements at the dinner in minute detail. How had she come to sit with Dante and had each of them sat at the place marked with their place card?

For the first time Lizzie remembered that Jackie had switched the cards so that Dante would be between them. She told that to the officers.

"Had anything been served when you sat down?" the sergeant asked.

Lizzie thought hard, trying to picture the place setting on the table when she arrived. It was a complex affair with multiple forks and other cutlery. "There was a roll on the small side plate," she said, "and a glass of red wine was already poured."

"Did Professor Zettler drink his wine or eat his roll?"

"He certainly drank at least some of the wine, we made a toast. I don't remember about the roll."

Edmund made a sound to catch Lizzie's attention and when she turned to look, saw an expression of concern.

The sergeant continued with his questioning. "I understand you were involved in a car accident two weeks ago."

She acknowledged that she was and described it at his request.

"Did you know the driver?"

"No, but my employer did. He was apparently a friend of Alison Kent's father."

They returned to the work that Lizzie was doing for Alison. Was it possible that Hockwold Bruce had tried to stop it by violence?

Lizzie explained the nature of their project, the journal, the Weaver's gifts to various churches, and explained that much of what she knew now she had learned since she was at the Chaucer conference with Dante Zettler. "I can't imagine any objection Hockwold Bruce could have had to any of it," she said. "If anyone would suffer by it, it would be Dante Zettler."

"Is there anything else that seems unimportant, but might lead us to information?"

Edmund spoke from behind her. "Tell her about the list with Bruce's name on it."

She described the list and the three names on the last line: Alison's father, Hockwold Bruce and Frederick Wickersham. "All of them are dead," Lizzie said. "Though Wickersham apparently has a grandson with the same name here in Oxford."

"Do you know him?"

"No, I've never met him."

"Would you recognize him if you saw him?"

She shook her head.

The policemen left the room and Edmund came to sit beside her.

"Lizzie," he said, softly but intensely, "you must realize that they think you might have been the target."

She looked at him with astonishment. "Don't be absurd, Edmund. I haven't done anything to make any enemies here."

He took her hand. "I'm sorry to have to remind you of this, but my brother tried to kill you over a secret that he thought you *might* uncover in the course of your research. Is it possible that you have stumbled onto something more here? Something you don't even realize yet?"

She quickly told him about the window and the gravestone in St. Martha's church. "There were clues leading to it, but they were so obscure—and they were put there by Alison's father sixty years ago."

"And yet you found them."

"But I honestly have no idea what they mean."

"Are you going to tell the police about them?"

"Should I? I can't believe it's relevant."

When the officers returned, the only questions they asked were where she would be in the days to come and if she wanted protection.

Edmund answered that she would be at his father's estate in Somersetshire and that it would not be a bad idea to have local police check on the place.

"Are you sure, Edmund?"

The police sergeant concurred. "It can't hurt to have the locals make a presence at the house," he said. "I assume you will be staying at the same location as Professor Kent?"

When she said that she was, it settled the matter. She and Alison were officially considered to be potential targets of one or more killers.

The solicitor spoke for the first time, asking if he could be kept up to date on the investigation, and was told that he would be. Through him, Edmund told Lizzie, they would know what was happening.

As she drove to Hengemont with Edmund, Lizzie expressed

her stunned confusion at the strange turn of events. "I still think this is all a big mistake," she said. "I simply can't believe that there is any plot against me."

"What about Alison?"

"It is more likely that she has enemies here than I, but even so, it is very hard to think how these threats could be related in any way to our project."

"But you have to admit that her enemies might have become yours since you started working so closely with her."

She had to concede that was possible.

She wanted to speak to Martin about it and as soon as they reached the house she called him. "This will sound like a strange echo of last year," she said, choosing her words carefully, "but once again things are happening around me that I can't explain."

"Are you okay?" he asked quickly.

She assured him that she was, and recounted her interview with the Oxford police.

"I'm glad you're coming to Newcastle," he said. "I miss you and no one will find you here."

"I'm glad I'll be seeing you in a few days," she said. "And I can't wait to see the mural."

"Should I come there?" he asked.

"No!" she said emphatically. "You need to finish the work. I know that this is no time for you to be leaving it with the dedication so close. Alison and I just need to put our heads together for a few days to see if we can't figure out what her father was up to sixty years ago, and then I am heading your way."

"Can you assure me that you are safe?"

"Of course I'm safe. I think there is a lot more being made of all this than is warranted."

Though it was late, the time difference allowed her to call Jackie when she finished her call with Martin, to tell her about her interview with the Oxford Police.

"My impression," Lizzie said, "is that they think that by switching those place cards at dinner, you saved my life."

"Someone meant the poison for you and not for Dante Zettler?" Jackie said, the surprise obvious in her voice. "But who?"

"That part isn't at all clear and I'm still dubious about the whole thing. I'm not convinced Dante couldn't have taken the poison in a drink or something else earlier that evening."

Jackie wanted to be thanked for saving Lizzie's life anyway, which Lizzie did with appropriate gratefulness.

"Believe it or not, being told that someone might have attempted to murder me was not even the weirdest thing that has happened since you left here." Lizzie described the whole of the day at St. Martha's with Kate.

"Let me grab a pen," Jackie said, "and then repeat all the names and dates you just mentioned. And send me whatever pictures you took in the church as email attachments. I'll see if I can add to what you know."

"Thank you, as always."

"Take care of yourself, Lizzie," Jackie said with a rare note of seriousness. "St. Pat's is a rather dull place without you, and Rose Geminiani is looking forward to a good story when you return."

"Even without knowing how this part of it will end, I think I can guarantee that."

Chapter 29

"The first thing you need to know are these dates," Jackie wrote in an email the next day. "Thomas Becket was murdered on December 29, 1167; his bones/relics were translated into a new shrine on July 7, 1220; and the shrine was destroyed in September, 1538 (I haven't been able to find the precise day). It can't be a coincidence that Brother Osbert Giffard's memorial stone has the year of Becket's death followed by the year his shrine was destroyed. Have you asked Alison yet what her father's Becket connection was, beyond having some of his relics?"

Lizzie printed out the message and brought it to Alison, who was propped up comfortably on an upholstered chair in the library at Hengemont. This was a familiar room to Lizzie, since she had worked there almost the whole month of January the previous year.

"It is wonderful to be able to see this garden coming into bloom rather than covered in frost," she said, walking to the tall windows. She turned when Helen Jeffries came into the room with a tray of coffee, another familiar sight from that previous visit.

Helen was always more formal when someone else was in the room, but she and Lizzie exchanged a warm look.

"I'm not sure what your friend Jackie means here when she asks what my father's Becket connection was," Alison said as she read the message.

Edmund had retrieved the Becket reliquary from the bank vault at Lizzie's request, and she had printed out the pictures she took of the window and the memorial stone in St. Martha's church.

She laid out two lines of evidence along the table. The top row had everything that related to the Weaver's pilgrimage: the journal, and photographs of the tapestry, the tomb in Wells Cathedral, the chalice at the Ashmolean that Jackie had linked to Shaftesbury Cathedral, the drawing of the window at Salisbury, and the image of Becket's shrine from the manuscript at Winchester. Lizzie briefly reviewed each piece for Alison, and for George and Edmund, who came into the room soon after she started.

"A truly remarkable documentation of a medieval pilgrimage," Lizzie said, "and a great book in the making."

Alison tried to thank her for all the work she had done, but Lizzie held up her hand and moved to the next row.

"This trail of evidence is related in some way, but as yet we don't know quite how."

She began with the Becket reliquary, removing the two lenses from the box. "One of these is marked 'StM 12/29,'" she said, "clearly referring to St. Martha's church on December 29, not coincidentally, I think, the date on which Becket was murdered. The other is marked 'CC 7/7,' which I think we can presume refers to Canterbury Cathedral on July 7, the date of the translation of Becket's remains."

The pages with the astronomical calculations came next. "These are worksheets for determining where to place a sun pointer in the wall of St. Martha's church, and also, again presumably, in Canterbury Cathedral. In each case the pointer illuminates a clue to something." She pointed out the Weaver's mark on both the page of calculations and the window. "Your father made the link between these two tracks of evidence by linking whatever he was working on to the Weaver's pilgrimage," she said to Alison.

She picked up the photograph she had printed of the memorial stone to Osbert Giffard and passed it to Alison. "This may be the most intriguing thing of all," she said, pointing to the dates on the inscription. "This clearly meant something to your father, Alison. Do you know what?"

"Sorry, my dear, but I don't," Alison answered.

"Two more things," Lizzie said, picking up the list of names and passing a picture of the window in St. Martha's church to

Alison. "This list may be as old as four hundred fifty to five hundred years," she said. "There are three names on each line, and the penultimate line has the names William Kent, Stephen Buckland and John Hockwold, whose names are all on the window your father donated to St. Martha's church."

"Buckland and Hockwold died in the war," George said, as Alison handed him the picture of the window.

"The last line on the list has the names William Kent, Hockwold Bruce and Frederick Wickersham."

Edmund interrupted. "That reminds me," he said. "I heard from my solicitor friend that the youngest of the Frederick Wickershams was picked up for questioning by the Oxford Police last night, but he was out of town the night of the dinner and isn't a suspect."

"I'd still like to speak to him," Lizzie said.

"The Oxford Police might have something to say about that," Edmund said.

"Well I'd like to speak to him too," Alison said. "I knew his father. I wonder if he would come here if I asked?"

"Before that, I need to go to Canterbury," Lizzie said.

Edmund looked at them incredulously. "Absolutely not!" he said. "To both suggestions. You neither of you seem to be giving enough credence to the danger you are in."

"The *potential* danger," Lizzie said, stressing the word. "How long can we just sit here without finishing our project?"

"I'd say until they catch Dante Zettler's killer and figure out what this is all about," Edmund said, clearly surprised that there was any question.

George backed up his son. "With what you've just described to us, Lizzie, surely there is plenty of work for you to do here for several days at least."

"But I don't have much time. In two days I am going to Newcastle for the unveiling of Martin's mural and then we leave five days after that."

She could not, however, deny George's point when she looked at the table strewn with papers. "Admittedly, there is an awful lot to do here." She turned to Alison and asked her how she would like to proceed.

"All that is really left of the pilgrimage is London and the road to Canterbury, and it can wait until we have processed this," Alison answered. "Even to some point in the future when you can come back, if necessary. You have already found so much more than I ever expected."

With that, Edmund left to return to Bristol, and George to some other part of the house. Lizzie and Alison began once again to go page by page through the Weaver's journal, identifying every time she mentioned making a gift to a church and then matching the artifacts to the locales. This was the first chance they had to look closely at images of the chalice that Jackie had identified at the Ashmolean Museum, and Lizzie opened the Museum's webpage to see the highest resolution photographs. The now-familiar floral design had been hammered into the silver of the chalice and a number of oval carnelian stones were set into it. The AW monogram of the Weaver was worked into a chain that wrapped around the base. The catalog information gave the date as "circa 1400," and a long list of owners going back to "probably Shaftesbury Abbey at the time of its dissolution."

"I can't believe how many times I have been in that museum and never had any idea this chalice was there," Alison said.

"Now that you know about it, we should make another visit to Oxford to see it."

"I have already been thinking that when our book comes out, we should try to get all these objects together at the college with the tapestry and the journal."

"It would make a wonderful exhibit," Lizzie said. "And there still may be more to add to it. Glastonbury is, unfortunately, probably a dead end on artifacts, so the next place on our list is Westminster Abbey in London."

"I have a colleague who can help us with that. He has done a lot of research on the writers buried there and is well connected at the Abbey."

"Excellent," Lizzie said. "And even without going to Canterbury Cathedral we might be able to start some research on their collection online." She told Alison Martin's theory that the Weaver's last gift might be an extraordinary example of her own work, rather than another commissioned piece. "So I think that we are likely looking for a textile there."

"She may have documented it at the end of the journal!" Alison said excitedly. "Hand me the manuscript!" She made a furious gesture with her hand, as if she could scoop the papers to her if she got enough air moving.

Lizzie gave her the journal and Alison turned immediately to the end. There was a series of pages with crosshatched patterns. Lizzie had never spent enough time with the original manuscript to study these and even now she didn't know how they were meaningful.

"This is a weaver's pattern," Alison said. "My grandmother showed me how to read one when I was just a girl. This shows how to set up the warp of the loom and the treadles to get the design you want. Here along the sides the Weaver has made notations about threads: scarlet and two different golds—I think one is actually a thin gold wire that was sometimes used in Medieval textiles."

"Is it the same floral pattern that appears on the tapestry and elsewhere?" Lizzie asked.

Alison looked up at her and smiled. "No," she said. "It is an all-over pattern of bishop's mitres alternating with her monogram, in gold on a red background."

"Like the fabric that wraps Becket's bones in that picture of the shrine?"

"Exactly."

"Did she make a piece of fabric specifically to wrap Becket's bones?" Lizzie looked in wonder at the image of the shrine, with its vibrant red and gold representation of that bit of fabric. "I wonder if it ever got used for that purpose?"

"I don't see how we could ever know. The bones were destroyed with the shrine in the sixteenth century. I'm sure if there was some textile in the grave it would have been destroyed as well."

Lizzie went to sleep that night still thinking about it. In two days she would take Alison's car and drive to Newcastle to meet Martin for the dedication of his mural. After that they were scheduled to return home within a few days. There was no time to go to Canterbury to search the archives. She returned to the library and sent an email to Jackie: "In the records of the Dissolute Shrine Destroyers, is there any mention of a textile in the grave of Thomas Becket at Canterbury?"

When the message was sent she thought of Tyler Brown, whom she had met at the Chaucer conference, and who worked at an historical society in Canterbury. He might be able to advise her on the best places to look for information. His business card was still on the table where she had left it for Alison: Tyler Brown, Archivist, Canterbury Catholic History Society. She composed another email. Without making any overture that might make him think that she was offering him the option of publishing the finished work, Lizzie asked if she could call him the next day to talk about resources available for research in Canterbury.

The next morning she received an enthusiastic response encouraging her to call him as soon as possible. There was also a message from Jackie with the subject heading: "Becket Bones Conspiracy," which she decided to wait to read until after she had spoken to Tyler Brown. Lizzie stepped out onto the terrace to make her phone call. It was a beautiful late-spring morning with all the features of the English landscape that inspired ballads and poems. In the foreground were buds and birds and fresh green leaves, down the hill toward the Bristol Channel were fluffy sheep, the occasional cow and cottages that looked idyllic from a distance. Beyond it all, a few ships plowed through the placid waters.

"Mr. Brown," she said, when the phone was answered.

"Is this Professor Manning?" was the reply.

"Please, call me Lizzie," she said.

After he had insisted that she call him Tyler, and laid on some pretty thick compliments about her presentation in Oxford, Lizzie got down to the reason for the call.

"As you know, Professor Kent is laid up with a broken hip and I am running out of time to get everything done that needs to be done for our project."

"How can I help?"

"Mostly with information, thanks. I'm looking for a good contact at Canterbury Cathedral, or sources of information on what happened to things that were stolen from the Cathedral at the time of the destruction of Becket's shrine."

"That is a special interest of my organization," he said.

Lizzie silently thanked her stars.

"Is there something special you are looking for?" Tyler asked.

"Something given to the Cathedral at the time of her pilgrimage by Alison the Weaver—the woman whose journal I described at the Oxford Chaucer Conference." She briefly described the items that had been given to the other churches along the path and the monogram by which they had been recognized.

"You didn't describe these things in your talk," Tyler said with interest.

"Believe it or not, most of them were only discovered in the last few weeks."

"And do you have a specific thing in mind that she might have given to Canterbury?"

"She described a textile design in the last pages of her journal, a pattern that alternates a bishop's mitre with her monogram, in gold on a red background. I think the gift might have been a piece of that fabric."

"I'll see what I can find out about it," he said. "Is there anything else?"

In the momentary silence that followed Lizzie felt he anticipated another scrap of information, but when she answered that there was nothing else he did not question further or express any sense of disappointment. She ended the conversation with a feeling of satisfaction. Tyler Brown had been a bit of a pest at the conference, but he sounded smart and reliable on the phone and, as Alison had said, he seemed to have his finger on the pulse of Canterbury. He would be a good collaborator.

She turned to Jackie's email. "Hi Liz," it read. "In looking at lots of different sources about Thomas Becket, I keep finding references to a rumor that his bones were not, in fact, destroyed with the shrine. The story is that the monks at Canterbury, knowing full well what the intentions were of the Commissioners for the Destruction of Shrines, replaced Becket's bones in the shrine with bones dug up from their own churchyard. Every now and then they find a mysterious skeleton at Canterbury Cathedral and have an argument about whether or not it might be Becket. I've found some other things that I think might be interesting to you, and I've written a little narrative to put it all together, which I will paste in below. Let me know what you think of all this.

Cheerio, etc., Jackie."

When Henry VIII went on his rampage to destroy the Catholic Church in England, the shrine of Becket was a particular target, because Becket had challenged the authority of his predecessor, Henry II. Three hundred sixty-eight years after the death of the archbishop, Henry VIII actually instituted posthumous legal proceedings against Becket and condemned him. Thereafter he was not to be venerated, called a saint, depicted in images, or described in books. As you already know, in 1538, at Henry's command, Becket's shrine was destroyed, and his relics reportedly burned and scattered in the wind.

In January 1888, archaeologists working on a survey project in the crypt of Canterbury Cathedral discovered an old skeleton. This, in itself, was not a surprise since church crypts are usually full of skeletons, but this one was unusual for three reasons: it was buried in the place where Becket had lain for the fifty years before being translated to the shrine; it had obviously been buried very quickly; and it had been buried not as a corpse, but as a pile of bones. Could Becket's relics have survived the destruction of the shrine? Could the monks of Canterbury, knowing that Thomas Cromwell and the Royal Commissioners for the Destruction of Shrines were on their way, have replaced Becket's bones with the bones of an ordinary mortal and moved the saint's bones to a safer spot? Could the Commissioners have balked at the thought of actually destroying the relics and collaborated with the monks to hide them?

A local surgeon, W. Pugin Thornton, laid out the bones and inspected them. A local dentist examined the teeth. The skeleton was that of a very tall man who had died at about the age of fifty a long, long time in the past. So far, much like Becket. Thornton was also a practitioner of phrenology, a popular pseudo-science of the period, and so he was also able to discern from the size and shape of the skull that the man who used it had been of 'large perceptive qualities, much intellect, indomitable energy, the power of arrangement and management, but unworthy of trust.' Still like Becket, if read from the Church of England perspective, and if you buy into the quackery of phrenology.

Thornton published a little booklet called *Becket's Bones*, which includes photographs of the remains. There is the skeleton, all laid out. There is the skull with a whopping big wound in it, as if made by a sword blade. Hmm, rather Becket-like. And there are the arm bones, connected to the hand bones, connected to the finger bones; and the thigh bones connected to the shin bones, connected to the ankle bones, connected to the foot bones. In fact, there are just too many dry bones to be Becket if one believes that many of his parts had to have been distributed during the great age of relics in medieval times. How could he still have two arms if his other three arms were in Italy and Portugal? (Okay, there was a papal bull about the spontaneous regenerative power of relics, but that *was* just bull.)

One source contemporaneous with the translation says that Archbishop Langton kept some of the small bones out at that time. That would be perfectly consistent with church practice at the time, especially since these were relics of unquestionable authenticity. There doesn't seem to be anything that would have prevented subsequent archbishops from opening the shrine either. Some sources say the bones were in a locked iron box inside the shrine, but there must have been a key to it. With all those kings from here and there visiting, who's to say that they didn't get their souvenir bone before they exited the church.

And even though the wound in the 1888 skull was whopping, the skull was all there. It's pretty clear from the testimony of eyewitnesses to the murder that the cap of Becket's skull was severed right off; and clear from the testimony of pilgrims, including Erasmus, that at least two parts of the skull were not in the shrine anyway, but were mounted in reliquaries for separate veneration.

But a lot of folks clearly wanted those bones to be Becket's. And if not those bones, then maybe some others buried elsewhere in the Cathedral. There are a few mysterious graves in the church, some of unknown origin, some of dubious provenance. Another skeleton, also buried in the crypt, was secretly exhumed and examined in the 1940s. This skeleton had no hand, which sounds more likely for a saint whose relics were scattered around, but there are still more questions than answers.

Asked about this recently, the dean of Canterbury Cathedral has said that 'the weight of evidence is that Becket's bones are not in the cathedral. The weight of evidence is that they were destroyed at the Reformation.'

The weight of evidence, the burden of proof, the ancient faith, the power of the thing. Dem bones, dem bones, dem dry bones.

"One last thing. There is an interesting book by John Butler called *The Quest for Becket's Bones*. He says that if Becket's bones were moved, the knowledge of their whereabouts has been kept through the years by a secret triumvirate—three men who pass on the information from generation to generation, bringing in a new member only at the death of one of the previous members. The information is only to be revealed when Catholicism is restored to its rightful place in England.

Look again at that list of names!"

Chapter 30

When we talked about this list the first time, Alison, you said that the last line was missing, and you speculated that it might possibly include you, Hockwold Bruce, and Frederick Wickersham, Jr."

"I know what you're thinking, Lizzie. There are actually *two* lines missing; we need another generation to bring us to the present."

Lizzie nodded. She had turned the list toward Alison and now she slid it back along the table to study it again. "Do you think it is possible that this list goes back to the time of the destruction of the shrine?" she asked, "and that these men kept the secret of where Becket's bones are hidden?"

"It is about the right age," Alison answered.

"Did your father ever say *anything* that would make you think he was part of something like this?"

"He spoke frequently about Becket," Alison said, "which never occurred to me as strange until now, and I was constantly inculcated with the important role our family played in maintaining Catholicism through the whole of the Reformation and the generations of persecution that followed." She was thoughtful as she tried to remember other details.

"Is it possible he was preparing to bring you into this club?" Lizzie asked.

Alison looked at her sadly. "And then lost his mind to Alzheimer's?" Her eyes welled with tears.

Lizzie returned to the list. "Clearly, men in your family have been involved in this enterprise, whatever it is, since the beginning." She read the first three names aloud: "William Kent, Thomas Bokland, Dunstan Hockwold. The first is obviously your ancestor, and the last is probably an ancestor of Hockwald Bruce. Whoever Bokland was, his descendents at some point changed the spelling of their name to Buckland and the last one was killed when a bomb hit London during the War."

"Perhaps he had no heir and my father consequently brought his friend Frederick Wickersham into the group."

"You said that the Wickershams were also Catholics?"

"Yes, with a history similar to ours."

"How did your father know him?"

Alison explained that they were friends at Oxford. "I think I told you that they were both avid amateur astronomers."

"Ah," Lizzie said. "That makes the sun pointer a particularly nice way for him to memorialize Buckland and Hockwald."

The two women spoke for some time about whether any of this new information was relevant to their project on the Weaver's pilgrimage and decided that it was not.

"We can't really be sure the list actually relates to Becket," Lizzie said, "though it certainly feels like it does. In any case it is much later than the Weaver's time."

"Is there anything you'd like me to do with it while you are in Newcastle?" Alison asked as Lizzie began to pack up her computer.

"I don't want to take you away from the work at hand," Lizzie answered, "but it would be interesting to find out what the connection was between the Weaver and that first William Kent on the list. It's possible your father traced that in one of those family trees we found."

"George is going to take me back to my house tomorrow to pick up some things I need. There are other genealogies there that I will bring back with me. I'll see if I can't answer your question."

"I'm surprised that George is letting you go back to your house."

"If you can believe it, a local policeman is actually meeting us there! It seems a ridiculous precaution to me, but I'm putting up with it to make George happy."

Lizzie stooped down to kiss Alison on the cheek. "I'm glad

you're able to get out for the day and I'm glad George is taking you."

Alison reached for Lizzie's hand. "When I first told you about George and me, and how our fathers forced us apart by clinging so fiercely to their religions. . . ." She swallowed several times.

Lizzie pulled her chair over and sat next to Alison.

"I don't know what I'm trying to say," Alison continued, her voice soft and filled with emotion. "Only that for years I buried the pain of that separation and fought the feeling that I should hate all of them, George and my father foremost. I lived with my father, I took care of him, I listened to his rantings—or mostly listened..." Her voice faltered. "Is it possible that he was trying to tell me something and I didn't listen because I was poisoned by that experience? That I didn't want to hear anything he had to say about the Catholic Church?"

Lizzie squeezed her friend's hand. "I don't know," she said, her voice almost a whisper. "But if it would help you to solve this mystery that concerned him, then let us do it. And George is in your life again and that can only be good."

There was a sound at the door to the library and the two women looked up to see George standing there. None among the three acknowledged that he might have heard some portion of the conversation that concerned him, and Lizzie soon after made her preparations to drive early the next morning to Newcastle.

"Are you sure you don't want an escort, Lizzie," George asked earnestly. "Edmund and I are both concerned about you traveling by yourself.

"No one even knows I'm going except the three of us, Edmund and Martin," Lizzie assured him. "If there is someone threatening me, he won't know where I am for the next few days."

Lizzie had planned to take Alison's car, knowing that Martin would enjoy driving it, but George insisted it drew too much attention and arranged for the rental of a much more pedestrian vehicle. She left at dawn the next day with a thermos of coffee and a lunch packed by Helen Jeffries, and drove the whole day, arriving in Newcastle in time to meet Martin for dinner at his hotel.

"Tell me everything that has happened!" they said, almost simultaneously; they began to answer simultaneously as well, falling easily into their long habit of conversation.

Martin demanded information on the case regarding the death of Dante Zettler, wanting to be reassured that his wife was safe. They had already spoken about this several times on the phone and Lizzie's certainty that it had nothing to do with her almost convinced her husband.

She then wanted to know everything about the mural. He was obviously pleased with the results and took her to see it long after darkness had fallen.

"We will put a cover over it tomorrow morning," he said, "so that the mayor can unveil it in the afternoon, but there is still some paint drying tonight." He pulled a large flashlight from his backpack. "You will get the full effect tomorrow afternoon when it is unveiled," he said, "but I want to show you some of the details that turned out particularly well."

Even in the dim light of street lamps and nearby buildings, Lizzie could see the arc of the big bridge that was familiar to her from the sketch Martin had made in his studio back home; she had driven across that bridge a few hours before. He ran the beam of light along the structure of the bridge, reproduced on the cement wall of the building in front of her.

"Look at this," he said, laughing softly. "There is graffiti on the bridge and the same guys who put it there reproduced it here. I love it!"

All of the details he showed her were the work of local artists, things that had not been in his original sketch. "Here," he said, illuminating a group of teenagers standing on a street corner. "This was done by a 13-year-old girl. So much talent. Look at the attitude in their postures, she just gets it."

They spent almost two hours, arm in arm, studying small aspects of the larger work. He described the experience of being in the city, of how warmly he had been received, and how impressed he was with the local artists with whom he had worked. "I have to do more projects like this," he said. "It is just so much more fun than doing a mural for a bank lobby."

A young man approached them. "Mr. Sanchez," he said.

"Ian," Martin said, extending his hand, "come see how

our work turned out." He introduced Lizzie. "Ian has real talent," he said, "which I hope he will develop."

The boy was clearly pleased with the compliment and told Martin how much he had enjoyed working with him and how much he had learned. He asked if he could introduce him to his mother the next day and Martin said he hoped that he would.

"I'm so proud of you," Lizzie said when they were alone again.

He kissed her.

"And where am I?" she asked. Her husband always put her someplace in every mural.

"You know I'm not going to tell you. It would ruin the surprise." He put an arm around her waist. "You'll have to wait until tomorrow when you see it in the light."

The next day was filled with festivities. After a breakfast with town officials and a lunch with more than a dozen artists who had worked with Martin on the painting, the party on the street began at which the mural was unveiled. When the mayor pulled the string that brought down the light fabric that covered the wall there was enthusiastic applause. Martin spent the next several hours being feted by the neighborhood.

Lizzie studied the finished mural from a seat in front of a pub across the street, a pint of cider on the table in front of her. The young man she had met the night before stopped to greet her and to introduce her to his mother.

"Have you met Martin yet?" she asked the woman. When she said that she hadn't, Lizzie pointed out to the two of them where her husband was. "Go there now," she said. "He is looking forward to meeting you."

The finished work was impressive. The colors were bold and the lines of the bridge moved across the wall, linking the various components together. There were a number of visual puns, and a fair amount of material that Lizzie hadn't seen before, either in the sketch at home or in the details the night before. Her eyes moved across and around the painting, admiring the artistry. There was a small church in the lower center of the wall and through the open door another mural was visible, a fresco on the wall of pilgrims on foot and on horseback. Lizzie smiled. They were characters from *Canterbury Tales*. She walked back across the street to look more closely. Martin had put her on horseback, with a broad-brimmed hat and scarlet socks. She was the Wife of Bath, and there was even a tiny monogram worked into the corner of her shawl: AW.

She felt his arm slip around her waist and turned. "I absolutely love it!" she said.

"I hoped you would," he said. "I wanted to tie our two projects together, and the Catholic church in this neighborhood is St. Thomas Becket."

"Though I'll bet they don't have such a fabulous fresco!"

"No, but I checked it out with the priest before I included it and have arranged for some of the local talent to paint one for him if it turns out to be popular."

The next minute he was called away again, but Lizzie continued to stand and look into the interior of the miniature church and to reflect on her relationship with the Weaver.

Chapter 31

Unlike Wells, Salisbury, and Winchester Cathedrals, which were all fronted by vast lawns, Westminster Abbey had very little open space from which to be viewed. It sat right in downtown London and traffic whizzed by, curving around the front and one of the sides, and separating the church from the Houses of Parliament and Big Ben across from its top end.

Lizzie was unwilling to go through London without visiting it and she convinced Martin that there could not be any potential danger if no one knew they were there.

"They must have cleaned the stone," Martin said as they walked across the street to the west entrance. "If I remember correctly, the last time we were here the building looked almost black."

"They do appear to have cleaned off the grime of the ages," Lizzie responded as she looked at Westminster Abbey gleaming white in the sunshine.

She explained that their primary goal for the day was the central tomb, the shrine of Edward the Confessor, King of England and son of Queen Emma and King Ethelred the Unready. That would have been the objective of the Weaver as well. Edward built Westminster Abbey and, as far as he was concerned, completed it in 1065. When he died in 1066 he received the burial place of honor at the high altar. That year also saw the ascendance to the throne of his cousin, William the Conqueror, who came over from Normandy in 1066 and was crowned in the newly completed edifice. Since that time, every coronation of an English monarch had taken place there.

The first translation of the body of Edward the Confessor

into a new tomb was in 1163, when Henry II and the then Archbishop of Canterbury, Thomas Becket, moved the body themselves. Edward had been canonized two years earlier, and his body was said to be wholly undecayed and intact. His clothes weren't even deteriorated—the ultimate evidence of saintliness.

A more elaborate shrine was built by Henry III, who also largely rebuilt the east end of the church during his thirteenth-century reign, in order to give Edward the Confessor a more stately and impressive resting place. A number of subsequent monarchs did their best to get themselves placed in close proximity to the tomb of the saint/king and to the holy relics which had been liberally strewed around his shrine, including a stone thought to have a footprint of Jesus Christ imprinted in it at the moment he ascended into Heaven, and a vial of his blood.

"This is the only shrine of a saint or a king," Lizzie said, "that escaped the destruction of Henry VIII's gang of marauders, though they did steal the gold and precious stones from it. It was rebuilt by his daughter, Mary Tudor, when she brought Catholicism back to England. It is the only place along the Weaver's pilgrimage path that still holds the bones that were venerated at that time."

"Do you think he was really saintly?" Martin asked. "Or was he just a king? Would he have become a saint if he were a humble poor man? There surely must have been a lot of people through the ages who were just as holy but never even became candidates for sainthood."

Lizzie didn't know. "Was it that he was a good *king*, a good *Christian*, or a good *person*?" she mused.

"I'm not convinced he had to be good at all," Martin answered. "He built this church. That might have been the first step to sanctification."

It cost an extra few pounds to come into the part of the Abbey where the royal tombs were, and Lizzie commented that the parade of monarchs, with all their good and bad qualities, contributed to the great appeal and fascination of Westminster Abbey. She looked around to see the effigies of royalty staring, pupil-less, into the canopies above them.

They ambled down the north aisle and Martin pointed out some of the extraordinary monuments along the way. He especially loved one of a couple looking remarkably relaxed in the effigies on their tomb. The wife looked like she had just fallen asleep, one hand resting lightly on her chest, the other on a book. Her husband lay beside her, resting up on one elbow and holding his coat of arms.

"I'm sure they must often have lain in bed this way," Martin said to Lizzie, "she reading, he in full armor admiring the family crest."

"Look at their poor children," Lizzie said. A son and two daughters were each represented in stone, kneeling on a cushion in front of their parents, each holding his or her own skull. She could hear Martin softly humming "dem bones, dem bones."

They went to the "Poets' Corner" to visit the grave of Geoffrey Chaucer, and Martin put his toe on the corner of the stone.

"Here is your old friend," he said. "Though I recall a conversation not so long ago when you said he was a creep. Do you still think so after the work you've done?"

"I hardly know what to think of him anymore, except that his work has inspired me to think, and I love how his words roll around in my mouth."

"Do you believe Alison's original contention that the Wife of Bath character is based on the Weaver?"

"Absolutely," Lizzie said without hesitation. "There are just too many commonalities to be coincidence."

"And was she as big a slut as he made her out to be?"

"No way!" she said, rising to the defense of the Weaver. "Though of course she would never have defined herself that way."

"So did Chaucer hate women or was he simply a man of his time?"

"The latter, I'm sure," Lizzie said. "And I think he can have had no idea that we would be standing here talking about him and his book six hundred years later."

They walked back out into the sunshine. "Is there anything else we need to do while we are in London?" Martin asked Lizzie.

"Let's go across the river to Southwark and see the spot where the opening of *Canterbury Tales* was set."

She suggested that they walk to London Bridge and cross there onto the High Street of Southwark, where the Tabard Inn had stood. They stopped in the middle of the bridge to look up and down the Thames.

"This was the center of the universe in Chaucer's day," Lizzie said, "and Thomas Becket's too. Both were Londoners by birth, both must often have crossed the River here. Becket was Chancellor, and consequently intimately involved in the commerce of the nation; Chaucer served as the Controller of Customs for the Port of London."

As they ambled across London Bridge, Martin asked Lizzie if she could recite to him that part of *Canterbury Tales* that was set there and she found that she had, in multiple readings, committed it to memory.

> *Bifel that, in that seson on a day,*
> *In Southwerk at the Tabard as I lay*
> *Redy to wenden on my pilgrimage*
> *To Caunterbury with ful devout corage,*
> *At night was come into that hostelrye*
> *Wel nyne and twenty in a companye,*
> *Of sondry folk, by aventure y-falle*
> *In felawshipe, and pilgrims were they alle,*
> *That toward Caunterbury wolden ryde.*

"Nine and twenty in the company?"

"And Chaucer's original idea was that each would tell two stories going there and two stories on the way back."

"But they never got there?"

"Nope. He never finished the book."

"Too bad," Martin said. "Just think of the fart jokes that were left untold!"

He asked her about the company of pilgrims. "If the Wife of Bath is based on the Weaver, then do you think the other characters are also based on real people?"

"One is certainly based on the host at the Tabard Inn, Harry Bailey, and one character is Chaucer himself. Their companions are generally thought to have mostly been born in the brain of Chaucer, but the people described are of types who must have been circulating around Southwark at the time, and I wouldn't be surprised if there were other characters based on people he knew."

"I remember the miller, the prioress, the friar, the Wife of Bath, of course, and it seems like a very mixed bag of clergy and commoners."

"Not all commoners, which is one of the things that makes it so interesting. There are multiple castes of English society represented among Chaucer's pilgrims. At the top is the knight who travels with his son as squire, and a yeoman servant. The franklyn owns an estate, and the reeve oversees the management of someone else's estate. There is a scholar, a doctor, a maunciple, who was something like a law clerk, and a bunch of middle class tradespeople. This is where the weaver Alison fits into the lineup, along with a tapestry maker, a dyer, a haberdasher, the miller, a cook, a carpenter, and a merchant." She added that there was also a sea captain, "like my stalwart companion, Kate Wentworth."

She described the independent middle class as a new phenomenon during Chaucer's lifetime. When he was a boy of about five, in 1348, bubonic plague—the Black Death—swept into England from the continent and killed so much of the population that the survivors found themselves with expanded opportunities. Serfs left the bondage of their feudal manor lords and moved around the countryside or even struck out for the city. In the period following the first wave of the plague, England changed dramatically. That was when hedgerows were planted to break up the land into smaller plots for yeoman farmers, independent tradesmen began to flourish in the cities, and the dominant language changed from French to English.

"If Chaucer had been born a hundred years earlier," she said, "his French-speaking party of pilgrims would have included the ecclesiastics and the knight, but none of the rest of the party. Certainly Alison would not have come to London as a professional weaver with an income of her own."

"Chaucer certainly exaggerates the different sensibilities

of his characters," Martin said. "I'm inclined to think that he probably based all his characters on real people. And the Tabard Inn was an actual place?"

Lizzie said that it was. "This street had a number of coaching inns, each one catering to customers headed in a different direction. If you were going east to Canterbury and the coast, the Tabard was your destination."

"I don't suppose that anything from it survives after so much time."

"No, I read that this whole neighborhood was destroyed by a fire in the late seventeenth century, though many of the coaching inns, including the Tabard, were rebuilt. I saw a photograph of it from the late nineteenth century, but it was torn down soon after that."

They wandered down the Borough High Street and could see in the names of alleys where the great old inns had been: the George, the King's Head, the White Hart, the Queen's Head, and the Spur. They went into the alleyway where the Tabard had been and found a loading dock with a sign on it that said "Tabard House." Lizzie couldn't resist going in.

"Is this where *Canterbury Tales* began?" she asked the woman who sat behind the counter, who had no idea whatsoever what Lizzie was talking about. She had never heard of the book, Geoffrey Chaucer, or the Tabard Inn.

"How extraordinary," Lizzie said as they walked back out to the street. "This must be the place. I'm surprised that Chaucerians haven't put a plaque up or something."

They found that the seventeenth-century George Inn had survived and went to have lunch there and steep themselves in the past. Lizzie got a map of the neighborhood from the desk.

"From Winchester to Guildford, Kate and I followed a path laid out by the historian Hilaire Belloc," she said. "His track is really sort of a best guess of how pilgrims might have made their way from Winchester to Canterbury, but no such guesswork is necessary to determine the route of Chaucer's pilgrims from here to Canterbury." She opened up the Ordnance Survey map of the Thames Estuary and placed it over the local map.

"Chaucer mentions specific places in the text. The trip began here in Southwark at the Tabard Inn. The pilgrims stopped to rest a few miles later at a place called St. Thomas's Watering. They traveled through Deptford then Rochester and Sittingbourne; they picked up some additional pilgrims at Boughten-under-Bleen, and ended just short of Canterbury at 'Bob-up-and-doun,' usually thought to mean Harbledown."

"Does the Weaver give the same itinerary?"

"She doesn't mention exactly the same locations, but then she mostly chronicles the places where she either made gifts or traded for wool. She wrote that she stayed overnight at Dartford and at Ospringe though, so it is definitely the same path as Chaucer's. The route seems to have been pretty standard."

Martin put his finger on the map. "This looks like a pretty big highway going the whole length of the route," he said.

"Yep," Lizzie sighed. "It's the major motorway from London to the coast, and it has been since Roman Times."

"It doesn't look like it would actually be much fun to walk."

She acknowledged that was so. "Kate said it would be better to follow Belloc's route, which looks like a lovely pastoral path. Unfortunately, these are the places mentioned by Chaucer and they aren't on that path."

"Well, if you have to end your pilgrimage early, it might as well be here."

"Actually, do you mind if we walk just a bit further and see if we can find this 'St. Thomas's Watering?'"

They put the Southwark map on top again and looked for anything that might indicate the place, but nothing in that direction and at that distance seemed like a likely candidate, though there were a number of streets named after characters or concepts from *Canterbury Tales*, including Tabard, Pilgrimage, Maunciple, Pardoner and Prioress Streets.

"Here's a library," Martin said, pointing to the open book icon just a few blocks away. "We could stop there and see if they know where it is."

At the Southwark Library, they were directed to the Local Studies Center and Lizzie was almost apologetic as she asked her question of the reference librarian, a man in his thirties with a friendly manner.

"I'm sure you must hear this all the time," she started. "I'd like to retrace the path taken by Chaucer's pilgrims in *Canterbury Tales* and wonder if you have a map of the route."

He told her that no one had ever asked him for that information.

Lizzie was surprised. "I was half expecting there might be a printed guide or something," she said.

He shook his head. "No. As I said, it's not a question I've ever gotten, though this district is called 'Chaucer.'"

"And I see that several streets are named after characters in the book."

"There was more of an interest in Victorian times, when that was done."

"Maybe you could help us find the first place mentioned," Martin said, stepping up to stand next to Lizzie at the desk. "Chaucer called it 'The Watering of St. Thomas,' or something like it, and it should be just a few miles down the road. We couldn't find anything on the Southwark Map."

"I have older maps," he said, clearly wanting to be helpful. After several minutes of looking at progressively older representations of the neighborhood, he located "St. Thomas's well" on a map of 1745 and put the appropriate part of it on the copy machine for Lizzie.

Lizzie took the old map and Martin the new and they ventured out along the Old Kent Road. In Chaucer's day this had been the agricultural outskirts of the city and even on the map of 1745 there was still a broad green swath through here, but the London metropolis had long ago bled into the countryside and there was no longer anything in the neighborhood that would have been familiar to Chaucer or the Weaver. Southwark had been heavily bombed during World War II and few buildings were older than the nineteenth century; most of them had been built in the post-War period of what Martin called "unspeakable architectural crimes."

With changes in the architecture had come other changes as well. The stretch of road that brought visitors along it into England since the Romans built it was now crowded with new immigrants. Flyers posted throughout the neighborhood advertised cheap phone rates to several African nations. There were pizza parlors, Indian, Chinese, Middle Eastern and Caribbean Restaurants, car dealers, insurance agents, furniture stores, bakeries, pubs, banks, barbers, butchers, newsagents, chemists, clothing stores, in an endless urban sprawl. Occasionally a straightforward English sign demanded "Queer Power" or "Victory to the Miners."

This was Martin's kind of place. He took much of his inspiration for his artwork from neighborhoods like this—where music blared out of cars and storefronts, graffiti covered buildings, small restaurants served food from distant places, and people sat out on the sidewalk on a nice day in folding chairs. He had been raised in a bilingual household in Los Angeles and always preferred urban areas to the countryside. Lizzie was glad he was with her today, as he chatted with people along the way in English, Spanish, and a comical improvised sign language when both of those failed him.

After an hour at a leisurely pace they neared the place that had been a stream or pond in medieval times, when pilgrims made their first stop. The modern map indicated a park at the site, Burgess Park, with a small lake. As they approached it, Martin put one hand on Lizzie's arm to stop her and put his other hand over her eyes.

"Prepare yourself," he whispered in her ear. "The watering hole is about to be revealed."

When he took his hand away, Lizzie saw a remarkable old pub, the Thomas A' Becket. It was disproportionately tall, with a wonderfully ornate roof-line, and appeared to be the last vestige of its age in the neighborhood, as if everything else had fallen down around it and it alone remained to welcome them to the first landmark on the path of Chaucer's pilgrims.

"Fabulous!" she said, taking Martin's hand as they crossed the street and into the pub.

It was cool and dark, and entirely without elegance or style or any pretensions to either. Two old codgers sat at the bar and Martin immediately hopped up onto the stool next to them.

"Is this the place that was known as the Watering of St. Thomas?" Lizzie asked the publican.

"Don't rightly know," he answered, "but it were famous as a boxing bar, and they used to 'ang people by the lake there."

"So you don't know if this is the place mentioned in *Canterbury Tales?*"

He shook his head. "Never read it," he said.

Martin ordered a pint of stout for himself and a cider for Lizzie.

As he poured, the barman turned to Lizzie. "You're interested in 'istory then?"

She nodded, anticipating some good nugget of local lore to follow.

He set the glass down in front of her and asked if she had ever noticed that the only statue in London free of pigeon shit was the one of Winston Churchill near the Houses of Parliament. "Yep," he continued, "My grandson noted that. He's interested in yer 'istory."

Martin and his new friends snorted with laughter; Lizzie smiled.

As they left the pub, Martin said that he thought that was a wonderful place to end her pilgrimage. Lizzie was not so satisfied.

"I mean *what?*" she said in frustration as they stood waiting for a bus to take them back to central London. "Two times today I felt like I went to the grail and found the cup empty. How can people go to work every day to a place specifically mentioned in one of the classic works of English Literature and never even have rubbed elbows with the fact?"

Martin patted her on the back. "Poor Lizzie," he said. "I know you must be frustrated not to make your way all the way to Canterbury, but didn't you tell me that Chaucer's pilgrims never got there either?"

She nodded, but felt more unhappy about the fact than she had at any point in the venture.

Chapter 32

There were messages on both their cell phones when they turned them on again back at the hotel. A reporter from the *London Times* wanted to interview Martin about the Newcastle mural, and arranged to have lunch with him the next day. Alison had left a message that her contact at Westminster Abbey had not found anything in the collection there with the AW monogram, but a voicemail from Tyler Brown made up for that disappointment. He had found something and wanted to speak to Lizzie about it as soon as possible.

She called him back immediately.

"I may have located that textile you described," he said. "I haven't seen it yet, but there is a description in an old inventory."

"Terrific!" Lizzie said in a burst of excitement. "That is fabulous news."

"There might be something at Rochester as well."

"Rochester?"

"Yes, it was a common stop on the pilgrimage trail."

Lizzie knew that it was. Chaucer's pilgrims stopped there, and it was mentioned in the Weaver's journal and depicted on the tapestry, but she had made no reference to having made a gift there and Lizzie had consequently not been concentrating on it for further research.

"Can you meet me there tomorrow and I'll show you what I've found? The trains there are very regular from London."

She agreed, and told him she would let him know what train she would be on.

Martin looked at her as she finished the call.

"I thought you weren't going to Canterbury," he said seriously.

"I'm not," she said. "I'm going to meet a librarian in Rochester who has been helping with the research. It may be the last piece of the puzzle."

"Do you want to check in with the Oxford police first? Or with Edmund's solicitor friend to see where they are on the case?"

"I'll talk to Edmund if you really think that's necessary, but I'm planning to just meet with this guy, see what he's found and then come back." She had now become convinced that she was in no danger, and she preferred not to act as if she was. In fact, if Tyler Brown was willing to give her a ride from Rochester to Canterbury, she was inclined to make a quick trip there. It seemed absurd to be so close to the final destination and not visit Canterbury Cathedral.

As the train rumbled out of Victoria Station the next morning, she referred again to her various maps, acknowledging the change in the landscape since the Weaver's day and imagining her on this same route six hundred years earlier. The train stopped in Southwark and Greenwich. Lizzie had done research at the Maritime Museum, and knew she could find a friendly reception, a cup of tea, and the relics of Admiral Nelson and Lord Franklin there. But the Weaver hadn't mentioned it and Chaucer had merely nodded at it, saying: "Lo Grenewich, there many a shrewe is inne," probably a snide reference to his wife, who lived there.

The Thames became increasingly industrialized as the train left London.

Big ships carrying oil and bulk cargoes, and containers filled with unseen goods, moved silently along the river. After Higham station the train dipped into a tunnel and when it emerged several miles later, Lizzie had her first glimpse of Rochester across the Medway River. In the distance was the solid block of Rochester Castle; the tower of Rochester Cathedral rose behind it, a familiar sight from the portrayal of it on the tapestry. Lizzie wondered why the Weaver had not thought to make a gift to the church here, but perhaps she had, and Tyler Brown had the evidence of it.

He was waiting for her when she disembarked and waved to her from beside his car, an old Ford wagon.

"Thanks again for all your help," she said, shaking his hand. "I'm eager to know what you have found."

"Have you been to Rochester before?" Tyler asked.

"Only through it on the train," she answered. "I'm glad to be able to see a bit of it before I go home."

"I can give you a tour," he said. "I was born and grew up here."

Lizzie felt the press of time and was keen to get down to business, but wanted to be polite. She said that she was interested in the castle and the cathedral and was somewhat relieved when he drove directly to the street that ran between the two great buildings.

"I wonder why the Weaver didn't make a gift here?" Lizzie mused as they got out of the car.

"There were no famous relics here," Tyler explained. "Local saints were of more interest to the men who ran this cathedral. They were genuine in their piety and not simply looking to attract a clientele of tourists."

"And yet I believe most pilgrims stopped here."

"It was a convenient mid-point between London and Canterbury," Tyler said. "The castle is particularly interesting," he added, steering Lizzie and the conversation toward it. "It is almost purely Norman, with very few changes or reconstructions over the years."

Lizzie was anxious for him to tell her what he had found regarding the Weaver's textile contribution to Canterbury Cathedral, and asked him about it as they walked onto the castle grounds.

"I found it in an inventory from the 1980s," he said. He continued to point out features of the castle. "Look at the bits of shell you can see in the mortar here," he said, picking at a small clamshell with his fingernail.

There was no roof on the castle. The square tower was divided up the middle by an interior wall, which gave a clear picture of how the rooms had been set up. They climbed a stone staircase to the top of the wall and out onto battlements where they stood on a ledge about three feet wide.

"I'm kind of surprised they let the public climb all over this," Lizzie said. "In the U.S. there would be barriers of all kinds."

"Wait till you see the view," Tyler said.

Lizzie stepped beside him and admired the prospect. They were as high as the top of the steeple of the cathedral across the street, and the entire building was visible below them. Beyond it was the course of the Medway, with its rail and road bridges to the north and the big motorway bridge to the south. The day was beautiful with a brilliant blue sky, light puffy clouds, and a clear view in all directions.

"From this vantage point there is absolutely no question why a castle would be built here," Lizzie said. "From here you could see everything coming to London from across the channel."

Tyler told her there had always been a fortress there since Roman times. "Rochester flourished for over a thousand years as the main stop on the road between London and the coast," he said, "but railroads and later highways bypassed it." He seemed wistful, even sad. "Sometimes bad things happen," he said philosophically.

Lizzie turned the conversation once again to the textile.

"Oh," Tyler said, as if he had just thought of it. "I have it!"

"What?"

"I have that piece of fabric you were asking about." He had a knapsack with him, which now he put on the wall of the castle. From inside it he withdrew a bundle wrapped in tissue paper.

"I don't understand," Lizzie said. "How could you possibly have it?"

Tyler gave her an impish look. Behind him Lizzie could see where the stone steps descended into the cavernous darkness of the castle interior.

She put her hand out to steady herself on the wall and found that there was a large gap in the stones there. For the first time it occurred to her that she had been careless and stupid to dismiss the possibility that someone might mean to hurt her. Tyler was nerdy and slightly built, and consequently she had never considered him a threat, but now she saw that though he was small he was wiry. She could see the sinews of his arms as he held the fabric to his chest. He could not, she told herself, actually be intending to murder her, but what was he doing with the Weaver's gift to Canterbury Cathedral?

"Why do you have that textile?" Lizzie asked again, attempting to sound nonchalant as she surveyed the stones around her. If Tyler attempted to push her, what could she grab, where could she step securely?

"I stole it yesterday from the treasury storage at Canterbury Cathedral," he said. His calmness unnerved her.

Lizzie tried to assess if he was more dangerous if he was calm or if he was discomposed. She wondered what her own response should be and decided that feigning ignorance would not be convincing; he was too smart for that. As she contemplated what to say next, he spoke.

"Do you know where they found this, back when it was discovered after the war?"

"In a grave with a marker for Osbert Giffard?"

"Yes!" he said. His hands twitched and moved possessively around the bundle. "How did you know that?"

"I found the clue left by William Kent."

He nodded. "Of course. Where was it, by the way? Dr. Bruce always wondered and Mr. Kent would never tell him."

"A church near Guildford."

"Really? How interesting, but it really doesn't matter." He set the bundle on the wall. "Do you know what is going to happen now?"

"You and I are going to struggle until one of us falls?"

He looked at her thoughtfully. "That's an interesting way to put it. I thought you might just say that I was going to push you off this tower." He shook a finger at her. "It was very stupid of you to come up here alone with me."

She agreed that it was. "I thought you could be trusted."

"I don't think so." He said, still shaking his finger. "I think you thought that I could be used for information and then disregarded."

"Nonsense. I would have given you a very nice acknowledgement in the book. But don't expect that now."

"You know you really are quite interesting and I am enjoying this conversation. It's a burden to have a secret and no one to share it with."

"I'm sorry to tell you that it isn't a secret anymore. My friend Jackie knows."

He laughed. "Oh yes, I remember her from the conference, she went after poor Dante Zettler with his pathetic notions of Chaucer."

"Yes, poor Dante."

"That was too bad about him," Tyler said. "He was just in the wrong seat at the wrong meal."

Lizzie steadied herself by putting a hand on the stone beside her.

"I can't believe you tried to kill me!" she said angrily. "What did I ever do to you?"

"It's not what you did, it is what you might find."

"And now I've found it and other people know about it, so the secret is out." She cursed herself for her stupidity and carelessness. Martin only knew she had gone to Rochester to meet someone, but she hadn't mentioned Tyler Brown's name. She hadn't told anyone else she was coming here; she never called Edmund as she'd promised.

"What do you think the secret is?" he asked slyly.

"That Thomas Becket is still buried in Canterbury Cathedral in a grave marked with the name Osbert Giffard." As she spoke she thought about the implications of that. If the Weaver's textile had once bound the bones together, then what was Tyler Brown doing with it now? Shouldn't it still be in the grave?

Tyler looked at her closely. "You are just beginning to realize that something is not right here, aren't you?"

"How did you get the textile?" she demanded.

"I told you, I stole it from Canterbury Cathedral."

"From a grave there?"

"No. You need to pay more attention to me." His tone was condescending. "I told you that I stole it from the storage area of their treasury. I work there often and am, I'm happy to say, quite a trusted colleague."

"You said it was found after the war?"

"Yes, it was in 1950 actually. Unfortunately, Hockwold Bruce was not in Canterbury at the time and didn't realize what had happened until later."

"What did happen?"

Tyler Brown sighed and looked up at the sky. "It was one

of those completely routine renovations that happen all the time in the Cathedral. They were working on the piping and in the process opened a few graves. There was an archaeologist there who said this textile was potentially important, and they took it from the grave and reburied the bones."

It began to dawn on Lizzie what had happened.

"Did they bury them in the same place?"

"No."

"Did they note where they went?"

"No." Tyler Brown shook his head sadly. "No, they did not."

"What about the Osbert Giffard stone?"

"It was moved to the center aisle and there is nothing under it."

"How do you know that?"

"Because Hockwald Bruce came into the Cathedral one night and lifted it up to see."

Lizzie considered pushing him off the tower in one of his thoughtful moments, but she was still having a hard time conceding that Tyler Brown was a murderer, and that on this lovely day he would actually try to kill her. It seemed too fantastic to be real. He was too elfin, too cultured; he didn't seem to be either a psychopath or a religious fanatic. How could he possibly be a threat if he wasn't one of those? She looked at his knapsack on the wall. There was a pointed stone near it that stood up higher than the stones around it. She calculated what it would take to slip the strap of the pack over his neck, but that seemed impossible. It would not take much to slip it over that stone, however.

She forced herself to keep the conversation going. "I assume Hockwald Bruce brought you into this triumvirate," she said.

"He did. I know you will think it sounds like a cliché, but he really was like a father to me. I loved him and I felt the honor of being invited into the Becket society." He described going to meetings with William Kent and Frederick Wickersham. "They were great old men," he said, "until Mr. Kent lost his mind, and then that idiot Freddie Wickersham came to a meeting at his grandfather's insistence, but he wasn't committed to the undertaking." He looked hard at Lizzie. "It is a vocation, really—a holy calling—and we didn't bring him into it when the old man died."

"But what was the use of continuing the society once Hockwold Bruce lost the knowledge of where the bones were?"

He turned on her angrily. "Don't blame Dr. Bruce!" he said fiercely. "He would have given his life to protect that information. It wasn't his fault. He fought tirelessly to restore the position of the Catholic Church in England." He was ranting now, about how the Catholic Church built all the great cathedrals and deserved to have them back, and how the relics of Becket were essential to rally people to action.

"Except that you don't know where the relics are," Lizzie said.

"I intend to find them," he whispered ferociously.

She tried to read his expression, a mixture of confusion and defiance.

"Ah," she said, "Hockwald Bruce never told William Kent or Frederick Wickersham that they were lost."

She resisted the temptation to scoff at him. He was getting angry and that made her position more dangerous. She asked him why Hockwald Bruce had tried to kill Alison Kent. "They were old friends," she said.

"Dr. Bruce wasn't sure how much she knew, but once she found the journal of that woman you call the Weaver, there was always the chance that she might reveal the secret either inadvertently, or by caring less about it than about her own work."

"And he couldn't just bring her into the secret, because there was no longer a secret worth protecting."

The two studied each other for several minutes, each calculating their own position on the wall and that of their adversary. Lizzie believed she had identified the best stones in each direction to grab or stand on if Tyler rushed her, but as the threat became more real she began to panic.

When he finally moved, he came at her with an outstretched hand and took her arm in a painful grip. She seized the front of his shirt with one hand and with the other grabbed at the wall behind her, desperately trying to find a handhold in one of the niches that had looked so reassuring earlier. The bundle of fabric went flying off the wall as she reached for the pack, and she was finally able to move her fingertips through the strap and slip it over the adjacent stone. This gave her something to cling to as she stamped her heel onto Tyler's foot and then brought her knee up hard into his groin. He released his grip and she pushed him as hard as she could.

He did not fall over the wall of the castle and onto the lawn below, but into the interior of the ruined shell, striking his head on one of the projecting ledges that had once held a floor, and then onto the stone pavement another forty feet below it.

Lizzie knew that he could not have survived the fall. She held tightly onto the wall and breathed in big frightened gasps, acknowledging the terrible perilousness of her position. She had maintained her calm through the whole of the peculiar conversation with Tyler, when time seemed to drag, but once the confrontation turned physical, events had moved in a swift blur. As she looked at his body crumpled on the pavement below, she began to sob and shake violently. For a moment she had a terrible flashback to the previous year at Hengemont, when she had found herself near to going off the roof before Edmund saved her.

She walked gingerly back to the stairs and then slowly descended, putting first her right and then her left foot on each step and keeping one hand securely on the wall at all times. By the time she reached the bottom there were two men kneeling next to Tyler.

One turned to her. "I'm sorry, your friend is dead," he said. "What happened?"

"He tried to push me," she said. "He's not my friend. Call the police."

"I already have, and the ambulance, but it won't help him."

She did not look in the direction of Tyler's corpse, but walked outside to find the bundle and then sat on the lawn and unwrapped the work done so long ago by the Weaver. The fabric was musty. It had lain in the shrine for two hundred years and in a grave for another four, but patches of bright scarlet color were still visible. The alternating monograms and mitres were still gold against the background, though the gold wire thread had broken in many places.

She rolled it up again and put the tissue paper back around it as the police arrived. Now she probably would need that solicitor, she thought. She called Martin to tell him what had happened.

"I'll come right there," he said anxiously. "Where will you be?"

"Probably in police custody," she said darkly. "Would you call Edmund and find out about that solicitor for me?"

He said he would do that and come directly to Rochester.

The young policeman was surprised at her assertion that Tyler Brown's death was not an accident but a murder attempt gone awry. She gave him the card she still had of the detective in Oxford, and then handed him the bundle.

"He said he stole this from Canterbury Cathedral," she said. There was no emotion in her voice. She felt listless, flattened.

Martin arrived, having taken a taxi from London, then Edmund with the solicitor, but the Rochester police were not inclined to hold Lizzie or to charge her with a crime after speaking to the police in Oxford. Edmund offered to take them back to Hengemont and Martin gravely accepted for them both.

Chapter 33

"Explain this to me again," George said, after Lizzie had told them the story of what happened. "Were Thomas Becket's bones destroyed at the time of the Reformation or not?"

"No," Lizzie answered. "Becket's bones were replaced in the shrine with the bones of a monk, Osbert Giffard, and it was *his* bones that were destroyed."

"And then your family kept the secret of where Becket's bones were hidden?" George turned to Alison.

"Apparently so," she said. "It seems that one of my ancestors was a monk at Canterbury at the time the bones were secreted. He came back to Bath with the reliquary and the secret, and passed it on to a nephew." She put a hand on Lizzie's arm. "My father had, in fact, kept a good genealogy of all the men involved, just as you thought, Lizzie."

"They must have moved the remains over the years, but always kept the name Osbert Giffard associated with the grave to identify them."

"And now the bones are lost?" George continued.

Lizzie had already told this part of the story more than once, but she described again how Becket's bones had been moved during routine maintenance of Canterbury Cathedral, and the Weaver's gift, the piece of fabric that could best identify them, had become separated from them.

"So they just got moved to a different place."

"That seems to be what happened. It is unlikely now that they will ever be identified."

"Does it matter anymore?" Martin asked.

They all looked to Alison for the answer. If the triumvirate had continued, she would likely now be one of the secret keepers. "I don't know," she answered. "How many bones do you need? I have one in this box here. Could it be used to restore Canterbury Cathedral to the Catholic Church? I hardly think so. Times have changed too much since the game started." She took a deep breath. "One thing I can say for sure is that this secret was never worth endangering Lizzie, or killing poor Dante."

George put a reassuring arm around her. "The Weaver is clearly the most interesting ancestor to you."

"Yes she is," she nodded. "And Lizzie and I have assembled a wonderful range of material to tell her story."

"I'm still intrigued by your father's interest in her, though," Lizzie said. "Why did he use her monogram on that church window in Guildford? And why did he think it was necessary to make that faux grave for Osbert Giffard there?"

George said that he thought he understood that move on the part of William Kent. "It was the war," he said, "the terrible devastation of the war. He was the only surviving member of the triumvirate and he was afraid that another calamity like that could wipe out them all. He wanted to leave a clue in a place that could be found by someone who was looking for it, and he wanted to associate it with his own family."

"The Weaver was well known to him through the *Canterbury Tales* connection, and his mother had shown him the Weaver's monogram," Alison explained. "The fragments of family trees are not all from my family, by the way. When Stephen Buckland and John Hockwold died in the war, my father tried to find their heirs, presumably to invite them into the triumvirate. Hocky Bruce was obviously a connection of John Hockwold, but he never found a descendant for Stephen Buckland, so he asked his friend Frederick Wickersham to join."

Martin was looking at the picture of the tomb in the illuminated manuscript. "This textile in the painting here, this is the one that was actually around the bones?"

Lizzie said that it was. "I held it in my hands," she said. "It still had some of that fabulous red color, and the gold."

"When we mount our exhibition we can include it," Alison said.

Martin continued to study the pictures of the gifts made by the Weaver. "She was really an extraordinary benefactor of artists," he said, "and a very talented designer. I can't wait to see this tapestry."

"Since we are going home in two days it will have to wait until we come back for the book launching."

"We could go tomorrow," he said.

"I'm afraid not," Lizzie said. "Tomorrow I need to go to Canterbury and finish the pilgrimage."

Chapter 34

There was no convincing her husband or friends that she should travel to Canterbury Cathedral by herself. Not only were they worried about her seeming too calm after her near-death experience, but they were all curious to see the place again with the information so recently learned. Even Alison was determined to go, announcing that she was recovered enough to travel in a car and a wheel chair. If she was going then George said he must also go, and consequently it was a party of four that traveled the next day to Canterbury.

They stuck to the motorways, bypassing the places Lizzie had stopped along the way. It was a very different view of England, more real in some ways. She knew that the vast majority of the population lived in urban areas, but clung to her romantic perceptions of the countryside.

In Sittingbourne they stopped at her request. "This is where the Wife of Bath told her story," she said, "her terrible story that has given me so much grief."

The town had a rundown look, and no visible surviving medieval architecture. Lizzie got out of the car and stood on the sidewalk next to it.

"Have you decided what it is that women most desire?" Martin asked, standing beside her.

"To finish their important projects and get them published!" Alison declared from inside the car.

"That works for me," Lizzie said. "Let's finish this!"

The modern road was now also the path of the ancient road, past Bleen and Dunkirk and into Harbledown, where they left the motorway. The exit ramp led to the top of a hill and around a gentle curve. Below them, Canterbury Cathedral came into view, shining blue in the distance, its towers rising above all the surrounding buildings.

Lizzie felt her throat grow tight when she saw it. Each of the great cathedrals along the way had a distinct color in her memory: Wells was a warm brown, Salisbury was white from every vantage point and all distances, Winchester was a solid grey, but Canterbury shone blue.

They crossed a road with a sign pointing to the "North Downs Way"—Belloc's Old Road from Winchester. When they got out of the car to walk the rest of the way, they were at a place where the Weaver had walked, and all other pilgrims, except the ones in *Canterbury Tales*. The book ended just before the party arrived at their destination, frustratingly frozen in time just outside the city.

Lizzie pushed Alison's wheelchair as they went through the west gate in the medieval wall and onto the main street of Canterbury. Many of the old half-timbered buildings leaned over the roadway. There was a pub called "The Archbishop's Finger" just inside the gate and Lizzie stopped. She touched Alison on the shoulder and pointed and they both laughed.

It was not far to the magnificent carved "Christ Church gate," and through it was the first close view of the Cathedral. Lizzie was feeling a combination of sensations, of which exhilaration, agitation and exhaustion were all a part. When Alison reached a hand up over her shoulder to touch Lizzie's hand on the handle of the wheelchair, Lizzie realized that her friend was feeling it too. This was not the end of their project, but it was the place where the Weaver's pilgrimage ended, and the journal that described it, and it was deeply symbolic to them both.

They entered the Cathedral and looked up the length of the long nave, which rose up and up to the empty space that had once held the shrine of St. Thomas Becket. Beyond it, at the very eastern tip of the cathedral was the "corona," or "Becket's Crown," the place where the severed cap of Becket's skull had been kept in a separate reliquary. The ceiling seemed impossibly high.

The party began a slow procession down the center aisle of the church. At one point Martin stopped and pointed down to the stone of Osbert Giffard; it was an ancient version of the one at St. Martha's church near Guildford. They passed the place where the altar had once stood, the site of Becket's murder. The name "Thomas" was carved into the stones of the floor.

The church was crowded with tourists, as it had been since medieval times. When the Weaver made her pilgrimage in 1387, she was one of 200,000 people who visited that year.

They approached the steps up to where the shrine had been and George and Martin each took a handle of Alison's wheelchair and lifted her from step to step as Lizzie followed them. The steps were worn into hard waves by the tread of millions of pilgrim feet.

At the top of the steps, the golden shrine of Henry IV and his bride momentarily drew their eyes away from the place that was the destination of the pilgrimage, and then there it was—a broad sweep of vacant tiles with a large candle burning in the middle

Lizzie put the brakes on Alison's wheelchair and stood beside her.

"I used to think that the power was in *the thing,* in this case the relics. But the absence of them is also powerful." She felt it was more effecting to look at the vast empty space in Canterbury Cathedral that had once held the shrine with Becket's remains, than it was to see the reproduction shrine of St. Swithun in Winchester, or even the real shrine of Edward the Confessor at Westminster, crowded in among multiple monuments.

George and Martin stood behind them at a distance. Lizzie had regretted that Edmund couldn't join them, but now as she stood with Alison, she felt the power of their pilgrimage together and did not feel that they needed the presence of men. She would rather have had Jackie and Kate here, a quartet of strong women who shared a bond with the Weaver, and she mentioned it to Alison.

"Let's do that," Alison said. "When our book comes out let's bring them here. By then I'll be walking again."

"I'd like that," Lizzie answered.

"And I think I'm going to abandon Geoffrey Chaucer as well."

Lizzie gave her a puzzled look.

"When I first read the journal I felt that I needed to somehow make a statement about the Weaver, that she was better than Chaucer depicted her, but that just doesn't seem important anymore. Her work can stand on its own."

"And the poor Wife of Bath never got to this spot, never felt the resolution of the pilgrimage that the Weaver did. Chaucer's pilgrims only got as far as Harbledown, without taking the last few necessary steps to bring them here."

Lizzie asked Alison if she was sorry that the relics were gone.

"They're not gone," she answered. "They are still here somewhere, we just don't know where."

"And that's good enough for you?"

"Absolutely. I think it would have been good enough for my father too. We will reveal what he knew in our book and people will argue over it, as they will argue over the Chaucer connection, and the dialog will continue and we will have done our job as scholars."

"Thank you for bringing me into this. It has been a remarkable experience."

"And so it is back to teaching for you?"

"Until George can find me another life-threatening historical research project."

"History is not for the faint of heart, is it?"

Lizzie laughed. "There is much to wrestle with when you take on the past, but I'd like for it not to be quite so filled with thrills as I have found it recently."

George came to take over as Alison's engine, and Martin stood next to his wife.

"Are you satisfied?" he asked.

She turned to him. "About what?"

"About the pilgrimage."

"I am," she answered, slipping her arm through his. "Belloc wanted to feel some powerful religious experience here, and even timed his journey so that he would arrive on the evening of December 29, on the day and at the hour of Becket's murder. He wrote that he feared to find, and then he did find, nothing but stones. It was all a huge let down."

"But not for you?"

"Not at all. I am feeling rather exhilarated, actually. I wanted to walk where the Weaver walked and now I have. I wanted to do a good job for Alison, and I have exceeded both our expectations in finding new and exciting information."

They paused and turned again to look at the empty space where the shrine had stood.

"What do you think the Weaver felt when she came here?"

"She had just found a new husband so I imagine she felt pretty good."

"And of course her fabric went around the bones of a saint." He paused. "But be serious, was she looking for the same spiritual fulfillment as Belloc? And was she more likely to find it because the bones of Becket were right here in front of her?"

"Those are questions I cannot answer," she said. "Alison the Weaver never wrote in her journal about her private thoughts. What I can say is that she was a talented artist and a patron of other artists, and I believe she had an adventurous spirit."

They stood silently. He resisted the urge to ask her about Tyler Brown and Hockwold Bruce and their violent attacks against her and Alison. He would never be convinced that their secret was worth killing to protect, even when they actually knew the exact location of Becket's bones.

Lizzie's thoughts were more philosophical. She thought of how many people had stood there over more than a thousand years, and she was pleased to be among the company.

Whan that Aprille, with his shoures soote
The droghte of March hath perced to the roote
And bathed every veyne in swich licour,
Of which vertu engendred is the flour; ...
Thanne longen folk to goon on pilgrimages...
And specially from every shires ende
Of Engelond, to Caunterbury they wende,
The hooly blisful martir for to seke
That hem hath holpen, whan that they were seeke.

Afterword:
The Author's Pilgrimage and Quest

In 1997 I walked across England from Bath to Canterbury, following a path that could have been traveled by Geoffrey Chaucer's character, the Wife of Bath. The story of this book was not yet born, but I was intrigued by the fact that Chaucer had created an extraordinarily interesting and independent woman in the character, and then mocked her as a fool. At the time we meet her in *Canterbury Tales,* Dame Alison has already traveled on pilgrimages to Rome, Bologna, Cologne, Santiago de Compostella in Spain, and been to Jerusalem three times! I began to ponder how differently she would be perceived if a historical model were found for her, and decided to make one up so that Lizzie Manning could have another research adventure.

My own research, both before and after my month of walking, followed much of the same path that I gave to Lizzie, and I incorporated some of it directly into this book. Dante Zettler's lecture on sources for the Wife of Bath's Tale, for instance, comes from Sigmund Eisner's 1957 book, *A Tale of Wonder: A Source Study of The Wife of Bath's Tale*. Other sources mentioned in the text are listed below; for a more complete bibliography, see my website at www.marymalloy.net.

Like Lizzie, I was given copies of both Hilaire Belloc's *Old Road* and Alfred Wainwright's *A Pennine Journey* before I set out on my walk, and I couldn't resist addressing them in this novel. Wainwright was such a sexist jerk that it was impossible to read his book (published in 1987!) without feeling that I was being thrown from the twenty-first century back into Chaucer's time in terms of attitudes toward women. The persistent question of how a woman should behave as a wife was still being addressed after more than half a millennium, and Wainwright had not traveled very far down the road to enlightenment. Here is what he wrote as he stared at a pile of rocks:

> A neat girl is to me as pleasurable a sight as a cairn of stones on a hilltop. To a young man seeking a wife, I would say that neatness is the first essential; a trim appearance, a dainty body, a precise outlook. Intelligence is the next virtue to seek, and it is a rare one; it is the comparative deficiency in intellect that makes woman's claim for equality with man pathetic. Next in importance is a sense of humour. But the girl who laughs loudly is to be avoided; look for one who smiles rather than laughs, whose heartiest guffaw is never more than a quiet chuckle. Good looks don't matter a great deal, and don't last, anyway; I have a partiality for blue eyes, to me they make the face look honest...keep away from the massive women, for they will go worse, and make you labour like a beast... If you picked blindfold, you could be pretty sure of getting a wife who would keep the home tidy, have your meals ready promptly, give you an amazing baby now and again, and be entirely devoted and faithful.

Poor Mrs. Wainwright!

When I returned from England, I went to visit my family and my sister Sheila told me to bring my slides along as she was going to arrange an English tea party where I could share them with all my close female relations. At the party were my mother, four sisters, the wives of my two brothers, my six nieces and my great-niece (who had been born while I was in England). Seventy-five years worth of women in my family; no men or boys were invited and I don't think we had ever been assembled in quite this way before. At the top of the invitation, in Old English lettering, was the question: "What Is the Thing That Women Most Desire?" (Obviously, Sheila had been reading The Canterbury Tales in my absence.)

I decided to make my own quest for the answer to that question which was so dominating my reading material, and several months later I started with the women who had been at this party. Here are their answers.

Mother: "Romance."
Sister #1: "Intimacy." (Not meaning just romantic love with a man.)
Sister #2: "Financial Independence" (Ability to travel, not to have to work.)
Sister #3: "Freedom."
Sister #4: "Balance." (Elaborating, she said that she meant a "balance between personal and professional fulfillment" or something like that. She was clear that she did *not* mean stability, which is, she said, "what you fall back on when you can't get what you really desire.")
Sister-in-law #1: "Love, and to be treated with respect and dignity. (Which is different than being loved and treated like a slut.)"
Sister-in-law #2: "Peace in my heart—and a pair of shoes that is equal parts cute and comfortable."
Niece #1: "Self-certainty." (Feeling totally at home in the world.)
Niece #2: "To be understood."
Niece #3: "Success."
Niece #4: "Mental and physical strength."
Niece #5: "Power and equality." (She also wanted to acknowledge that the answer would be different for every woman.)
Niece #6: "To be independent."

As a control group of one, I decided to ask my Aunt Theresa, who is a nun, and could therefore be expected to answer the question without regard to relationships with men. Her answer: "Love."

"You were meant to be my control group," I told her. "I thought that since you are a nun you wouldn't answer 'love.'"

"I wasn't answering as a nun," she said. "You asked what 'women most desire.'"

"Okay," I said, "so if you were answering as a nun, what would you say."

"Love."

We both laughed.

"It doesn't just mean love of a man," she continued. "It can be love of God, love of family."

I then asked my mother-in-law, who answered "stability." When I asked her this question we were at a lecture and one of her friends was with us. The friend interjected that she was surprised that "love" would not be every woman's first answer. "If I was widowed though," she added as a second thought, "I guess I might say stability." (My father-in-law had died about nine months previous to this conversation, and the comment was not made thoughtlessly, but with the understanding of intelligent friendship.) My mother-in-law thought about it a bit more and changed her answer to "Love, *and stability.*"

Peg Brandon, who accompanied me through much of my walk across England, said that "partnership" was what women desired—a relationship with equality. Soon after we talked about this, she was at the dentist's and decided she should ask her hygienist, whose instant response was "a husband who vacuums." On greater reflection she said that a woman wants "good health for her family." On still greater reflection she added, "not to have to work." I was then inspired to ask my own hygienist and on my next visit to the dentist I asked all three of the women who worked in the office. Their answers were "love," "to be loved," and "good health."

Another of my friends to whom this question was addressed actually submitted her answer in writing.

> What do women really want? They want a lover who makes them laugh.
>
> No seriously. I've thought more about your question, and here's my answer: What women really want is independence. We (at least, I) want to not have to ask anyone's permission to be the person I want to be (career-wise, choosing motherhood or not, being someone's wife or being single, choosing men or

choosing women as my sexual/life partners)—and I don't want to have to beg society's pardon for my choices, either. To quote Virginia Woolf, one *does* need "a room of one's own and five hundred pounds a year"—one does need independence—to be able to choose one's life course. Call it independence, call it self-determination. I prefer "independence," because it implies the financial means and social means of putting self-determination into practice.

Feeling I needed a wider test group, I determined to ask a women from every continent. The women surveyed ranged in age from fifteen to seventy-seven, and had children ranging in age from newborn to fifty-four. They represented women who were single, married, widowed, divorced, remarried; working, looking for work, retired from work; their occupations included lawyer, social worker, sea captain, student, artist, housewife, teacher, museum curator, writer, musician, waitress, dental hygienist, receptionist, librarian, nurse, nun; the level of education ranged from high school student to Ph.D.; four of them had faced life-threatening bouts with cancer (and none of those four answered "good health").

Several of the women I surveyed asked if theirs was the right answer, and I told them about the "mastery over her husband" response. Invariably they laughed. "Good joke, but what is the *real* answer," they'd say. The nearest that any came to an answer that even resembled the one in the Wife of Bath's tale was "a husband who vacuums." They all want self-determination and love in some balance. They do not wish to dominate men, they just do not want to be dominated *by* them. In fact, what they want is exactly the same things that men want.

Except men like the beastly Wainwright, of course. He really does believe that men must have mastery over women.

> There is the grotesque female who screams for equality with men: give her all the privileges she demands and let her demonstrate her right to be considered an equal, if she can; then at least she may creep

quietly back to the kitchen where she belongs. Her protest is not against lack of opportunity: it is man's dominance she resents. Man's dominance is not of mushroom growth; it has been developing through the ages, and his gradual expansion has seen inculcated in him qualities which the ladies might possibly acquire when they have spent as long a time in apprenticeship, not the least of these qualities being a sense of fair play, to which at present they are strangers.

What do I want? A world without Wainwrights!

I am going to give the last word in this book to my great-niece, who was born while I walked across England and is now fourteen years old. When I asked her what she thought women most desired, she asked if she could submit her answer in writing and put a great deal of thought into it. "A woman most desires to contribute something unique to society, or to expand the boundaries of a certain field. She seeks individuality and to, at some point, with something, stray off the common path."

Though I spend much of my time thinking about the past, I am pleased to think that this is the voice of the future.

Sources Noted in the Text

(For a more complete bibliography, see www.marymalloy.net.)

Hilaire Belloc. *The Old Road* (London: A. Constable, 1904).

Francis J. Child. "The Knight and the Shepherd's Daughter" (Ballad No. 110), *English and Scottish Popular Ballads* (Boston: Houghton Mifflin, 1898).

Steve Connor. "Wife of Bath's Hectic Sex Life Should Have Been Cut," *The Independent* (27 August 1998), p. 89. http://www.independent.co.uk/news/wife-of-baths-hectic-sex-life-should-have-been-cut-1174278.html

Ralph Adams Cram. *The Ruined Abbeys of Great Britain* (New York: Churchman, 1905).

Sigmund Eisner. *A Tale of Wonder: A Source Study of The Wife of Bath's Tale* (Wexford: J. English, 1957).

Robert Frost. "The Road Not Taken," first published in *Mountain Interval* (New York: H. Holt and Co., 1916).

Alfred Tennyson. *In Memoriam* (Boston: Ticknor and Fields, 1856).

Alfred Wainwright. *A Pennine Journey: A Story of a Long Walk in 1938* (London: Joseph, 1986).

Acknowledgements

In England, the Gould family (Joan, Ron, Elizabeth and Annah) provided me with a place to stay and four sounding boards for ideas when I made the original pilgrimage; the street on which they lived in Chelsea gave me the title of this book. Peg Brandon walked with me and inspired the character of Kate Wentworth; Erik Zettler won the opportunity to name a character in a fundraiser and offered up his brother Dante (who gets my thanks and apologies); Kit Ward first suggested that I might build a novel on the framework of the walk; Deborah Harrison and Liz Maloney were perceptive readers of the manuscript ten years apart.

While this book started with a walk, the writing of it was completed on a "Sea Semester" sailing cruise from Tahiti to Hawaii. Thanks to my comrades Steve Tarrant and Jan Witting for their patience and their willingness to give me expert advice on navigation and optics.

I am, as always, grateful to have a family of such intelligent readers. Thanks to my husband, Stuart Frank, and to Mom, Kathy, Sheila, Pat, Tom, Peggy, Jen, Julie, John, Laura and Sally for your support and comments.

The Author

Mary Malloy is the author of *The Wandering Heart*, the first Lizzie Manning Mystery, and four maritime history books, including the award-winning *Devil on the Deep Blue Sea: The Notorious Career of Samuel Hill of Boston*. She has a Ph.D. from Brown University and teaches Maritime History at the Sea Education Association in Woods Hole, Mass., and Museum Studies at Harvard University.

About the Type

This book was set in Plantin, a family of
by the work of Christophe Plantin (1520-1589.) in 1913, Frank
Hinman Pierpont of the English Monotype Corporation directed
the Plantin revival. Based on 16th century specimens from the
Plantin-Moretus Museum in Antwerp, specifically a type cut by
Robert Granjon and a separate cursive Italic, the Plantin typeface
was conceived. Plantin was drawn for use in mechanical typeset-
ting on the international publishing markets.

Designed by John Taylor-Convery
Composed at JTC Imagineering, Santa Maria, CA